PROTECT *My* HEART

rock U
book 5

ONE
GABE

I stood at the window in the large family room of my parents' home in North Scottsdale, taking in the pool, then the large patch of lawn surrounded by palo verde and mesquite trees, and finally, the stables where Mom's Arabian horses were stalled. I caught my reflection in the glass, my curly blond bangs hanging past my cheekbones and my blue eyes lighter than usual with the sunshine streaming in. I'd been growing my hair out little by little and so far, Dad hadn't complained too much about it at Easter dinner. At some point, I'd have to start living my own life and stop caring about what he thought.

"Gabe, how much longer are you staying?" Mom asked.

I turned from the window to face her, noting her short curls, almost as light as mine, her blue-eyed gaze raking over me, a glass of red wine swirling in her hand. "Not much longer. I have to get home and study." With Easter dinner over, I had no reason to hang around. Not when Dad was home.

She stepped toward me, her long white dress billowing around her legs. "How are you doing?" She tucked an unruly curl of my hair behind my ear, then locked her gaze on mine, her brows wrinkling. "I mean really."

"I'm fine, Mom. Really." I forced a quick smile. "School is going great—"

"You know that's not what I'm asking about." She sipped her wine and studied me. "Are you dating anyone? I don't like you being alone." She pursed her lips. "You should at least be dating."

I puffed out a breath and glanced behind her. Dad was nowhere to be found. Maybe he was already in his study, working on the case that was causing all the trouble. Why he wouldn't tell me about it specifically was beyond me. I *was* going to law school. It wasn't like I wouldn't understand. "I'm not alone. I'm in the band house with the guys. I see uh... people." *Random hookups more like, but how do you say that to your mom?*

"Those boys you live with are good for you, I know. Especially Milo?" She arched a brow. "Nothing going on there?"

"No." With a soft chuckle, I pinched the bridge of my nose. "He's just a friend, Mom." Why did she always fixate on him? We had become best friends, but there was nothing there and I was pretty sure Milo had a crush on someone he wasn't telling anyone about. I let my gaze meet hers. "Silas asked Cash to move in, so we'll have another guy there in June."

"So, Silas found someone, but not you?" Her gaze searched my face.

"No, you know Dad would go ballistic. I don't need that kind of headache and I have too much studying to do anyways. Law school isn't exactly a cake walk and you know Dad expects me to graduate first in my class." My gaze fell to the set of cream, tufted couches behind her, surrounded by gold and marble tables. No amount of opulence or money ever made my dad happy. He always wanted more...and having a gay son? That was not part of his master plan.

She brushed a hand down my arm, tilting her head. "I know, but I want you to be happy, too. I just...if you find someone, we can hide it from him."

"I know." I twisted my lips. If Dad walked around the corner and heard any of this, we'd both be in big trouble. But hiding things from him had become a way of life. I leaned in close and whispered in her ear, "Let's not talk about this here. I'm doing fine. Let's leave it at that." I ticked my brows at her. "Where did Aiden run off to?"

"Oh, he wanted to help brush the horses down, so he's out in the stable with Jed." The corners of her lips curled. "He loves those horses almost as much as I do."

"Good. Then he's not going out and getting into trouble tonight, I hope." I grinned. "He'll be twenty-one in six months. I wish he'd wait to go to the frat parties and stop the underage drinking." With a shake of my head, I chuckled. "Last time I had to pick him up, he almost puked all over my car."

She hooked a brow at me. "Ah, but I seem to remember you doing the same thing. Only it was marching band parties."

"Yeah, but I was more responsible about it. I knew my limit and didn't overdo it." I sighed. Aiden, my younger brother, was always a troublemaker and drove Dad crazy at times. It was probably why Dad pressured me to succeed even more. "Anyways." My gaze caught on Dad strolling down the hallway, past the columns and into the room. *Speak of the devil.*

Dad halted and narrowed his brown eyes at us, his thick graying hair cut short on his head. "Oh, I thought you'd left already, Gabe." He pulled at the cuffs of his blue paisley button-down.

I threw a glance at Mom, who turned around. "No, but I

was just about to." I stepped past Mom. Maybe if I left now, he'd leave me alone.

He grabbed my arm. "I'm glad you haven't gone yet."

With a sudden stop, my gaze met his. "Okay." My pulse quickened. I wasn't sure I liked the tone of his voice.

He pressed his lips together, then said, "There's been another threat against the firm and my client. I'm going to need you to move back home, so we can protect you."

"What?" Mom held her fingers over her open mouth.

I shot a look at Mom, my heart aching. I didn't want her worrying about me. "No, I'll be fine. The security cameras we installed a few months ago will alert me to anything—"

"Gabe, this is serious. I'm going to hire some security guards for the house." His gaze hardened and his grip strengthened over my bicep.

I yanked my arm away, my chest tightening. "Dad, I have a life and the band is getting popular with the casinos. Plus, I have another month of classes and it's a forty-five-minute drive from here. It doesn't make sense for me to move home." Not to mention having to climb all the way back into the fucking closet if I moved back here with *him*. No fucking way was I doing that. "Why don't you tell me what's going on?"

He glanced at Mom, then focused on me. "I can't tell you. It's too sensitive and if the wrong person—"

Lowering my brows, I said, "I'm not going to blab to anyone. My roommates don't even know the real reason I paid to install the security cameras at the house." I glared at him. No, the perfect alibi had arisen with Silas' ex stalking him. "I can talk to Remy and get a full-on alarm system installed at the house."

"But what would you tell your roommates?" Planting a hand on his hip, he smirked at me. "I thought the girlfriend situation was under control?"

My gaze dipped, then met his. "I don't know. I'll think of something." Mia, Silas' ex-girlfriend, had also been a great cover for the fact that all my friends were queer.

"And what about when you're on campus or out playing in the clubs with your band?" Mom stepped toward us.

Great, I didn't need her to be on his side. "Mom, I can't hide for a just-in-case scenario. I have a life." I shifted my attention to Dad. "I have to finish out my classes if you want me to graduate on time and start taking cases at the firm." There, that would fix him. Even if I didn't want to work at his firm. But I had a few years to figure a way out of it.

"Fine, then I'll hire someone to keep you safe." He lifted his chin, looking down on me.

"No, you won't." I darted a glance at Mom. How the hell could I deal with a guard at the band house? How would I keep my big secret from Dad then?

"Oh, honey, do you really have to do all that?" Mom squeezed his forearm. "Let him add to the alarm system at his house. I'm sure he's safe on campus and he does have his friends all around him. You know Silas took down that shooter, so I'm sure he's capable of helping Gabe out."

I peered at her. What, did they think Silas was going to keep me safe? I quirked the corner of my mouth. If it would keep Dad from this train of thought, I wouldn't say a word.

He pressed his lips into a grim line, then focused on me. "Fine. For now, I'll let this go. You'll need to watch yourself if you're out alone. Do you hear me? And beef up the security system at the house. Just tell your friends your father wants it, and you don't know why."

"Sure." I hugged Mom, kissed her cheek, then gave Dad a brief hug. "See you both soon and say goodbye to Aiden for me." I strode out of the house. What the hell was I going to tell the guys?

AFTER PARKING MY BMW 540i, my birthday present for making it to twenty-one, in the garage, I strolled through the door and into the kitchen of the band house, then tossed my keys on the cream Formica counter by the stove. This house was nothing like where I grew up. It was an old bungalow in Tempe, built in the mid 1980s and it looked every bit of it. I didn't think the old white appliances had ever been replaced and our sectional sofa, which Silas and Cash were getting cozy on, was a haggard leather thing that had come from Axel's parents when he'd moved in as a sophomore with Caleb and Milo. Between that and our black IKEA coffee tables, it said *college students* all over it. "Hey."

Silas twisted his dirty-blond head of hair, cropped at his shoulders, and smirked at me. "Hey, how was dinner with the fam?"

As I dropped into the end of the sofa, Cash smiled at me, his blue eyes twinkling, and his brown hair mussed on his head. He was edged into Silas' side with his legs curled up beside him and a bright, rainbow-colored t-shirt stretched across his chest.

"It was fine, the usual." I patted Cash's foot. "How did Silas do, meeting your whole family today?" I knew Silas had been a nervous mess and Cash had six brothers and sisters to meet, all from foster care.

"He did great." Cash pecked Silas' cheek and ruffled his hair. "Didn't you, hun?"

Silas' cheeks flushed. "Yeah, his brothers were all really cool. We watched a Diamondbacks game and that helped break the ice."

"A Diamondbacks game?" I chuckled, shaking my head. "Since when do you watch baseball?" I sank into the couch and flung my arm over the back cushions. I'd shoot the shit with them until I figured out how to tell them about the security system bullshit.

Silas lowered his brows. "Since it was on, and they were all watching it. I know about baseball." He tilted his head and picked at the hem of his shirt. "A little bit." He smirked at me. "Okay, I know a home run when I see it."

"You did just fine." Cash rubbed Silas' chest.

"How's Mia doing? Did you hear from her? Wasn't she supposed to see her mom for the first time since the...since she was in the hospital?" I winced. For some reason, none of us wanted to say what she had done was a suicide attempt, even though that was what it had been. Her mom had been emotionally abusive to her, and after leaving the hospital Mia had decided to seek treatment and stay away until she felt strong enough to face her.

"Yeah, we heard from her. She's like a different person. I'm really proud of her for doing the hard work with her treatment program." Silas glanced at Cash.

"She said it went well with her mom today. They're going to take it a little at a time." Cash dipped his head, then met Silas' gaze. "She said her mom is going into therapy with her."

"What? How do you know that?" Silas lifted his brows.

"I...talked to her on the phone?" Cash spread a mischievous grin over his lips.

"You did? When?" With his mouth dropping open, Silas stared at him.

"When you were watching the game. It was boring, so I called her from a back bedroom." Cash held his head high. "I want to help her. I know what it's like to go through what she's going through. She needs all the friends she can get."

"Jesus, Cash. Sometimes I can't believe how kind you are." Silas shook his head, clucking his tongue. "She was my crazy, stalker ex and here you are, helping her."

"You're a good guy, Cash. Silas is lucky to have you." I squeezed Cash's ankle. Guess I wouldn't be using Mia being out of treatment as a reason for extra security. I'd go with what my dad told me. "So, I guess I have to install an alarm system on the house."

"What? Why?" Silas shifted his stare to me and tightened his arm around Cash.

"My dad told me to. He won't tell me why, exactly." I pursed my lips. I hated lying to them, but it was sort of the truth.

"What's going on, Gabe?" Silas curled the edge of his lip. "Got a hot dude following you around that you're not telling us about?"

I choked out a huff. "No." *I wish.* I should tell them some of it. My dad wouldn't know. It wasn't like he ever saw or spoke to my friends. "My dad's law firm is trying a case, and he says there's been threats. I think he's being overly cautious."

"Threats? Like what sort of threats?" Cash lowered his brows. "Gabe, are any of us in danger?"

Were they? Shit, I hadn't thought of that. "I-I don't think so. I think the threat was only on my dad and his firm. I don't know. He won't tell me very much about it." I huffed laugh. "Shit, he was thinking about sending a security guy to the house to keep an eye on me."

"Oh, fuck. That's not good." Silas rubbed his lips with his index finger and thumb. "How the hell would you keep your queer ass a secret with one of his guys lurking around?"

"Exactly. I talked him out of it and told him I'd add some extra security to the house instead." I glanced at the table, my stack of books where I'd left them this morning. "I'll text Remy and set something up with him. I'm sure he could use some extra side money." And Remy had been installing security systems in high end homes for years now. He knew his shit.

Slapping my thighs, I rose from the couch and stepped to my books. I needed to get some reading done.

"Gabe?" Silas twisted on the couch to face me.

"Yeah?" I tugged my phone out of the back pocket of my jeans to text Remy. Hopefully Axel wouldn't ask a bunch of questions, too.

"What should we do if your dad *does* send a hired gun over here?" Silas twisted his lips and glanced at Cash.

"What do you mean?" I tapped on my phone.

GABE

> Can you install an alarm system on the band house and if so, when could you do it?

The three dots popped up.

"I mean, do we all have to pretend not to be queer? How would that work?" Silas furrowed his brows.

"No, of course not. It's okay for me to have queer friends and roommates. Dad just can't know that *I'm* gay." I watched my phone. How would this work, though? I'd have to be really careful. Fuck, Dad won't send anyone over here. This line of thinking was stupid and unnecessary.

REMY

> Sure, I can come over after work tomorrow. Let me know exactly what you're looking for and I'll pick up what we need from Home Depot.

GABE

> I'll look at some things online and text you later. Thanks!

REMY

> Anytime.

9

Okay, that was settled. I glanced at Silas, still facing me from the couch. "What?"

"How the fuck are you going to explain to some goon that all your friends are queer, but you're the only straight guy?" He raised his brows.

"Yeah, Gabe?" Cash twisted around, grabbing the back of the couch, and kneeling on the cushions.

I blew out a breath. "It's a non-issue. I shouldn't have said anything. I'm sure the security system will make my dad happy. Remy's coming over tomorrow to install it." I'd look up a kick ass alarm system and let Dad know it would be installed tomorrow and that should be the end of it.

"Gabe, can I ask you why you're not out to your dad?" Cash wrinkled his brows, watching me.

I snapped my gaze to Cash's and shrugged. "It's just easier this way." How could I explain it to a guy like Cash, who only seemed to see the good in everyone? "We decided, my mom and me, that it would be better not to tell him. My dad can be..." I dipped my head, my chest tightening, then focused on Cash. "He can be an asshole when he doesn't get what he wants. And what he wants is a perfect, smart son to work with him at the firm and eventually take it over from him." I pressed my lips together. "My mom just wants to keep the peace for as long as we can. Right now, with me living here and still in school, it doesn't really matter."

"But Gabe, have you ever had a boyfriend?" Silas tilted his head while he studied me.

Through a huffed laugh, I said, "No, not really." I gave my head a quick shake and fingered the edge of my book. "I don't have time for that shit anyways. I'm expected to graduate at least *summa cum laude*."

"What the fuck does that even mean?" Silas furrowed his brows. "I mean, I've heard of it, but..."

"It means I need a GPA of at least 3.8. It's around 3.95 right now and I intend on keeping it that way." I dragged my gaze to meet with Silas'. Why *was* I doing this to myself? Was I overcompensating for being gay? Did I think somewhere deep inside, he'd accept me better someday if I was a smart, successful gay son and not just a gay son?

"So, but your mom doesn't care?" Cash cocked his head.

"No, she doesn't care." I sucked in a breath. "Neither does my brother." I knew what the next question was. I might as well spill it before they even asked. "My mom caught me..." I grinned as the memory of that day swept through my mind. "She caught me giving head to a guy in the stables at home when I was a senior in high school."

"Stables? What?" Silas lifted the edge of his mouth. "You have horses and you never told us?"

"They're my mom's horses. She breeds and sells Arabians. It ends up being a tax write off against my dad's business and my mom loves it, so it's a win-win for them." I glanced at Cash, knitting his brows, then focused on Silas.

"Damn, dude, we studied a case like that in one of my corporate tax classes where the IRS tried to tell a couple with an Arabian horse farm that they couldn't deduct the losses from their farm as a business and the couple won in court and got their deductions. I'm assuming your mom runs it like a business?" Silas pinched his lips. "But a BJ in the barn? And your mom saw it? Dang, that's harsh." He chuckled.

"Yeah, but she was sort of cool about it. She said, and I quote, I'd burned her eyes out and she'd never be able to unsee it." I huffed a laugh. "She didn't care so much about me being gay and she told me at some level, she already knew it." I glanced at my book, now open to the chapter I had to read. "Anyways, me and my mom talked after the guy left and decided it would be better not to say anything to my dad. I was about to move out for college, so I didn't really care."

"And who was the guy?" Cash rested his chin on his hands, crossed over the back of the couch.

With a soft snort, I shook my head. "Fuck...a guy from my high school band." Let the teasing begin.

"Oh, no." Silas snickered. "A horn blower? You got a thing for them, don't you?"

"Stop, but yeah. He played the trumpet. He had strong uh, lips." I gave Silas a sly grin. Damn, I didn't even think I could remember the guy's name. Where had he gone to school after that?

"Learn something new every day." Silas turned around to face the other way and Cash did the same.

"Wait." Cash twisted around again. "Did the guy get off, at least?"

"Yeah, we finished." I nodded my head. The guy was hot. There was no way I was going to let that incident stop us. "Mom left us alone after the initial viewing."

"I don't think I'd be able to keep going after something like that." Silas scoffed. "No way."

Cash settled in next to Silas again. "Yeah, me neither."

"Yeah, well, I was...young." With a smirk, I rose up from the table with my book. "I'm going to get some reading done. See you all tomorrow." I'd give them some space and I wasn't going to be able to focus on my reading with them out here anyways. I stepped toward the hallway to the bedrooms. "Where's Milo?"

"I don't know. Out somewhere. You know how he is." Silas twined his fingers in Cash's and kissed his knuckles, then gazed into his eyes. "If he comes home before we go to bed, I'll tell him about the security shit."

"Thanks." I walked to my bedroom and turned on the overhead light in the ceiling fan. I should probably have a conversation with Milo about this mess tomorrow.

TWO

JEREMY

It was a sunny Wednesday afternoon and I sat on a bench at the park by the law office building in North Scottsdale, eating a Subway sandwich, people-watching. A few children played on the colorful playground equipment further into the park, past some tall Sissou trees and the grass area, their moms sitting at concrete picnic tables along the edge. I hoped they didn't think I was some sort of pedophile sitting here. I chuckled. I'd been reading too many law cases. I didn't fit the profile at all.

My phone buzzed in the front pocket of my slacks, and I set my sandwich, wrapped in paper, down next to me. A FaceTime call from Grant, my best friend, scrolled across the screen. I answered the call and held the phone to my face, catching my image on the screen and shaking my long, almost black bangs off my forehead. My eyes looked a lighter shade of brown in the sunshine out here.

"Hey, what's up, Jeremy?" Grant gave me his signature charming smile, his brown hair cut short and his hazel eyes beaming at me.

"Hey, got your haircut for the police academy?" I sat back on the bench and stretched my arm across the back of it. He'd always had short hair, but this was the shortest I'd seen it and it looked really good on him.

"Yeah, I did." His smile faded. "You sure you still want to study law and not join me? I could probably put in a good word for you."

I glanced at the playground, then focused on him. "Yeah, I'm sure. My boss at the firm assigned me a case to research a few weeks ago. It's way more interesting work than I was doing and I'm learning so much. It amazes me every day how incredibly smart and driven he is." I sighed. "No, trying cases is my future. No one should get away with a reduced sentence for a technicality like the asshole who killed my dad." My chest pinched. The civil suit we'd filed hadn't been enough. It shouldn't be that way.

"Well, your dad inspired the hell out of me, too. He was a great detective." He worried his lower lip. "The two year anniversary is coming up, isn't it?"

"Yeah." I breathed in deeply. Seeing Grant doing the program I'd trained for my whole life was good and bad. But I'd made my decision not to follow in my father's exact footsteps, instead taking a different route and becoming a lawyer with my degree in criminal justice. I'd been accepted into law school, but then had taken a deferral so I could get my finances under control and pay off some of my student loan debt. Again, thanks to Kevin and his firm.

"How's your mom?" Grant's warm smile returned with a vengeance.

"She's doing great. It's Simone I'm worried about. You know, with her quitting school after my dad died." I rubbed the palm of my hand over the ache in my chest. It was amazing how much carnage one drunken driver could cause to a family. And the guy basically walked. Heat flared in my chest.

"I saw her a few weeks ago tending bar at Talking Stick casino. She seemed happy and she looked like she was making bank. There was this band playing that night that had the whole place rocking." Grant glanced at something beyond his phone, then came back.

"Really? What band was that?" I picked at the bread of my sandwich and stuffed a pinch of it into my mouth.

"They were called, *Knot Me*. They do all that pop-punk stuff. It was insane. You should have come with me." He flashed a grin at me.

"Yeah, well, I wish I could have rescheduled my protection training. It sounded like a fun time. Besides, my student loan debt won't pay itself off." I picked another piece of bread off my sandwich and ate it. If all went to plan, I'd be working too much to have any free time.

"I understand. You'll get there, Jeremy. You're a good guy with a great heart. Anyways, guess we'll both be working hard and won't have a lot of time to hang out," he said.

"But when we get to the end of this, it will be worth it." Soon enough, I'd be hanging out with Grant again. I glanced at my sandwich. I needed to eat up and get back to work. "Anyways, it was nice catching up. I have to finish my lunch and head back to the office."

"I hear ya. I'll keep in touch. Let me know if you get the side hustle going you were talking about. Especially if it involves a hot celebrity detail in town." He winked at me.

"Uh-huh, right. I doubt it. I'll probably end up doing some work as a bouncer at a bar on the weekend or something." I sighed. I'd started that program back when I thought it might help me be a better police detective. I mean, it wouldn't hurt, right? I needed to slow down and stop overdoing everything.

"See you, Jeremy, and take care of yourself." He waved into the phone.

"Yeah, you too, Grant. Have fun in the academy." I gave him my most cheerful smile, then stopped the call. Picking up my sandwich, I scanned the area again, then bit into it. Who knew, maybe I would get lucky and get picked up for a celebrity event?

AN HOUR LATER, I sat at my desk inside a short-walled cubicle, my laptop monitor open to a case analysis on Lexus-Nexus. I'd been doing some research for Kevin on waste management, and in particular, who was the responsible party when a contractor dumped toxic waste from a manufacturing facility. Kevin hadn't told me too much about the case, but it clearly was the biggest one in the firm right now. I clicked to the next page.

Kevin strolled to my cube, his graying hair cut short and his brown-eyed gaze narrowing. He tapped on the wall of my cubicle. "Jeremy, can I talk to you in my office?" He pressed his lips together.

"Yeah, sure." I clicked to pop up my login screen on my monitor, then stood up and rubbed my slacks down over my thighs. "I'll follow you." I walked past a smirking Samantha, the senior paralegal who'd been training me, and into Kevin's large, corner office.

Kevin shut the door behind me, then took a seat in his black leather desk chair, behind a mahogany desk and in front of a massive bookshelf with the old leather-bound law books most firms had done away with. His office had some killer furniture in it, contemporary but imposing. Was it to impress his clients and scare his adversaries? Maybe, I wouldn't put it past him.

The man was as much about the show as he was the strategy behind winning a legal case.

I dropped into one of two tall wing chairs facing his desk and folded my hands in my lap, then glanced out a wall of windows and over the front courtyard of the building. We were on the sixth floor and the view spread all the way out to the McDowell mountains. "What can I do for you, sir?"

He shifted in his seat, then tented his fingers over the closed laptop on the desk. "I'll be direct. I have a job for you and I'm willing to pay you very well for it." His gaze locked onto mine. "Samantha tells me you've completed your body-guard training?" He lifted his brows.

"Yes, executive protection training, really." My pulse sped up. This was not what I was expecting. Could one of the clients be a celebrity I didn't know about? Grant was going to shit himself if that was the case.

"Okay, and you have a black belt in Brazilian Jiu-Jitsu, correct?" He side-eyed me.

"Yes, my dad got me into that at a young age." I pursed my lips. I should probably leave out *why*. Me being a small kid who got bullied wasn't something he'd care to hear about right now. Thankfully, I'd grown during college and with my workouts, I'd filled out a lot.

"I'm going to tell you something, but it's confidential information." He leaned his chair back and exhaled a long breath, glancing out the windows, then focused on me. "We've been getting threats." He lifted his chin. "I've been getting threats regarding the case between Desert Solar and TRS Waste, the company they contracted to remove some of their more...hazardous materials from their facility up in North Phoenix."

"Threats? What kind of threats?" I leaned forward in my chair, planting my elbows on my knees. This was serious business. Who the hell would pull something like that on a *law firm*?

"I can't go into it with you. We've got a team of investigators collecting evidence for the case, but for now, I need to protect my son." He pressed his lips together. "As you've probably heard, he lives down in Tempe and is going to law school at ASU. I need you to keep him safe."

I widened my eyes. Holy shit, he'd trust me with something like this? "Of course, but um..." I wasn't even sure what to ask. "H-how, what do you want—"

"I don't want it to be obvious that I've hired a bodyguard for him and you're about his age, so it won't look suspicious when you both are together all the time. I'm sure people will think you're just another friend of his." He looked me up and down. "Though I think all of his friends are band types, you know, dyed hair, tattoos and piercings, all of that."

"I-I have a tattoo. For my dad. Right here." I held up my inner forearm to him, the tattoo I'd gotten for my father of the word *dad* in script and a dove taking flight on full display. Kevin knew about my dad. I'd told him about him in my interview for the firm. It was my reason for changing course and Kevin had admired me for it.

"Oh, yes." He furrowed his brows and dipped his gaze to his laptop, then opened the lid. "Anyways, I expect you'll need to pack a bag or two and stay with him until we can get this sorted out. The house he's in has multiple bedrooms and people come and go, so I'm told. I'm sure there's space for you." His gaze met mine. "I'll prepare a contract to pay off your student loans, so you can start fresh and get into law school sooner." He curled the corner of his mouth. "And of course, you'll still be getting your regular salary here." His gaze grew hard. "We need to keep this hush-hush. Only tell people on a need-to-know basis, only people you and Gabe trust." He shifted in his seat. "I can't have the bad guys thinking their tactics are working."

"I understand." Holy fuck, the rest of my student loans erased? I fought to keep from smiling like an idiot.

He breathed in deeply, his gaze softening. "I'm sure nothing will happen. These people are probably trying to blow smoke up my ass, but my son will be the next head of this firm and I can't risk anything happening to him," he said, "And he's unwilling to move back home."

"Yes, sir." I nodded. "When do you want me to start?" My heart pounded in my chest. This was fantastic, but also a little nerve wracking. What if something happened to his son on my watch? I'd potentially lose it all. I pressed my lips together. Nothing would happen. I'd make sure of it.

"Can you start tonight?" He fixated on me. "Gabe doesn't know anything about this, and I don't want him to. He'd only try and find a way out of it if I told him." He rubbed his chin. "The bastard is smart. We have to ambush him." He gave me a smirk. "If he tries to keep you from doing your job, call me and let him know you're calling me." His smirk widened. "I do hold the reins to his credit card and his college fund."

"Of course, sir. Consider it done." What sort of a son would turn down his father's protection? It didn't make sense. Maybe he was one of those entitled rich boys who didn't know what was good for him. I was already forming a picture of him in my mind, but I guessed I'd find out what he was like soon enough. "Is there anything else I need to know?"

"Yes, I have a file here with addresses, phone numbers, his class schedule, everything you'll need and probably information you won't need." He leaned to the side and opened a top drawer on his desk, then pulled out a file and held it out to me. "Go through it, memorize it, whatever, until you feel comfortable enough to face him in person."

I grabbed the file from him. "Of course." I could outwit this guy. I just knew it. He didn't have a chance.

———

LATER THAT AFTERNOON, I'd gone over the file on Gabe Johnson, tenor drum player for ASU's marching band and the drummer of Knot Me, the band Grant had seen at the casino, where my sister worked. The world was a small place.

After packing a large duffle bag with my things, I sat at the dinette in my Scottsdale apartment and called Grant. He was going to lose his mind when I told him my new assignment and level of pay. I couldn't wait to tell him. The phone rang a few times, then clicked.

"Jeremy, long time no talk," Grant chuckled.

"Yeah, I know, right?" I grinned like a lunatic. "You'll never guess what happened after I talked to you today." I straightened in the chair and stretched my long legs out in front of me.

"You're going to be in close quarters with a hot actress?" He huffed out a snort.

"Uh, no, but close enough." I sprang forward in my seat, planting my elbows on the table. "My boss wants me to do security for his son and he's going to pay off my student loans and give me my regular salary. Can you believe it?" I lifted my brows.

"Who is this son and why the hell would they pay you so well? How much trouble is this guy in?" His voice raised.

"Uh..." Shit, I hadn't thought of that. What if there was way more to it and the job was really dangerous? "He's a band geek and a law student at ASU and he plays drums in that band you saw at the casino." I dropped my smile. "The son isn't in trouble, but my boss was threatened by someone because of the case they're trying." I hung my head and clamped my mouth shut. I wasn't supposed to be telling anyone about that. I'd already failed my assignment.

"Interesting...Do they have the police involved?" He drew in a deep breath.

"I-I don't know. Listen, all this shit is confidential, so don't say anything to anyone. Just...I was excited to be getting my loans paid off." I knitted my brows. I had to keep my mouth shut about it from now on. If anyone asked, I was doing a special assignment for my boss and that was it.

"Hey, you know you can trust me," he said. "But I'm worried about you. This sounds like it might be dangerous, based on the amount you're getting paid. Let me know if you need anything and don't get yourself hurt." He tsked. "Please don't get hurt for this guy."

My chest warmed. "You know I won't. I can handle myself." I drew a circle on the wooden table with my index finger. I had all the training I needed for this. I could do it. And if someone was out to get Kevin's son, then I'd protect him for him.

"I know. You're a badass and big as a house." He chuckled. "Take care of yourself." He sighed. "See you later?"

"Yeah, but probably not until after this assignment." I straightened in my chair, my gaze landing on my duffle bag. "I should probably head out. The son should be home right now studying." I still had to stop at the store to get a cot or something in case Gabe's house was full. Hopefully I could find a longer cot, so my feet didn't dangle off the end. I should probably bunk with Kevin's son as well. I blew out a breath. And I had to find a way to ambush Gabe and get him to understand my protection wasn't a choice.

"Okay, then, bye," he said.

"Bye, Grant." I hung up the phone, stood up, then grabbed my duffle.

I DROVE TO THE GRAY, single-story bungalow in an older Tempe neighborhood full of tall trees and parked on the side of the road, then perused the home. It was nothing special and certainly not something I'd expect a rich kid to be living in. The lawn sprawled out in front of the walkway to the front door and the lights were shining out of a large front window. Security cameras were mounted on the corners of the roofline. They'd see me coming, maybe already saw me sitting out here.

The silhouette of a young man strolled from one end of the window to the other with a plate in his hand.

Was that Gabe? Maybe he was just sitting down to dinner. Perfect. I glanced around my car. I should leave my duffle, my gun and the cot inside it for now. First, I had to get in the house and make him see I had to stick around. "Mmm-hmm…" I stepped out of my car, locked it, then strolled through the grass to the entryway and knocked on the front door.

The door swung open, and a young man stood there, his curly blond hair a mop on his head, his light blue eyes peering at me, his face impossibly perfect. "Can I help you?" He shifted his weight, jutting out his hip. Black skinny jeans stretched tight over his legs. His shoulders and arms were well muscled under his gray polo shirt. Must have gotten the physique from playing those drums and marching in the band.

I slid my tongue over my lips, my mouth going dry, my heart pattering in my chest. This was it. "Hi. Are you Gabe?" I stepped forward, planting my hand on the door and my booted foot just inside the jamb. He couldn't shut me out now.

"Uh, yeah?" He furrowed his brows, then his eyes widened. "Holy fuck." He slammed the door on my boot.

THREE
GABE

I held the door against giant guy's shoe. Fucking hell, Dad did it and got me a bodyguard. No other way to explain a muscled dude in stylish, black athletic attire coming to my door looking for me. I winced. Did the guy have to be so fucking good looking on top of it? The dark straight hair falling over his sultry fucking eyes...*Fuck me.* He could have been Henry Cavill in Superman, except with longer bangs.

Milo waltzed out of the hallway in his pink sweats and stopped. "Uh, what are you doing?"

I glared at him. "Nothing. Get out of here. Go back to your room." That was all I needed. The gayest gay man in the house standing right there. Okay, Cash was a close second. But fuck, why couldn't Silas have been home tonight and not at work?

"Gabe, you need to let me in. Let's talk." The booted foot inched into the room and the door swayed toward me.

"No. Go away." I pushed on the door with my shoulder. I didn't want to hurt him, but what the hell else could I do?

"Who is that, Gabe? Do you need help?" Milo jogged

toward me and pressed on the door with his hands. "Talk to me, man."

"My dad sent a bodyguard, like I told you he might." As the door edged toward me, I gritted my teeth. God damn, this fucker was strong.

"Listen, I don't want to break your door, so how about you just let me in, and we'll talk? I don't have to stay..." Fingers wrapped around the edge of the door.

"Damn it." I couldn't take the guy's fingers off. He was too gorgeous. "Okay, fine." I looked at Milo. "Let go when I do, okay?"

Pursing his lips, he nodded.

"Okay, I'm letting go in one, two, three," I called out. We both freed the door and stepped back, Milo standing behind me.

Giant guy flung the door open and strutted into the room, panting, and perused the place, then raked his fingers through the long, thick bangs hanging over his forehead. His gaze landed on Milo, then swung to me. "Oh, um..." He winced. "You're Gabe, right?" He pointed at me.

"Yeah, I'm Gabe." Reaching behind me, I pushed Milo further back, then upnodded at the guy. "Who are you?"

"The name's Jeremy." He held out his hand.

I stared at his hand while Milo pressed up against my back, then whispered in my ear, "He's fucking *hot*."

Turning my head and through my teeth, I said, "I know. Shut up." I let my gaze roll over Jeremy from head to toe, stopping at the generous bulge in his black Adidas sweatpants. My dick woke. Dad did this on purpose. He was trying to out me or kill me, one of the two.

Jeremy cleared his throat and jabbed his hand at me. "It's only polite to shake hands when you meet someone."

"Yeah, okay." Slumping my shoulders, I shook his hand.

"Can I get you a drink or something, too, while we're at it?" I smirked at him. Damn, I'd been expecting a bodyguard to be an older guy, not someone my age. *And not so fucking hot.*

"Sure, that would be nice." Jeremy strolled into the room, scanning the place as if he were taking inventory of our things, then dropped into a corner of our couch.

"Milo, can you please, *please*, go back to your room while I handle this?" I grabbed his hands and shook them between us, my gaze locking to his. I had to get this guy to leave somehow, and I didn't need Milo saying something that would out me to him. Even though we'd talked about it, Milo was always a wild card with this shit.

"Yeah, sure. Call for me if you need me. Like if he's gay or something and looking for a quick threesome?" He arched a brow at me, creeping a sly grin across his lips.

"Stop it." I chuckled, despite myself. No way this guy was gay. Questioning? *No, Gabe.* I freed Milo's hands, then walked into the kitchen and pulled out two bottled waters from the refrigerator. "Okay, so tell me why you're here. I already know my dad sent you." I handed him a water, then sank into the other end of the sectional, watching Milo sneak off down the hallway to the bedrooms.

He twisted the cap off his water, then took a sip. "Yeah, I work for your dad, doing legal research for his firm. I also happen to have training as a bodyguard and have a black belt in Brazilian Jiu-Jitsu, so your father hired me to protect you." He wrinkled his brows. "He really loves you."

I stared at him, a stuttered chuckle erupting from my throat. "He does, huh?" What a load of bullshit. But of course, he loved me, at least the me he thought I was. He was still an asshole. "So how long do you need to stick around here for you to see that I'm not in actual danger?" I looked around him. The guy hadn't brought anything with him. Hopefully this was just a house call. "I beefed up the security system on the house already." I drank some water. "I can show you that if you need to see it."

He scratched his forehead. "Yeah, well..." He glanced behind him. "Was that one of your roommates?"

"Yeah, his name is Milo." I breathed in deeply. I shouldn't give out any more information than I had to.

Leaning forward and in a soft voice, he said, "There've been more threats. I'm not really supposed to say much more than that. Your father would like me to stay here until his people get a handle on things."

"What?" I barked out a laugh. "You can't stay here. There's no need." I waved my arms around me. "As you can see, there's nothing going on here. We have cameras, a kick ass alarm system and I'm not alone in the house." I lowered my brows. "My other roommate took down the gunman in the Guitar Center shooting. He's pretty badass." I hated to use Silas this way, but Jeremy, hot as he was, had to go.

He nodded. "Yeah, I know about that. But I made a promise to your dad, and I need to honor that promise." He set his water on the table and crossed his arms over his chest. "You have to believe me when I tell you you're in real danger here."

"Yeah? Just me? What about my roommates?" I stared him down. "You going to protect them, too?" This whole thing was insane.

"If I need to, yes." He leaned back into the couch, fixating on me, his jaw muscle bulging. "Sounds to me like your badass roommate wouldn't need my protection though." The edge of his lips quirked.

I huffed and looked around me. There had to be a way out of this. How would Dad even know if Jeremy stuck around here? Maybe there was a way out. My gaze snapped to his. "How about we both agree to tell my dad that you're doing a fine job protecting me and you can just go on a vacation or something? Wouldn't that be cool?"

He uncrossed his arms and threw me a glare. "No, that would be lying and probably stealing. I have more morals than that." His gaze softened. "Besides, if something did happen to you, I'd be to blame." He gritted his teeth. "I won't have that. I came here to do a job and I'm going to do it." Under his breath and turning his head, he mumbled, "Entitled..."

Heat pricked my chest. "What did you just say?" I jumped up from the couch, planting my hands on my hips, and glared at him. "Say it to my face." I hated being called entitled. I worked fucking hard to get where I was, with or without dad's money.

His gaze locked on mine. "I said, *entitled*." He stood up, towering over me, even from the other side of the coffee table. "You're obviously used to getting your way and having whatever you want. Why the hell else would you turn down your dad's protection when your life may be in danger?"

"My life is in danger?" I widened my eyes, my heart skipping a beat. Jeremy obviously knew a lot more than he was letting on. Why hadn't Dad told me about it? Did dad trust this guy more than me? "Tell me what's going on. All of it." I scoffed and paced into the room, then faced him. "Did Dad call the police? Why isn't there an officer here instead of you?"

He dropped his gaze. "No, the police are not involved, and I can't tell you everything. It's confidential and Kevin, uh, your dad doesn't want the perps to know he's taking action on the threats. He thinks it will give them a hand up."

"Perps? Are *you* a cop?" Who the fuck was this guy? I studied him. He could totally be a cop, but his hair was too long.

"No, I'm not. I wanted to be, but that changed." He pursed

his lips. "Just let me do my job, okay? Is it that hard?" He held his palms up.

Silas flung the front door open, wearing his red Target t-shirt and tan trousers, and strolled into the room. "Who's car is that out—?" He halted next to me and stared at Jeremy. "Who are you?" He swiped his long bangs off his forehead, his gaze raking over Jeremy's tall, muscular frame. Arching a brow, he flicked his gaze to mine and flashed me a sly smirk. "Horn blowers are big these days."

"Not now, Silas." I slapped his shoulder.

"Ow, fuck." He flinched and rubbed his shoulder. "Who is he then?"

Through my teeth, I said, "He's a bodyguard my dad sent here to protect me." God, I hoped Silas didn't say anything stupid. But we'd talked about this, and he knew better.

"Oh, okay." Silas dropped his backpack next to the couch and stepped to Jeremy with his hand out. "Name's Silas. Nice to meet you."

Jeremy shook his hand. "Jeremy. Nice to meet you, too." He freed Silas' hand and peered at me. "Your friend knows how to properly greet someone."

Silas choked out a laugh. "Dude, what happened?"

Walking around the end of the couch, Jeremy said, "He wouldn't let me in. I almost had to break your door down." He smirked at Silas, then turned it on me.

"Jesus, Gabe." Silas dropped a hand on my shoulder and squeezed. "Don't worry. We got this." He gave me a knowing look.

What the hell did that mean? I glanced out the front windows. If Silas was home, that meant Cash might be on his way, too. How was I going to explain away all my queer friends without outing myself? "Yeah, well, Jeremy was just leaving, right?" I flung Silas' hand off my shoulder, grabbed Jeremy by the elbow and tugged. "Right? Leaving? I mean, no one's going to try anything with all these guys here." I tugged again. It was like trying to move a concrete statue.

Jeremy yanked his arm free. "I told you, I'm staying." Pursing his lips, he glared at me.

Silas sputtered out a laugh and slapped his thigh. "Where are you staying? In Gabe's bed? 'Cause we only have three beds in this house and two of them are taken." Covering his mouth with the back of his hand, he chuckled.

"I..." Jeremy knitted his brows. "I brought a cot. It's in the car. I'll bunk in Gabe's room. It's better that way in case someone comes in at night."

"Are you shitting me right now?" I lifted my brows, my jaw dropping open. I had to sleep in the same room with him? How was I going to hide the boners? 'Cause they were sure to happen. He was really taking this job seriously. "How about you sleep on the couch. It's really comfortable." I gave him my best smile. I'd show him I wasn't *entitled*. We still needed to have words over that remark.

"I don't know." Silas sauntered into the kitchen and pulled out a beer from the refrigerator, then snicked it open. "He should probably bunk with you, Gabe. You wouldn't want the bad guys to sneak in through your window in the middle of the night and kidnap you while Jeremy was sound asleep on the couch." With a tick of his brows, he sipped his beer.

Jeremy quirked the corner of his mouth. "See? Your friend has some sense."

With a stomp of my foot, I said, "That's what the alarm system is for. Anyone opens that window at night and the whole place will go off with sirens and lights and the police will be notified immediately." Fucking Silas. I wanted to kill him. Now was not the time to be fucking with me.

"Oh, yeah." Silas tossed me a coy grin, then strolled to us

and patted Jeremy on the shoulder. "You don't want to sleep with Gabe. He snores like an old man with sleep apnea." He leaned in close to Jeremy. "And he farts. The guy's bedroom smells like something died in it in the morning. Stinks up the whole house." He snickered.

"Silas..." I said through my pinched grin, fisting my hands. At the next gig, I was going to cross the wires on his damn guitar pedalboard. That'd fix him.

Dipping his head, Jeremy chuckled and shifted his weight. "Yeah, okay. Guess I'll have to get some air freshener and some ear plugs." His gaze met mine.

My heart faltered. Damn, he had a gorgeous smile. "So, you don't need to sleep in my room. We have the alarm system, and the couch will work just fine."

Jeremy glanced at the couch, twisting his lips. "I still think it would be better if I stayed in your room. I'm here to do a job and I don't take that lightly." The edge of his mouth lifted.

The fucker knew he'd won. Damn it. I sighed. We'd gone from him leaving to him staying in my room with me. "Have it your way." With pursed lips, I strode to the coffee table and grabbed my water bottle. "I have to study now. Are you going to sit around and watch me do that, too?"

"After I get set up." Jabbing his index finger at me, he said, "And don't try locking me out when I go to get my things. I don't want to have to call your father."

"And what? Tattle on me like a child?" I scoffed. He had no idea how much I disliked the man, how much I'd rather not do his bidding.

Jeremy hooked a brow. "You're a feisty one. I like feisty." With a snicker, he strode toward the door.

My gaze snapped to Silas and a slow smirk spread over his mouth. What sort of a comment was that? Was he queer?

Stopping with his hand on the doorknob, Jeremy turned.

"Don't lock me out. It won't work." He opened the door and left.

"Holy shit, dude. What are you going to do?" With a grin, Silas lifted his brows. "God damn Superman is going to be *bunking* with you and probably wiping your ass for you when you take a shit, by the sound of it."

Blowing out a breath, I raked my fingers through my bangs. "I-I don't know. Is Cash coming over tonight?" At least Cash hadn't moved in yet.

"No, I have studying to do." Silas knitted his brows. "Why?" His eyes grew wide. "We are not going in the closet for this guy. You have to tell him your roommates are queer."

I dipped at the knees and pressed my palms together over my chest. "Oh, come on, Silas. Can't you spend some quality time with Cash over at his apartment? Just until I find a way to send Jeremy home?" I could probably convince Jeremy I wasn't queer if I had only one queer roommate, but two?

"We have a gig on Friday. How are you going to explain it then? All the guys will be there. You can't ask them all to hide who they are." With a tsk, Silas drank his beer.

"I'll get rid of him by then. I'll call my dad and convince him that this is overkill. All I need is a few days. Please, Silas? This guy works at my dad's law firm." My chest pinched. Could I really pull this off? I'd never been able to get my dad to change his mind about anything. But maybe with Mom's help, we'd get him to call off his hired gun.

Silas huffed, then side eyed me. "Fine. I'll hang out at Cash's tomorrow and pretend to be straight tonight." He drank more beer. "He better be gone by Friday night."

"He will. I promise." I strode to him and gave him a quick hug. "Thanks, man."

"Yeah, yeah." He chuckled. "Though, it might be worth it

to be home just to watch the comedy show of you pretending to be straight with a guy who's serious jerk-off material."

I shook my head. "Yeah, this sucks and not in a good way."

Jeremy opened the door with his shoulder, a folded cot dangling from one hand and a large duffle bag in the other. After entering the room, he kicked the door shut. "Where's your room?"

"You moving in?" I stared at the duffle bag. He had to have enough clothes for weeks in there.

"Maybe." A smirk tugged at Jeremy's generous lips. "Depends on how well you behave."

Silas spat out his beer, laughing. "Fuck." He wiped his mouth with the back of his hand.

I flashed my eyes at Silas, my pulse quickening. "Don't say it." This was bad, very bad. "It's over here." I led Jeremy down the hallway and into my room. My queen-sized bed was pushed into the corner, but it still didn't leave a lot of space for a cot with my desk at the other end of the room.

He scanned the room, rubbing his chin. "I'll set up the cot next to your bed. Otherwise, it'll be in the way of the closet." He leaned the cot up against the side of my bed and plunked the duffle bag next to the closet doors.

Great, he would be right beside me. This would be torture. My gaze landed on his tight, round ass as he bent over to unfold the cot. My cock stirred and my breath quickened. I had to get out of here. "I'll uh, let you get set up while I go and get some reading done." I bolted from the room and into the main room, shaking my head at Silas. "Don't you have studying to do?"

"I do. Just waiting for the shit show to end." He sipped more beer, then grabbed his backpack and ambled to the kitchen table.

I plucked my book from the dinette and made my way to the couch, then sat down. How was this going to work? Would I get any reading done with Jeremy around? Silas knew to keep his mouth shut while I was reading.

Jeremy strolled out from the hallway with a gun holstered to his hip.

"Oh, hey, why do you have a gun?" I waved my hand out in front of me. This was not good and possibly triggering for Silas.

With a quick turn in his seat, Silas glared at Jeremy. "Dude, this is a firearm free house. Have some respect and put that thing out in your car or something."

Jeremy stopped, his brows furrowing. "If someone breaches the house with a gun, I need to be armed."

"I thought you were a ju-ju-shitsu champion or something?" I stared at the gun. I didn't think I'd ever seen a real one up close. I'd never had need of one.

"Dude." Silas shook his head at me. "It's Jiu-Jitsu." He stood up and stepped close to Jeremy. "This is our house and there are some things you'll need to compromise on. This is one of them. If we get an indication the gun is needed, then by all means bring that sucker out. But for now, I'd appreciate it if you kept it in your shit, or out in your car."

Jeremy parted his lips and stared at Silas. "Yeah, okay. But if we see anything suspicious on the cameras, it's coming back out."

"Fine." Silas walked to the table and sat down, then fished out his laptop.

Milo peeked from the hallway. "Can I come out now, Gabe?"

"Shit, yeah." I'd totally forgotten he was still here. I huffed a breath. "Sorry," I mumbled.

Milo looked Jeremy over, his gaze stalling on the gun. His breath caught.

"Don't worry, I'm putting it away for now." He patted Milo

on the shoulder and gave him a warm smile, then walked toward the bedrooms.

Heat flared in my chest. Did he *like* Milo? Could Jeremy be queer after all? Surely Dad wouldn't have hired a gay bodyguard. My pulse quickened. Did Dad know about me? Was he pretending not to? I glanced at the book in my lap. How the hell was I going to focus on my reading with all this shit going on? I had to try.

"I'm going to get a snack, then back to my room to draw." Milo strode into the kitchen and pulled down a box of Frosted Flakes cereal from a top cupboard, along with a bowl.

"Sure." Silas typed on his laptop, peering into the screen.

Jeremy made his way out of the hallway again, this time with a book in his hand and no gun on his hip. "Thought I might as well read, since everyone is studying." He dropped into the corner of the couch and propped his bare feet up on the coffee table, then opened his book.

I cocked my head, studying the book. The title read, *Letters to a Law Student*. I furrowed my brows. "Wait, are you in law school, too?"

With his gaze finding mine, he said, "Not yet. I was accepted last year, but got a deferment, so I could get my finances in order first." He pursed his lips.

I glanced at my book, then watched Milo pour milk into his cereal. "I guess you already know I'm in law school." I worried my lower lip. "How old are you?"

"Twenty-five." He peered at me. "I graduated with my criminal justice degree last year, but worked for your father on and off to keep the student loan debt at a reasonable level."

Maybe I *was* entitled. To him, at least. "Oh." I nodded, then opened my book to the chapter I needed to read, more shit about contracts. I wanted to offer to help him when he got into law school, but we weren't friends and probably wouldn't ever be. Dad was paying him to be here with me. I needed to remember that. I glanced at Silas, watching us with his incessant smirk on his face, his cheek resting in his palm.

Milo stepped to the couch and leaned over Jeremy's shoulder. "Interesting. I'm going to school for art. Going to be a graphic artist." He gave Jeremy a coy grin, fluttering his lashes at him.

"Really? Being able to do art is such a gift. I always wished I could draw." Jeremy glanced at me. "But law is really my thing."

My chest prickled. Was Milo hitting on *my* bodyguard? The little shit. I threw him a glare.

"Anyways, I'm going now." Milo gave me a knowing grin, then sauntered off, swaying his hips as he left.

Jeremy raked his teeth over his lower lip, his brows dipping for a heartbeat. "I have to ask...Uh, is he um—"

"Yeah, he's gay." Silas sniggered, then typed on his laptop, shaking his head.

"Oh." Jeremy nodded and met my gaze. "Just so you know, I'm cool with it."

"Good." I pursed my lips. Would he tell Dad about Milo? Did it really matter? "My dad doesn't know I have a gay roommate."

Silas tossed me a glare.

I scratched my forehead. I was going to fuck this up. I better keep my mouth shut. "Anyways. I need to get back to my book." I stared at the words, but my brain refused to process them.

Jeremy cleared his throat, opened his book and sank into the couch. "Don't worry, I won't say anything." He turned a page in his book. "Don't think he'd care either way."

My chest pinched. He obviously did not know my father all that well. With a deep breath, I settled in and started reading.

FOUR

JEREMY

After fixing my cot along with the thin blanket I'd brought and a borrowed pillow from Gabe, I snuck a peek at Gabe's slender body gliding under the covers of his bed, the muscles of his back flexing over his pajama bottoms and the girth of his arms and shoulders. Heat tingled low in my belly. What the hell was wrong with me? He was just a guy like any other guy.

I climbed under my blanket and laid my head on my pillow. Except no, he was Kevin's son. And yeah, I was getting those weird feelings around him that I had around guys I admired. Did I admire Gabe though? Maybe, but probably because I admired his father so much. He must be like Kevin in some ways. I peered at him, as he fluffed his pillow.

His light-blue gaze met mine and I looked away, my heart skipping a beat. I didn't know what to think of him and now I'd be spending all my time with him. I had to keep whatever this was in check and not let it affect the job I was here to do.

He cleared his throat. "I'm turning off the light now."

"Okay." My voice was rougher than usual. I turned on my

side to face the mirrored closet doors. Shit, I could still see him behind me. His bed was higher than mine.

Turning the switch on the lamp, his gaze slid over my body, and he snuck his lower lip between his teeth, then darkness fell on the room.

I pulled the blanket up under my chin and closed my eyes, the image of him burned in my memory.

"Hey, Jeremy?" He asked.

"Yeah?" I rolled to my back. It was safe to look now. I could barely see the outline of his body in the ambient light.

"Are you going to come to school with me tomorrow? I mean, how does this work?" Sheets ruffled beside me.

"Yeah. I need to stay by your side. We don't know when and where these people could make a move." I stared toward the ceiling. He was going to have a problem with that, I was sure of it. For some reason, he had a problem with everything I did. Did he hate me or something? I'd tried to be as nice as I could be.

"Even to my classes?" His shadow shifted in the dark as if he were rising up, onto an elbow, and looking down at me.

I rolled toward him. "Yes, even to your classes." I huffed. Here we go.

"I don't know if my professor will allow that," he said.

"They'll allow it. As long as there's an empty seat and I'm not disrupting anyone, they won't care." I tucked my hand under my pillow. He was doing his best to find a way out of this again. Not going to happen. I had done my research before coming here. "And if a professor does have a problem with it, I'll talk to them privately and explain the situation."

"Shit." He dropped into his pillow.

"Why are you so against this? It's not that big of a deal." I huffed. This was getting old. In another situation, if we'd met in class, we might have become friends.

"It is. It's violating my privacy and the privacy of my room-mates and I don't think it's necessary." He puffed out an exhale. "What did they threaten to do? Can you at least tell me that? Am I going to be kidnapped or something?" He choked out a laugh.

Shit, even I didn't know the answer to that question. I furrowed my brows. Maybe if I told him yes, he'd shut up about it and behave. "Yes, they threatened to kidnap you." I held still.

His breath caught. "Seriously? What about my brother? Does he have a bodyguard, too?"

"I-I don't know. I never asked and your dad never said anything about him." As my gut tightened, I tensed my lips. I hadn't thought about the brother. I'd have to call Kevin tomor-row, give him an update at some point and let him know what I'd told Gabe. But how else would I get Gabe to work with me on this?

"Aiden's not exactly careful. He better not be a target." He huffed. "Damn it. Now I can't sleep." The ruffling of sheets filled the room, followed by a thump. "Find out if Dad got him a bodyguard, too," he said. "Aiden's the one who really needs one."

I clenched my jaw. Fuck, I'd said the wrong thing. They didn't cover these types of discussions in my protection services classes. It had been all about risk assessment, how to disarm someone and how to shield the client. "Gabe, I'm sure your dad has it under control. He's a good man and he knows what he's doing."

He barked out a sharp laugh. "Yeah, right." He rolled over, putting his back to me.

Heat prickled in my chest, and I pursed my lips. Obvi-ously, Gabe and his father had some sort of falling out. Maybe that was why he was so hardheaded against me being here. I wasn't going to get in the middle of it. No, I was here to protect him and that was it. "Goodnight." I clenched my eyes shut.

"Goodnight."

THE NEXT MORNING, after an uneventful breakfast of cereal, I sat quietly in Gabe's car as we drove to his parking lot on campus in downtown Phoenix, where the law buildings were located. Of course, Gabe had a parking pass in the coveted *A* lot. Guns weren't allowed on campus, even with a concealed carry permit, so I had to leave it at home. Not that Gabe would have allowed it, but I wouldn't have told him, either. I'd be extra diligent in surveying our surroundings instead.

As I climbed out of his fancy BMW, I scanned the parking lot around us. Students milled about, chatting, and locking up their vehicles before walking toward the campus buildings. "What class do you have first?"

"Contracts. It's what I was reading last night." He locked the car and slung his backpack over his shoulder. "It's sort of boring." He walked to me and patted my shoulder. "Make sure you don't nod off. It's not a good look." He smirked at me, his sunglasses hanging low on his nose.

"I won't fall asleep." I scoffed. He couldn't help but fuck with me. I followed him to a modern glass building with a sprawling courtyard in front of it, housing patio tables and desert plants. This was pretty different from ASU's regular campus. The sign on the building read, *Sandra Day O'Connor College of Law*. My heart fluttered. Someday, hopefully sooner rather than later, I'd be entering this building as a student and not a bodyguard.

Gabe opened a glass door for me. "After you." He waved me inside.

I stepped into the foyer of the building, an open space with a slanted glass ceiling showing off an opening to the blue sky in the center of the three tall main buildings. "Wow, this place is nice." I stared up, then caught myself. I was supposed to be looking for threats. With a sigh, I perused the area, assessing the students and faculty around us. A muscled young man passed by us, his rounded ass swaying as he walked. Dang, was he a football player, maybe?

Gabe leaned in. "I highly doubt someone is going to attack me at the college of law. I mean, think about all the lawyers walking around here?" He waggled his brows at me.

"Or, the perps will think you'll have your guard down and have this place scoped out." I locked my gaze to his. Fuck, his eyes were so damn blue. My heart faltered.

He stopped walking and faced me. "Dude, do you have to use that word? It sounds...weird. You're not a cop and this is not a crime drama." He chuckled. "Come on. I don't want to be late." He strode off and I jogged to catch up with him. Turning his profile to me, he said, "We're sitting in the back, so hopefully nobody notices you." He flicked a lock of curly hair off his forehead.

I watched him walk, the way his hips swayed in his snug white trousers, then his strong shoulders pulling his tan polo tight. Heat stirred inside me. I liked looking at him. Did I admire his body, too? Why though? I had to stay focused on my assignment.

We took a seat at the back of the room, angled up like a small auditorium, and the class filled in with most of the students sitting toward the front.

He slid out his laptop from his backpack and turned it on, then rested his chin in his hands. "Bored yet?"

A professor stood at the podium, scanning the students.

"No. In fact *I* might learn something." I leaned back in my desk and spread my legs out in front of me. I could be doing double-duty here. Someday I would be taking this class for real.

His gaze ran from my shoes up my legs, then up my chest and met my eyes, his tongue sweeping over his lips. With a jerk, he parted his mouth and grabbed hold of his keyboard. "S-sorry."

I leaned in, warmth rushing up my neck. "For what?" I knitted my brows. He did that sometimes, looked at me as though he could see inside me. It was a little unnerving. This was the first time he'd acknowledged it.

"N-nothing. The class is going to start. Be quiet." He flashed me a glare and held his index finger over his lips. "Ssh."

I rolled my eyes. Whatever. I did not understand him. Not at all.

THE OTHER CLASS WAS UNEVENTFUL, and now we sat at a bistro table by the window of a small pizza place down the street from the law buildings with the large slices of pizza and sodas we'd ordered. I took in the stark white walls of the restaurant and the red chairs pulled up to the wooden tables, almost full with students. The pizza must be pretty good if it was so crowded.

Gabe sipped from his straw and ticked his head in the direction of a man walking down the sidewalk. "So, what about that guy? Do you think he might be a perp?" He chuckled and ate a bite of his pepperoni pizza.

Glancing at the man, dressed in a suit, I said, "No, I don't think so." My gaze narrowed and focused on Gabe. "Why are you asking me that?" And why was he using that word after teasing me for it?

"You're the professional. Shouldn't you know just by

looking at someone if they're shady?" He waved his hand in a circle "I mean, look around in here. There's got to be one or two shady people you've got your eye on, right?" He offered me a smirk.

With a low scoff, I looked around us. "Everyone looks like students to me." Here we go. It was like he was *trying* to piss me off. It wasn't going to work. I sipped my soda. "I mean, nothing says entitled law student more than a designer leather backpack and Gucci sunglasses." I lifted the edge of my mouth. There, threw it back at him.

He dropped his mouth open, his fingers holding the straw in his soda glass. "My mom got me these sunglasses for my twenty-first birthday." He glanced at his black leather back-pack. "I've had that old thing forever."

"Still..." I widened my smirk. "Canvas not good enough for you? Is the world a little rosier with those sunglasses?" I was on a roll now. I straightened in my seat and bit into my sausage pizza, the tang of the sauce filling my mouth, the crust soft, but crunchy. The pizza in this place was damn good.

"It might be." He leaned across the table, his blue eyes twinkling at me like I'd just started a challenge. "Maybe you'd be able to see danger coming at us a little faster if you didn't have all those scratches on your cheap ass plastic sunglasses." He flicked my folded sunglasses, resting beside my plate.

I leaned in, my face so close to his, his breath whispered over my cheek. "Maybe I have x-ray vision. I *am* Superman, remember?" Yeah, I'd heard the remark his friend had made before I'd shut the door to the house to get my stuff.

Gabe's eyes widened and his breath snagged. "Shit, are you? You certainly have Superman's hearing." His gaze drew to my lips, then snapped up. He arched a brow. "Are you?" He flicked his tongue at his upper lip.

My pulse quickened and my stomach flipped. What the

hell? I lurched back into my seat, wrinkling my brows, toying with the edge of my plate. Was he flirting with me? Was I flirting with him? I snuck a glance at him, then focused on my pizza. "I'm not Superman. Why would your friend even say that?" I'd left right after I'd heard it, too worried Gabe was going to lock me out if I didn't get back as soon as possible.

"Silas likes to tease people. If you hadn't noticed with all the shit he told you about me." Gabe ate another bite of his pizza, then wiped his fingers on his napkin. "Tell me a little bit about yourself, you know, since we're just sitting here eating lunch before my next class," he said, "We've got time to kill."

I puffed out a breath. "What do you want to know?" I drank my soda down, then ate my pizza. I was sure he wasn't really interested in me and my life.

"How long have you been working for my dad and how well do you know him?" He eyed me.

"I've been working for him, oh, for about three years total. I'd done some summer internships at the firm and after I graduated with my criminal justice degree, he hired me on full time until I could..." I flashed my eyes at him. I'm sure Gabe knew nothing about student loan debt. "Until I could pay off some of my student loans."

"Yeah?" Gabe stuffed pizza into his mouth and chewed, peering at me as if thinking hard on what I'd said. "So, what do you do for him, besides pretending to protect his son?"

I winced. This was serious and he had to stop making jokes about it. "I'm not pretending." I straightened in my seat, throwing him a quick glare. "I have a certificate in executive protection. It was a lot of hard work."

"Yeah, okay. So, why would you do that if you want to ultimately be a lawyer?" He sipped his soda.

"Originally, I was going to be a detective, like my father. I thought it would give me a leg up." I pursed my lips. Had this turned into an interrogation, or did he really care?

"So, your dad's a cop?" He ate more pizza, focused on me.

"Was." I bit my lower lip, a familiar ache flooding my chest. I wasn't sure I wanted to say any more.

"Was? So, did he retire or something?" He wiped his mouth with his napkin.

"No, he died on duty. Wrong way drunk driver on the free-way." I fisted my hand next to my plate.

"Shit, I'm sorry." He covered my fist with his hand, the warmth sparking up my arm and down my spine. "Tell me more."

My gaze cut to his. This was weird. I'd never had a guy friend hold my hand like this. But oddly, I didn't want to pull away, either. It felt natural. I stared at our hands. "H-he was on duty, and he saw the drunk first, so he tried to pull him over before he hit someone." I shook my head. "I don't know exactly how it happened. No one really does, but the drunk hit him instead at a high rate of speed. Maybe the drunk fled, but Dad was in an unmarked car. The drunk got off with two years and probation over some technicality. He was rich and had a good lawyer." I clenched my jaw, my heart pinching. Why was I telling Gabe all this?

He squeezed my hand and rubbed his thumb over my knuckles. "That sucks. That's the sort of thing I'd like to see stopped. Maybe laws have to change or maybe we need better prosecutors. I don't know yet." He freed my hand and sat back, combing his fingers through his curly bangs. "So, you decided to go into law instead to try and change things?"

"I did." I rubbed the palm of the hand he'd held. Gabe was smart, I'd give him that. He was going to be great at interro-gating witnesses. He'd gotten me to open up like it was nothing and I didn't do that with just anyone. I ate the last of my pizza, then washed it down with soda. "So..."

"So." He gave me a warm grin. "Looks like both of us are on the same page when it comes to the law." He cocked his head. "You still didn't tell me what you do for my dad."

"Research, mostly, right now. I'm working with one of his senior paralegals." I relaxed my shoulders and scanned the restaurant, much of the lunch crowd finishing up around us.

"When do you think you'll start law school? How much longer do you have to pay off your loans?" He sipped the rest of his soda through his straw, making a crinkling sound.

My heart stuttered. It didn't feel right to admit to him how much his dad was paying me to sit here with him. "Uh, don't know, really." I focused my attention out the window and to the street, watching a woman walk her dog down the sidewalk, the dog stopping to sniff at the base of a spindly tree. The reality was, I might be joining Gabe here at this college next semester.

He stood up from his red chair. "Okay, well, better get to the next class." He sighed as he bent over to pick up his backpack, then slipped his sunglasses onto his face.

Plucking my sunglasses of the table, I said, "Yeah." Shit, I should get a new pair of sunglasses. Now I was going to notice all the damned scratches. I followed him out of the restaurant.

WE'D GOTTEN BACK to the house in the late afternoon and none of Gabe's roommates were home. After turning off the alarm at the door leading into the kitchen from the garage, we both strolled inside the main room. "I'd like to see the video from the cameras. Can you give me the login for the app?" I probably should have checked this yesterday, but I'd been too busy convincing Gabe I needed to stay and do my job.

"Sure." Gabe dropped into the couch and planted his backpack on the floor next to him. After giving me the login, he tipped his head back and stared up at the ceiling. "If you see anything, show me."

"Yeah." I logged into the app on my phone, then sat down next to him. This way, if I did see something, I could just hand my phone to him. I perused video after video, but wasn't seeing anything I could point to as suspicious.

"See anything?" He lifted his head and met my gaze.

"Not yet, but there's quite a few videos to go through." I tapped play on a video of a man running down the street, obviously a jogger.

"I'm going to the bathroom." He fished his phone out of his backpack, then strolled into the hallway.

I smirked. Guess he might be in there a while if he'd taken his phone. I scrolled through a few more videos.

A minute or so later, Gabe's muffled voice rang out from the hallway. "It's stupid. There's no reason for it!"

"What the hell?" I set my phone on the coffee table, then jogged to the bathroom door in the hallway. He was still in there. Who was he talking to?

"Dad, please, he needs to go," he said.

My eyes grew wide, and I swallowed hard. Was he talking to his father about me? Why did he have such a problem with me being here? I hadn't gotten in his way or anything. I leaned my ear up against the door and listened, my heart thundering in my chest.

"The house cameras have shown nothing. No one's tripped any alarms and even Jeremy didn't see anything suspicious at school. Whoever is threatening the firm doesn't have any interest in me."

Gabe really didn't know anything. I pursed my lips. If

Kevin told his son more, maybe he wouldn't be so against me being here.

"Because it's disruptive. Not just to me, but to my room-mates, too. You do remember that I have them, right?" Something bumped inside the bathroom.

"No, he's nice enough. It's just..." He huffed. "I don't need a babysitter." Tapping filtered out of the room. "I have a gig tomorrow night at Talking Stick casino. The place already has a bunch of security, so he's not needed. But I'm telling you, you're wasting your money on this."

He had a show tomorrow night? Why didn't he tell me? My gaze scanned the hallway. He was right that casinos already had a lot of security. But they weren't looking for same kinds of things I'd be looking for. Hopefully Kevin would understand that.

"Fine. If it's so important for me to have a bodyguard, I hope you have one for Aiden, too." His breath hitched. "Shit, okay."

The door swung open, and I stumbled into the room, falling into Gabe, throwing my arms out around him.

His ass hit the counter and his head dropped back toward the mirror.

"Shit." I grabbed him up to stop his fall, putting one hand on the back of his head and holding him to my chest, and righted us both.

He relaxed into my hold and breathed me in, his cheek pressed to my shoulder. My heart faltered and sputtered, and heat tingled over my skin. What was happening? I didn't want to let him go. "You okay?" This could have been much worse if his head had hit that mirror.

He tipped his head to peek up at me, his arms folded between us. "Now I am." He gave me a soft grin. "Guess you heard all that?" He pushed me away from him.

I dropped my arms to my sides and stepped back, his warmth leaving my body. "Uh, yeah, sorry. Didn't mean to eavesdrop." I stared at the floor. What was this feeling? I didn't think it was admiration anymore. It was on some deeper, physical level. I'd never let myself go there before with a guy. I snuck a peek at him.

He watched me with narrowed eyes, then brushed his hand over my forearm and tilted his head. "It's okay, I'm sure it's in the job description, huh?"

My skin tingled with his touch and goosebumps broke out over my arm. I pulled it away and rubbed it. "Yeah, part of the uh...job description." I stepped from the room. What the hell was he saying? My mind was on overdrive. I didn't like guys, I didn't. Did I? But I dated women. I was happy with women.

"Come on. We need to talk about something." He grabbed my elbow and led me to the couch. "I hope I can trust you."

FIVE

GABE

My father was an unrelenting bastard, and no amount of reason was going to change that. I sighed as I led Jeremy to the couch. We needed to have a *come to Jesus* talk. I'd somehow have to find a way to explain my bandmates without outing myself. But fucking hell, if the guy didn't smell as good as he looked. And he was so fucking strong. He'd saved me from a possible head injury. He was all the things I liked in a guy. But he was definitely straight, and way off limits. I had to stop touching him like he was one of my friends.

I sat down in the middle of the couch and Jeremy dropped in next to me. "So..." I glanced at him, a lock of his straight dark hair falling across his forehead and over one of his sexy as hell dark eyes. My heart skipped a beat. It was impossible to look at him and not want him. How much longer could I put up with this?

"Tell me about this show your band is doing, so I can prepare for it." He toyed with a fold in his jeans.

I smirked. Poor Jeremy thought *that* was the talk we needed to have. "There's more to it than logistics."

His gaze snapped to mine, flickered to my lips, then rushed back up. "What do you mean?"

Heat flared in my balls and my dick twitched. What the fuck? I'd thought I'd seen him look at my mouth a few times today. Was he straight? Of course he was. I turned to face him. "Listen, my bandmates are all queer. All except for me." I lifted my brows.

He widened his eyes as his forehead wrinkled. "*All* of them? Even Silas?"

With a nod, I said, "Yeah, even Silas. He has a boyfriend named Cash." I let my words sink in for a few heartbeats. "In fact, all the guys have boyfriends except for Milo."

"And you're the only straight one?" He looked me up and down, his gaze narrowing.

"I am the only straight one." Was he buying this? He didn't strike me as stupid, but he also didn't strike me as someone who'd been around a lot of queer guys before, either. "Do you have a problem with that?" I'd hit it from that direction.

"I...no, of course not. Who someone loves is their own business." He stared out across the room. "H-how did you end up—"

"It's a long story. We all met freshman year at a frat party, and we all clicked. When we discovered we'd all been in bands, we decided to start our own. Well, Caleb and Axel, the guitar and bass players, were already friends and had been in a band together in high school." I sighed. I wasn't about to tell him it was our queerness that had brought us together. "Some of the guys are bisexual, like Silas, Caleb and I think Devin, our singer, but Milo and Axel are gay."

He scratched his cheek. "And your dad doesn't know, right?" He faced me.

"Yeah, he doesn't know, and I don't want him to." I huffed out a long breath. "You won't say anything, right?"

"Gabe, I'm not here to disrupt your life and whatever messed up dynamic you have with your father. I'm here to do a job." He clamped his mouth shut.

My heart stung. *Here to do a job. Right.* He only saw me as his client, nothing more. He was being paid to be here. "Yeah, okay." I made to get up.

He tugged on my arm, pulling me back down. "I'm sorry, that didn't come out right." He furrowed his brows. "I was thinking today, if we'd met some other way, we might be friends, you know?"

I stared at him. "Friends?" I focused on his plump lips and the sharp edge of his jawline. Oh, I could be a lot more than friends with him. *Get yourself together, Gabe.*

His attention drew to my mouth. "Yeah, friends. I'll probably be going to school with you in the fall." His throat dipped with a hard swallow as his gaze rose to meet mine. "I can still do my job and get to know you, right?" He worried his lower lip. "In fact, getting to know you more might help me protect you better."

I ticked my brows. He had a point. But fuck, if I stayed on this path, I'd be moving into crush territory, I knew it. "S-so, we should uh, get to know each other, I guess." God, I was in trouble.

"Tell me about this show tomorrow, so I can prepare for it." He lifted his chin and settled further into the couch.

I drew a deep inhale. "Okay, so we get there a few hours early, load all our shit up through the back hallways of the casino, then after the sound check, we usually eat dinner together in the bar. There's not much more to it than that."

He gave me a smirk. "My sister works as a bartender there."

"She does?" I blinked a few times. I'd gotten to know all the bartenders at this point. "Who is it?"

"Simone?" He gave me a shy smile.

It figured. She was tall, had long dark hair and was beautiful. "Damn, guess good genes run in the family." I chuckled.

"Oh? You got a thing for my sister?" He tagged my shoulder, then pointed at me. "She's off limits. She doesn't need an entitled rich boy with daddy issues in her life." He smirked at me.

"Oh really." If only he knew. "Don't worry, it's not her I'm into." I covered my open mouth with my fingers. *Shut the hell up, Gabe.*

"Yeah? Then who?" His smirk faded.

"I'm not saying a word." I shook my head. I'd said too much already. I was not crushing on Jeremy, I was not. Especially after he'd opened up to me about his dad and his feelings on the law. But we had so much in common. I slumped my shoulders. "Anyways..."

"When you're onstage, are people allowed to get close to you?" He lowered his brows, then brushed the lock of hair from his forehead.

"Uh, we don't encourage it or discourage it. Sometimes it gets pretty crazy, depending on the crowd." I leaned in close. "I'm the drummer though, so it's not like people can get to me. They'd have to pass Devin, Silas and Axel for that."

"Oh, yeah." He bit his thumbnail, peeking at me. "I'll talk to Simone about it. She might know some things that would be helpful."

"Sure." I looked him over. How close was he to my dad? I'd never seemed to have gotten it out of him. "So, tell me something."

"Yeah?" His gaze met mine.

"What are your thoughts on my dad?" I arched a brow. "If you think he's a dick, you can say that. *I* think he's a dick."

He turned to face me. "He's not a dick. What I've seen of him, he works hard and he's smart. He's been more than fair to me and the people who work for him. I look up to him. You should, too." He pressed his lips together.

I scoffed a laugh. Jeremy hadn't seen the real man, the man whose wife and sons lived in fear from. "Okay. Well, obviously he treats you better than he does me." I slapped my thigh, then rose up from the couch and stretched, my shirt pulling up to expose a swath of skin over my stomach.

Jeremy squirmed on the couch, his gaze locking onto my belly button. His tongue darted out to flick over his lips. "I'm sure he uh, he uh..." He shook his head and looked away. "I'm sure he means well."

"Yeah, if you call grounding your son for a week for getting a *B* in a seventh-grade class well-meaning." I dropped my arms. Speaking of good old Dad, I should hit the books.

"He did that?" Lowering his brows, he stood up next to me.

"Yeah, he did that. It was a standard punishment in my house. My mom tried to protest, but the man can yell pretty loudly when he wants and knows how to strike fear into people with his words." I scowled. "It's not fun watching your mom cower from a man who's supposed to love and protect her, afraid to open her mouth and speak her truth." I fixated on him. Would his opinion of Dad change now? Probably not. Dad could charm the hell out of people, too.

"Yeah, he can be formidable. But I always thought it made him a good lawyer." He touched my arm as if to comfort me, but then stopped. "I'm sorry if he was harsh to you. Maybe you're not as entitled as I thought."

"I'm not." I studied him. Had I gotten through? "Punishment for staying out five minutes past the time I had to be home at night was being grounded to my room with the door taken off its hinges." My chest tightened as the memories flooded my mind, his rage over the smallest of things. "And I'd lose my phone." I planted a hand on my hip. "One time I was late because our bus got back late from a marching band field show. There was no way I could have done anything about it."

"Seriously?" He clenched his jaw. "I can't imagine him being that way. I mean, he's a little strict in the office, but not like that."

"His employees are not being groomed to replace him as the head of the firm." I shook my head, huffing. "They don't have to be the perfect son." My gaze snapped to his. I should drive home my concerns now. "Perfect sons don't have queer friends. You get me?" I poked at his ribs.

He jerked back. "Yeah, I get you. You don't have to worry about it. When I call him, we're only going to discuss the case and anything nefarious I might see around here." His breath caught. "Queer people are not nefarious." He curled the edge of his mouth. "In fact, I'm looking forward to seeing you all play in the band. My friend saw one of your shows at the casino and said you were great."

With a grin, I said, "Yeah? Well then, you're in for a treat." I scanned the couch for my backpack. "I need to study now, so do whatever you want."

"Can I watch some television?" He pointed at the TV, sitting on a wooden console across from the couch.

"Yeah, sure, have at it. I can read with my headphones on." I grabbed my backpack off the floor and dropped it at the dinette. I could rest a little easier now knowing he wasn't going to go and tattle to my dad about my friends.

An hour or so later, I lifted my gaze from my book for the thousandth time to watch Jeremy. He'd made himself comfortable on the couch, lying across it with his arm curled under his head at the corner, propped up by throw pillows. I should text the guys about our conversation now that he wasn't watching my every move.

I opened our group text on my phone, then typed.

GABE

> Good news. I had a talk with my bodyguard, and he's cool with you all being queer. He's not going to say anything to my dad.

AXEL

> Dude, I heard he's hot. Like Superman hot.

I smiled.

GABE

> Yeah, he is. But he's straight.

SILAS

> You sure about that? He was looking at you like you were a giant sausage he wanted to wrap his buns around.

With a soft snort, my pulse quickened and I peeked at Jeremy. Could he be? No, Silas was fucking with me.

GABE

> Stop it. He's straight.

MILO

> How do you know? Did you ask him?

AXEL

> I'm sure you can turn him. Look at what I did to Remy?

REMY

> I was already bi before we got together.

CALEB

So, he's cool with us being queer? He's not a homophobe?

GABE

He doesn't seem to be.

ERIC

Milo is right. You should ask him, but in a roundabout way. You can ask if he's had any long-term relationships or something.

GABE

Good idea. I'll bring it up when the time is right. I think he wants to be friends, since he might be starting law school in the fall.

I stared across the room. Friends. Did I want to be friends with him after this? I supposed I could be. If I could keep my hands off him.

AFTER DINNER, I washed up for bed in the hallway bathroom. Silas had made plans to stay with Cash tonight and Milo was drawing in his room. I'd been trying to figure out a way to ask Jeremy about his past relationships all night, but the opportunity never arose. Did it really matter?

I strode into my room and stopped.

Jeremy was already in his cot with his law book open, reading, his bare chest with the hint of stubble on full display. God, I loved it when a man shaved his chest. I ran my gaze down every ripple in his abs and over the peaks of his nipples, my mouth watering. I could do some damage to that body with my tongue. My cock woke and lengthened. Damn it. Don't think about those things.

"Is the book any good?" I climbed over his feet to get into my bed. I knew a lot of students had read that book at some point, but I'd started in on the advanced books. I'd always known what I was in for with my father partnering in the firm.

"Yeah, it's pretty interesting." He flipped the front cover to his face and peered at it a moment. "I'm really looking forward to being in those classes you're in for real." He snapped the book shut and placed it under his cot, then turned on his side, tucking his hands under his pillow, his gaze finding mine.

How could I get him to talk about his past relationships? Was now a good time? I lay on my back and stared up at my ceiling. I could start with what to expect at the gig. "So, I get hit on sometimes at our gigs. Don't think everyone is out to kidnap me, okay?" I rolled to my side to mirror him. I just had to turn the guys down tomorrow night and somehow force myself to flirt with the girls. Shit, I hadn't thought about that.

He parted his lips. "Yeah, I suppose so." Sucking in a breath, he snapped his brows together. "You're not going to hook up with someone tomorrow night, are you?" He wrinkled his nose.

Narrowing my eyes, I said, "I don't know. Is that a problem?" Why was he making a face like he'd eaten something sour? "Normally, if the right person came along, I would." And that was the truth. I had to have some kind of sexual outlet for fuck's sake.

"You think you can keep it in your pants for one night?" He scoffed and turned his back on me. "I mean, I'm supposed to be with you pretty much at all times and that would be... awkward." He batted at his covers, then kicked them off his feet. "Your dad didn't want it to look like I was your bodyguard to outside people. He wanted it to look like I was a friend who was hanging out with you. If you go and find a hookup, I can't do my job and how would we explain to some rando girl what was going on?"

Shit, was he pissed about this? "I don't know. Are you expecting me to give up my sex life while this is going on?" Where the hell was he coming from? Why would we have to explain anything to a potential hookup?

He let out of soft growl. "Would it kill you? I've had to put my life on hold to do this job, too."

That was my in. "Oh? Do you have a girlfriend waiting on you or something?" My chest pinched with heat. Why did that thought bother me so much? Of course, a guy like him, looking like he did, had a girlfriend. Why hadn't I thought of it before?

"Not right now." He bunched up his pillow under his head.

"So, but you had one?" Okay, so he was single now. But he dated girls. But so did Silas for a long time and look who he was with now.

"Yes, I've had girlfriends. A few of them." He choked out a sigh. "How is this relevant to the conversation?" He rolled over to face me again, his gaze raking over me, then snuck his lower lip between his teeth.

"I don't know. Guess I was curious. I haven't uh…had any long-term relationships." Shit, I'd almost outed myself. What kind of woman was he interested in? I wanted to know all about this now. But it was getting late, and I'd answered my big question.

"Why? You're a good-looking guy. And rich. Seems to me girls would be falling all over themselves to be with you." His gaze softened.

Oh, my fucking God, what I wanted to say right now. But no. I clenched my jaw for a heartbeat. "I haven't had time. I've been focusing on the band and my studies."

"What about in high school? Surely you had time for a relationship then?" He knitted his brows, his gaze focused on my mouth, then he licked his lips.

I blinked. Why was he looking at me like that if he was straight? "I didn't have time in high school, either. My father made sure of it." I rolled to my back and stared up at my ceiling, plunking the heel of my hand on my forehead. How could I find out if he were queer, but not gay? "So, you don't have a problem with my friends being queer. Have you ever been around queer people before?" I'd hit it from that angle.

"Not really. I don't have any queer friends anyways. I mean, I've been acquainted with some." He breathed a deep inhale. "Why? Will there be a lot of queer people at your show tomorrow night because the rest of the band is queer?"

I chuckled. "Yeah, there probably will be. Every once in a while, we play at The Club on Mill." Had he heard of that bar? I turned my head to watch his reaction.

"The gay bar by the ASU campus?" He lifted his brows. "I don't remember them having bands in there."

I shifted to my side. Now I was getting somewhere. "Have you been to it?"

"Sure. My last girlfriend loved going there. She liked the music and the vibe of the place." He dipped his head over his pillow. "I told you I don't have a problem with queer people." His gaze locked on mine. "I..." He pressed his lips together. "Nothing." He rolled to his back. "It's getting late, and we have a long day tomorrow. How about we get some sleep?"

What the hell had he been about to say? I stared at him. "Yeah, sure."

"How about we make a deal. Keep your dick in your pants tomorrow night. Okay?" He flicked a quick glare at me.

I shook my head and chuckled. "Okay, fine. I'll introduce you to people as my friend. I can flirt, though, right?" I tongued the corner of my mouth. He was really bent out of shape at the thought of me hooking up. But then, it was probably because of his job and nothing more.

"Yeah, whatever." He punched at his pillow and settled in. "Goodnight."

"Goodnight." I turned off the lamp on my nightstand and closed my eyes. Tomorrow night was going to be very interesting.

THE DAY of classes had gone quickly, now it was evening and we were all at the back of the enormous casino. After the brief introductions of Jeremy to the the guys, we unloaded our gear. It was nice to have Jeremy around to help. He was strong as an ox, a fact that my dick had taken notice of with the show of his rippling muscles under his blue polo shirt. I followed Axel into the stark casino back hallway while Jeremy pushed a load of our things on a cart behind us. I could see on Axel's face he was dying to get me alone, so he could snark on Jeremy.

Axel glanced behind us, then leaned in, covering his mouth with his hand, his black hair framing his deep blue eyes, the hint of eyeliner rimming them. "Damn, dude, how are you not walking around with a constant boner with this guy?" He ticked his brows.

"How do you know I'm not?" I hooked a brow. Frankly, I'd had one of the best shower jerk-off sessions ever this morning, fantasizing about Jeremy's thick lips wrapped around my cock. My dick twitched. It wasn't smart, but I had to do something.

With a snicker, Axel's gaze dipped to my groin, then flicked back up.

I tagged his shoulder. "Did you have to look?" I snuck a peek behind me at Jeremy, shaking a lock of black hair off his forehead as he pushed the cart.

"Did you ever find out if he's at least questioning?" He adjusted the bullet belt wrapped around the hips of black, tattered skinny jeans.

"He's not gay. He's had girlfriends. I-I think he's straight." I hung my head, an ache filtering into my chest. I was not crushing on him, I was not. Or was I? Fuck me.

"Yeah, well, I knew Remy my whole life and thought he was straight. You never know." He patted my shoulder. "Why don't you try flirting with him and see what happens?"

My gaze snapped to his. "Because he's not supposed to know I'm gay. He reports back to my dad, remember?" Oh, things were always so easy for Axel. He never gave a shit what anyone thought about him. Wonder what he'd have done with a father like mine? I hefted open a metal door leading into the bar and the hum of the slot machines filled the air.

"Thanks." Jeremy flashed me a grin as he pushed the cart past us and toward the stage.

"Did I tell you his sister works here?" I held the door while Caleb, Devin, Milo and Silas walked through, everyone dressed up for the gig.

"No, you didn't. Damn, man, you're already going to meet family?" He freed a soft snort.

"Yeah, right. I don't know what he's telling his sister. The plan was that we would tell people we were friends, but I'm sure he trusts his sister enough to tell her the truth." I watched Jeremy unload a speaker cabinet with Caleb directing him.

"Who is it? His sister." Axel scanned the opulent bar.

"Simone, the bartender." I lifted my brows at him. She'd been the one who usually waited on us when we'd ordered our food before the gig.

"Oh, yeah. She's gorgeous...for a woman." He nodded, rubbing his chin. "I can totally see them being siblings."

"Shit." My heart lurched and I grabbed Axel's bicep.

"What if she knows I'm gay?" I thought back through our other gigs here. Would she have seen me with anyone? I licked my dry lips, perusing the bar area, the white leather barstools, the marble bar top and the blue glow underneath it, then all the liquor bottles lined up on a shelf, lit up from underneath. Was she here already? As far as I knew, Jeremy hadn't contacted her yet.

"She might infer it from the fact that the rest of us are queer, but you've never been here with a guy that I can recall." Axel flung his arm around my shoulders and set his forehead against mine, grabbing the nape of my neck. "Settle down. I don't know why you're being so weird about this. Do you really think Jeremy would out you to your father at this point?"

"I-I don't know." I stared at the floor, my heart racing. I'd hidden my sexuality from Dad for so long, it terrified me now to think he might find out. "I don't think he'd out me on purpose, but he might slip. I mean, I've almost slipped up a few times already." I shook my head. "No, it's better if he doesn't know." I pressed on my chest and breathed deeply, attempting to steady my heart.

Jeremy's gaze caught mine from across the room and he pursed his lips.

I shrugged off Axel's arm. I should probably tone down the affection with my friends while he was around, too.

SIX
JEREMY

I set the speaker cabinet down and peered at Gabe with his friend, Axel. Axel had a hold on Gabe that looked way more than friendly. My gut tightened. I knew Axel had a boyfriend, but damn these guys were chummy. Much more than I was with my friends. Was this what it was like to be queer? But Gabe was straight, right?

I shrugged off the thoughts and walked into the bar area. I'd texted Simone earlier today to let her know I'd be here. I'd left the details to discuss when I saw her. But right now, I needed to update Kevin on the situation with Gabe and I'd had no time today. Taking a quick glance in each direction, I strode into the now empty hallway behind the bar and tugged my phone out of the back pocket of my jeans, then dialed Kevin.

The phone rang a few times and picked up. "Hello? Jeremy?"

"Yeah, this is Jeremy. I'm finally alone, so I can give you an update on things." I drew a deep inhale. This assignment was nothing like I'd thought it'd be.

"Good. Where are you now?" Papers rustled in the background. Kevin must still be at the firm.

"Gabe has a gig tonight at Talking Stick casino, so we're here. He's setting up his gear with his bandmates and I'm..." I looked down the hallway. "I'm in some sort of service area behind the bar. Alone."

"So, have you seen anything suspicious?" Kevin asked.

"No. There's been nothing on the cameras at Gabe's house and Gabe's only gone to class or studied at home with his roommates. I did finally meet his other friends tonight." I combed my fingers through my bangs and leaned my back against the wall. "They know what's going on. We can trust them and there was no way not to tell them." These guys were way too close to believe Gabe had some old friend come out of the woodwork to stay with him. "Any news on the threats?"

"No, they seem to have gone silent. Just be careful out there at the casino..." He exhaled. "We're dealing with a mob from Philly."

"What?" I dropped my mouth open. Were mobs still a thing?

"That's all I'll say. The contractor Desert Solar hired is headquartered there and it looks like they decided to try their hand at high-tech manufacturing waste and failed." He huffed. "You don't need the details. That's all part of the case I'm working on."

My pulse kicked up. This was serious. I could be way outnumbered. "Okay, but these people, like, do drive by shootings and behead people, don't they?" I winced. The only thing I knew about the mob was from *The Sopranos*.

He chuckled. "I don't think anyone's going to get beheaded." He clucked his tongue. "The threats are more low-key. Just keep your eyes out for anything and let me know as soon as you see something, okay?" he asked. "This is probably just a scare tactic and nothing more. But we have to be cautious."

"Yeah, okay." I took a hard swallow. "Should I tell—"

"No, don't say a word to anyone about what I just told you. Gabe needs to finish out his first year at law school without this distraction. This is his most important year, and I don't want anything upsetting his grades." Rapping sounded through the phone. "I uh, have to go. I'll talk to you soon." He hung up.

I stared at my phone a moment, then tucked it into my jeans' pocket. This whole thing was way more serious than I'd thought. I'd have to keep a close eye on Gabe tonight. I should go and find Simone now and see what help she could give me. I walked into the bar and perused the area.

Simone stepped into the bar from the casino with a box in her hands, her long, dark hair past her shoulders and fake eyelashes fluttering around her eyes, the same brown color as my own.

I jogged to her. "Hey. Can I help you with that?" I gave her a smile, taking in the short black dress hugging her tall frame. That looked a bit too revealing for my younger sister, but I wasn't in charge of her.

"Yes, please." With a grin, she handed me the box. "Good to see you, Jeremy." She rubbed her hands together.

"Same. Damn, it's heavy. What's in here?" I hefted the box in front of me and strode to the bar, then set it on the bar top.

"Liquor. It's not even all the way full." She stepped around to the back of the bar and opened the top of the box. "So, you have to tell me what's going on." Flashing her eyes at me, she plucked out a bottle of vodka and placed it under the bar.

I hopped onto a barstool and rested my elbows on the bar top. "I'm doing a special assignment for my boss at the law firm." I could trust her. She was my sister after all.

"You are?" She picked out a bottle of whisky and put it

away. "And what is this assignment? Are you getting intel on someone?" She gave me a sly grin.

I leaned in. "No, I'm working as a bodyguard for my boss's son. I guess there's been some threats with a case they're working on. So, I'm getting to use my executive protection certificate already." And that was all she really had to know.

"Good. Is this job paying enough to make up for what you paid for the class?" She put another bottle away.

"It is and then some. I'm getting all my student loans paid off." I sat back and crossed my arms over my chest, a grin sweeping over my lips.

"Are you shitting me?" She stopped with a new bottle in her hands. "That's great. Who are you having to guard?" She glanced out at the band, running cables and moving their microphones around. "One of the guys in the band tonight?"

"Yeah, the drummer, Gabe." I planted my hand on the bar top. "Hey, think you could get me a water?" All that moving of equipment had made me thirsty and I certainly couldn't drink tonight.

"Sure." She grabbed a glass from under the bar, then filled it with ice and shot water into it from a soda gun. "Here." She set it on the bar top. "So, Gabe..." She tapped her finger to her lips. "He's a good-looking guy. Never seen him with a boyfriend or anything like the other guys."

"He's straight." I sipped my water.

She erupted in a sharp laugh. "What? No, he's not." She shook her head. "Jeremy, it's pretty well known that all the guys in the band are queer."

My heart fluttered, then heat crept through my chest. Gabe wouldn't lie to me about that, would he? "He told me he's straight. Are you sure?"

She stopped and tilted her head, peering at me. "Well, I always assumed he was. Every one of his friends are. Like I said, I've never seen him with a guy here." She pursed her lips. "But then I've never seen him with a girl, either."

"He doesn't have time for relationships." I drank my water, watching her over the lip of the glass. Was I being duped? But why? I'd made it clear I didn't have a problem with queer people, and it wasn't like I was going to tell his dad, knowing what I knew now. I glanced at him, sitting behind his drum kit, fiddling with something on a cymbal. Was that where these weird feelings were coming from? Did I sense he was gay?

"Okay, he doesn't have time, but his friends do? Seems sort of odd, doesn't it?" She poured maraschino cherries from a jar into a square container.

"He's going to law school. It's not easy. His dad is kind of hard on him, too." I stared at my glass. I'd have to watch how he handled himself when people hit on him. I should be able to tell if he was into men, women, or both. My chest tightened. I didn't much like the idea of him flirting with people though. He had to be careful right now. Who knew if someone would come in here and hit on him to gain his trust and then try and hurt him?

"Jeremy." Leaning over the back bar, she tapped the bar top next to my glass. "Hey, what's going on inside your head? Did I just blow your mind or something?"

I darted my gaze to hers. "No, why would you say that?

"How long have you been guarding this guy and thinking he's straight?" Her lips curled with an almost smile, then she dropped her mouth open. "Wait, do you have to sleep with him, too?"

"Not in the same bed, but yeah, sort of. If someone breaks into his room in the middle of the night, I have to be there." I wasn't going to admit how much I liked sleeping next to him, listening to his rhythmic breathing, knowing he was so close I could reach out and touch him. Fuck, and sometimes I did, just for a second. It was like my mind was possessed by him in the middle of the night when I couldn't sleep. "Plus, there are no other bedrooms I can sleep in. It's a full house."

She side-eyed me and smirked. "Jeremy, is something going on?"

"Like what?" I lowered my brows, fixating on her. Could she see it? Were the weird feelings I had for Gabe seeping out of me? Maybe since we were siblings, she had some sixth sense.

Shrugging a shoulder, she said, "I don't know...you just seem off. Are you doing all right?" She wiped a sink in the back bar with a white towel.

"Yeah, I'm doing fine. Great, even. When this assignment is done, I'm going back to law school and getting it started. I'm sure to have a position at the firm after I graduate." I gulped my water down. I had that to look forward to. Then Gabe and I would be at the college at the same time. My heart warmed. I'd still see him. We might be friends. Maybe we could even study together.

"That's great. I'm happy for you." She looked out across the bar, then focused on me. "I'm making such good money here, I don't know if I'll go back to school. Not for a while at least." She twisted her lips.

My gut clenched. I wasn't going to bring up Dad. Not tonight. "Sure, you do what you need to do for yourself." I scanned the room. The band was doing their sound check, testing mics, and strumming guitars. Gabe tapped on his snare a few times and laughed at something Caleb said.

I leaned over the bar top. "So, as far as keeping Gabe safe tonight, what can you tell me about this place?" Surely she knew all about security here.

She stopped wiping the back bar and met my gaze. "There are cameras everywhere, and I mean everywhere. If someone gets unruly, they eighty-six them in seconds. I have a button under the bar to call them, too, if I need. It's only happened once." She glanced in each direction. "I think your guy, Gabe, will be pretty safe here. Just keep an eye out and if you see anyone suspicious, let me know and I'll just say they need to go and out they'll go." She gave me a quick smile. "Does that work?"

"That's perfect." I tapped the bar and stood up. "Thanks, sis. I'll let you know if I need your help." She was giving me a leg up if a mob thug did come in here. They'd have no idea I'd have my sister helping out. I looked at the guys on the stage, all stepping off and walking toward the bar. "I think they're getting ready to order their dinner."

"Tell them I'll be right with them." She flashed me a smile, then grabbed a handful of menus.

I met Gabe by the stage. "So, what now? Dinner?" I was starving.

"Yeah, we're going to pull a few tables together. The wives are all on their way, too." He waved for me to follow him, and we strolled to the guys, pushing round tables together inside a long booth area.

What the hell did that mean? Groupies? As my chest heated, I grabbed his arm and tugged him back to me. "What do you mean by wives?"

He chuckled. "That's what we call the boyfriends of the guys in the band. They all usually sit together at our gigs, so we started calling it the band wives table, and oh...fuck." He dipped his head, then focused on me. "It's just a term of endearment, that's all. Everyone is friends."

"Oh, okay. I thought..." I shook my head. "Never mind."

A group of four guys strolled into the room, all chatting with each other, one dressed in a colorful get up. "Is that them?" I pointed.

"Yeah." Gabe slid out a seat at the end of the table. "Sit

down and relax. None of these guys are nefarious." He huffed out a chuckle.

I gave him a thin-lipped smirk. "Yeah, okay." Now he was fucking with me.

After being introduced to everyone, I dropped into the chair Gabe had offered and watched them all. Gabe had simply introduced me as Jeremy, not as a friend or his bodyguard, but I was pretty sure they all knew the truth. My gaze scanned over the tables at them. They were openly affectionate —kissing, giving each other absent touches, holding hands, and it was obvious they really loved each other. I'd never been exposed to anything like this. It was as enlightening as it was beautiful.

Gabe sat to my right and Milo sat to my left with Cash next to him. "So, Milo, you play the keyboards?" I should strike up some normal conversation. People were starting to filter in, and I needed to look like I belonged.

Milo turned to me, wearing a pink sequined crop top that glittered in the bar's low lights. "I do." He smirked. "Which means I play piano, too. Just like Elton John." He lifted his chin.

"Oh, Elton John? Don't you love his outfits?" Cash looked Milo up and down. "I bet we could add some yellow feathers to the hem of that shirt and really kick it up a notch."

"You think?" A wide smile swept over Milo's lips. "I think we need to go shopping. I need some new clothes and I love your style."

"Oh, Jesus." Silas, sitting next to Cash, huffed and shook his head. "At least we're not playing dive bars anymore. You can get away with that shit in a casino."

Cash's eyes grew wide. "Oh my, yes. Big feathers. We can do you up like one of those Vegas showgirls."

Milo squealed.

"No, no we are not turning this into a drag show." Silas scoffed. "Stop it, you two. This is a pop-punk band. Act like it."

"You let Devin wear what he wants." Pouting, Milo dragged an index finger across the table.

"That's different." Gabe patted Milo's forearm. "Devin's got the whole androgynous thing going on and it fits our image. I don't think Vegas showgirl does. That's all I'm saying."

I dragged my gaze to the other end of the table where Devin sat, his black shirt open, exposing long, chain necklaces. I'd seen the short-pleated skirt he was wearing over black leggings when I'd met him and wasn't sure what to think of it. I tapped Gabe's forearm and leaned in. "So, Devin dresses like that for the stage?"

Gabe knitted his brows. "No, man, he's gender fluid."

"What uh, what does that mean?" I bit my lower lip. I was way out of my element here.

He came in closer, his breath brushing my cheek. "He sort of flows from one gender to the other, yet he's not one or the other. That's the best way I know to describe it."

A shiver raced down my spine. Gabe was so close. I turned my head. My lips grazed Gabe's and my breath caught.

Gabe flung himself backward in his seat and covered his mouth with his fingers, his eyes wide.

My lips tingled and heat sparked low in my belly. What the hell was going on here? Was being with all these queer men fucking with my head? And why was Gabe acting all put out after our lips touched? He didn't have a problem cozying up with his bandmates.

Simone came to the table and handed out menus. "Hello boys. I already know what beers to bring you, so I've got those coming up." She stepped toward me. "Cash, I'll get you one of those ciders you like." She stopped behind me and placed her hand on the back of my chair. "More water, Jeremy, or do you want something else?"

"Uh, soda water this time." I glanced at Gabe, then focused on Simone. "You two already know each other, so I guess I don't have to introduce you."

"Yes, I've already met your sister. Simone is the best bartender in this place." Gabe gave her a warm smile.

"Thanks, Gabe." She squeezed his shoulder.

"Wait, *that's* your sister?" Silas pointed at her. "Damn, man. You both are stunning."

Warmth filtered up my neck. Silas was bi, so of course he'd notice Simone's beauty. But me? "Uh, thanks, Silas. I think." I rubbed my forehead.

Milo squeezed my forearm. "Yes, stunning like Superman." He fluttered his eyelashes at me.

"Shut up, Milo." Gabe said between his teeth.

"I-I'll be right back." As I stood up, my chair groaned across the floor. I needed some air and a few minutes of quiet so I could think. This was all coming at me so fast. Gabe would be okay for a few minutes with all his friends around him. I ambled into the casino, the bright lights flickering on the slot machines, the dinging all around me. This wasn't much better. My gaze caught the restroom sign and I beelined for it.

I strode inside, stopped at a sink and splashed water on my face. As the cool water dribbled down my cheeks, I looked in the mirror. Gabe's striking reflection hit me, and my heart jolted.

"Are you okay? What happened?" Wrinkling his brows, Gabe planted his warm hand on my shoulder as I twisted around to face him.

"I'm fine. Just needed some air." My traitorous gaze landed on his plump lips. I wanted to kiss him. *I wanted to fucking kiss him*. He was so close. Was he queer, too? What would he do if I just...My jeans tightened.

"Jeremy." He grabbed my chin. "Look at me. Is something wrong? Did someone drug your water or something?"

I blinked a few times. "What? No." I hung my head and stepped back, leaning my ass against the counter. Fuck, I had a boner. I clasped my hands over my groin. Jesus fucking Christ, I was queer, too. No other way to explain this shit.

"Damn, the way you were acting, I thought maybe..." He wrapped his arm around my shoulders. "Are you sure?"

"Yes, I'm sure." I leaned against him, my body craving him, need flaring up my spine. My cock twitched in my jeans. Oh yeah, if nothing else, I had a queer dick. A soft chuckle erupted from my throat. I couldn't stop it.

"Why are you laughing?" The corner of his mouth twitched with an almost grin. "I fail to see what's so comical."

I shook my head. I had to come up with an answer and fast. "It's nothing, really. I haven't been sleeping very well. Maybe I'm just tired and punchy."

"We have a late night tonight. Maybe you should go home and get some sleep?" He slid his arm from my shoulders and planted his hands on his hips, looking me over from head to toe.

Locking my gaze to his, I said, "No, I have a job to do, and I'll do it." No way was I leaving him here by himself. What if something happened? What if he ended up with someone? My chest prickled. "I'll ask Simone for some coffee."

"Yeah, okay. Well, come out and order some food, too." He took a step toward the door. "Are you coming?" He raised his brows.

"Yeah, I'm coming." With a quick exhale, I swiped a paper towel from a holder in the counter and wiped off my face, then tossed it in the trash. "Let's go eat."

An hour or so, some coffee and a burger later, the place was filling up to capacity. People were lined up at the bar to order drinks and two more bartenders had joined Simone, all hustling.

I sat at the tables we'd pulled together, all the guys engrossed in each other, then a man with short, dark hair and a tight button-down shirt walked up behind Gabe and placed a hand on his shoulder. "Hey, long time, no see."

Gabe twisted around. "Oh, shit, hi. How are you?" He glanced at me and stood up.

The man threw his arms around Gabe and embraced him, then held him out, keeping his hands on Gabe's shoulders. "So, you ah—"

"No, not tonight." Gabe rubbed the back of his neck, then ticked his head in my direction. "You should meet my *friend*, Jeremy." He gave a stuttered laugh. "Jeremy, this is um...this is Oliver. He's in marching band with me." He glanced across the table at Silas and glared at him.

Shaking his head, Silas snickered and ran his finger over the lip of his beer glass.

"Oh, nice to meet you." I stood up and shook Oliver's hand. "What do you play?" The guy was built and good looking. Maybe he was another drummer like Gabe?

"The mellophone. I also play the French horn when I'm doing the regular band and not marching." He smirked at Gabe.

I stared at him a moment, Silas' words rolling around in my mind, *horn blowers are big these days.* My gaze cut to Silas, who hooked a brow at me, a devious grin on his face. There was some inside joke there.

"Anyways, Oliver, I didn't know you were coming out

tonight. Did you bring some friends?" Gabe grabbed him by the elbow and led him toward the bar.

Where the hell did he think he was going? Puffing out a breath, I followed them through the crowd.

Oliver stopped and leaned in close to Gabe's ear, his hand resting on Gabe's hip.

Throwing his head back, Gabe laughed and swung his arm around Oliver's waist.

What the fuck? Was Gabe gay? Was Oliver one of his regular hookups? Heat bristled in my chest, and I stomped to them. "Hey, Gabe." Grabbing his shoulder, I flung him around.

He dropped his mouth open and stared at me. "What? We're just getting him a drink. I was going to hang out with him until his friends got here."

"Fine, but you shouldn't walk off like that. You know it's not..." I glanced at Oliver, crossing his arms over his wide chest, and eyeing me up and down. Oliver couldn't find out who I really was. "It's not cool to leave me back there. Maybe I want a drink, too." I forced a grin. I sounded like a child.

"Yeah, sure, but I thought you had one back at the table?" Gabe faced Oliver. "Come on, let's see if I can get you ahead of the crowd over there. I'm sure we'll get fast service from Simone." He threw a knowing grin at me, then led the way to the bar.

We huddled at the end of the bar where Simone was working, Gabe at the front with his elbows resting on the bar top and me squeezed in next to Oliver with people all around us. I didn't like this Oliver guy. He was too...I didn't know what, but I didn't like him. I pursed my lips and scanned the people around us. I was here to do a job and I had to remember that. But no one looked out of place. I edged in closer to Gabe, attempting to shield him.

My chest pushed against his back, and I took in the floral

mix of his shampoo, his hair tickling my cheek. I was starting to like this scent a little too much. Heat shivered over my skin.

Gabe shifted and his ass pressed against my waking dick. *Oh, hello.* Ever since the bathroom incident, the damn thing had a mind of its own. My cock lengthened behind my front pocket.

Twisting in front of me, Gabe furrowed his brows and his gaze found mine, then dipped to my mouth. "What uh...what's going on? Do you have to be this close?" As his gaze rose, his pupils flared.

Shit, could he feel my hard on? I rocked my hips back. "This place is packed." I glanced at Oliver, glaring at me. Apparently, he didn't like me much either. But why? I hadn't done anything to him. "We need to get drinks and go." I lifted my brows. He should know this wasn't a safe situation to be in.

A woman with long, wavy blonde hair sat at a barstool next to Gabe. "Hey, you're the drummer in the band that's playing tonight, right?" She offered him a coy smile.

"Yeah, I am." Gabe waved at Simone and she upnodded at him, then poured two beers at a time.

"You're hot. Are you queer, too, like the rest of the guys?" She bumped her shoulder into his and flicked her tongue over her lower lip.

"I, uh..." Gabe glanced from Oliver to me, then said softly, "No, no I'm the only straight guy." He pursed his lips.

Oliver's gaze snapped to Gabe. "What did you say?" A smirk teased his mouth.

"Nothing. Never you mind." Gabe waved him off, then focused on me. "Why won't your sister come down here?"

"So, what are you doing after this?" The blonde planted her elbow on the bar and her cheek in her hand, fluttering her thick black lashes at him.

"I'm uh, I'm going home. It'll be really late, and we have to pack all the gear up and bring it back." He bit his lower lip, his brows knitting.

"But *I* can wait to go hang out after all that. I'm free all night." Oliver edged in closer to Gabe, attempting to push me aside.

That was it. Who the hell was this guy? "He has shit to do. Didn't you hear him? He's busy."

Oliver dropped his jaw open and turned to me in the crowd. "Who are you, his mother?"

With my chest clenching, I fisted my hands and said, "No, but I—"

"Hey, stop it. What the hell, man?" Gabe glared at me and slowly shook his head. "Stop, both of you." With a scoff, he faced the bar. "Simone, we need drinks and fast!"

"Sorry, Gabe. Beer and?" Simone watched us while she grabbed a bottled drink from the cooler in the back bar.

"Beer and a white wine for my friend, and I think Jeremy needs another soda water." He hung his head, then rubbed his eyes. "This night is insane."

I blinked a few times and huffed out a breath. I was out of control. What had gotten into me? I whispered into Gabe's ear. "I'm sorry, I'm just trying to—"

"Keep me safe?" He turned his profile to me. "Or keep me from hooking up with someone?"

Gaping, I stammered, then said, "Keeping you safe." But was I really?

SEVEN
GABE

I knew a boner when I felt one on my ass and Jeremy had one just moments ago. I'd almost lost my shit, but I didn't call him out on it. No, that would have been a dick move. I bit at my thumbnail, watching Simone pour our drinks. What the hell was going on between us? If I'd have known he was queer, it would be simple. He wanted me. The signs were there, and I wasn't stupid. Was he questioning maybe? Could being here with all my friends, seeing them with their boyfriends, be normalizing feelings he'd kept buried? God, I could only hope. But was it right to do anything with him? My dad would freak the fuck out.

Simone dropped off our drinks. "Here you go." She was gone, taking more orders.

"Here" I twisted at the bar and handed the soda water to Jeremy, then drank my beer and glanced at Oliver. I had to ditch him, and fast. "When are your friends getting here?"

Oliver picked up his wine and sipped it. "They're here. I just got a text." He held his phone to his face with his other hand.

"Okay, well, I'll leave you to them. I'm going to have to get up onstage any minute." I slid by Jeremy. "Come on." I needed to get out of here before the blonde woman started in on me again. Flirting with a man I could do. A woman? A shudder worked over my spine. No thank you.

Jeremy followed me, weaving through people, back to the band table and we took up our original chairs.

"How much longer?" I looked at Silas. We might need to get started a little early with how packed the place was already getting.

"Axel was thinking we should head up there in like, ten minutes?" Silas glanced at Axel, who flashed all ten of his fingers at us, nodding. "Yep, so be ready."

"We're doing my song first, right?" I drank some beer down. It had been my turn to add a song to the set list and it was perfect in so many ways.

"Yeah, we got it down in practice last week. And I know Milo can't wait." Silas smiled at Milo.

"I finally get to show off a little." He bumped Cash's shoulder and smiled. "We're doing *Black Parade* by My Chemical Romance."

"Oh my God, I love that song!" Cash grabbed Milo's hand, held it up between them and they both squealed.

"Figures you'd pick a song about a marching band, horn-blower lover." With a snicker, Silas rolled his eyes.

"Silas? Fuck off." I chuckled and glanced at Jeremy, studying us. He was way too quiet. I leaned in close. "Hey, you okay?" He was getting the same look he'd had before he ran into the bathroom. Maybe he'd be better off with a beer. One couldn't hurt, right?

"Yeah, I'm okay." He hung his head, his black bangs falling into his face. "I uh, I like that song, too." His gaze met mine and his brows wrinkled. "Did you pick it because of your dad?"

As my chest pricked, my breath caught. Damn. I'd only known him for a few days, and he'd already figured that out. "Yeah." I slid my fingers up and down the condensation of my beer glass. But he knew the man, so...

The blonde woman from the bar stepped to our table. "Got room for one more?" She grabbed an empty chair from the next table over and slid it next to mine, then dropped in. "We didn't get to finish our conversation.

Milo, Cash and Silas all stared at me.

Oh, fuck. I was in for it now. "Yeah, guess not." I sucked in a deep breath. I had to at least try and flirt with her. With my best grin, I faced her, planting my elbow on the table. "So, you need a drink?"

"Sure, that would be nice." She shimmied in closer to me.

I snuck a peek at Jeremy. Was he going to buy this?

Frowning, he released a soft huff. "Don't you have to get up onstage soon? Do you really have time for this?"

"Hey, we have a few minutes, don't we?" She brushed her fingers up my arm, her blue eyes twinkling. "How about a shot?" She waved a waitress down. "Miss? Two tequila shots and make it quick. He has to start the show."

"Of course." The waitress strode off.

"You do like tequila, right? I mean, who doesn't?" She shrugged and glanced at Jeremy. "Oh, do you want—"

"No, I'm not drinking tonight. I'm the designated driver." He pursed his lips.

"Oh, okay." She edged in closer to me, her flowery perfume invading my senses.

I leaned back a bit. "So, what's your name?" Wasn't this how straight people started off a hookup?

"My name's Amelia, but most people call me Amy." She giggled, fluttering her eyelashes at me. "What's yours?"

"His name is Gabe. You ever been in a marching band by

81

any chance?" Silas smirked at her, rubbing his hands together in front of his face.

"No, why?" She hooked a brow.

"Oh, 'cause Gabe's in ASU's marching band, and he tends to like people who play, what is it? Wind instruments or brass?" Silas cackled. "He likes people who blow."

Jeremy, Milo and Cash erupted in laughter.

Oh, my fucking God. "Silas, will you stop?" Shaking my head, I breathed in deeply. At least Jeremy was having a good time at my expense.

Planting an elbow on the table, she leaned in. "Yeah, I blow. Most guys tell me I'm great at it." She curled the edge of her plump, red lips, then planted a hand high up on my thigh. "I've got all the moves."

I flicked my gaze to her hand. How could I get it off me? And God damn, she was not shy at all. "Uh, good to know."

Jeremy's smile dropped. "Hey, don't you have some friends here?" He pushed her arm, moving her hand from my thigh.

"Yeah, they're over at the bar still." She flapped her hand toward the bar, then planted it on my thigh again. "They'll wait."

The waitress dropped off our tequila shots and left.

"Oh, great." She picked one up and handed it to me, then picked up her own. "Come on, hook our arms while we drink it."

"Uh, hook our arms?" I stared at her. Where was the salt and lime? "I don't uh, don't usually do these shots without the training wheels." Was she trying to kill me?

"Here." Jeremy snatched my shot and tipped it back, then hissed. "He's gotta play and can't be too drunk." He curled his lips in a satisfied smile.

"Hey, that's not cool. That shot was for him." She pointed

at me. "Who *are* you anyways? His boyfriend?" She glared at Jeremy.

"Maybe." He lifted his chin, his gaze darting to me, then focusing on her. "What if I am?"

"Dude..." Silas hung his jaw open and the whole table turned and stared at us.

Jeremy grabbed my hand and kissed the back of it. "There, you satisfied?"

"Superman is gay?" Axel hopped out of his seat, barking out a laugh.

I stared at Jeremy, my chest warming. Holy fuck, was this real? No, it couldn't be. He was just *protecting* me by getting rid of this girl.

"Gabe told me he was straight though." She set her shot on the table and crossed her arms over her chest, then narrowed her eyes at us, nodding slowly. "I get it now. You've got a thing for Gabe and haven't told him yet."

Jeremy's eyes rounded and his gaze crept to mine. "Um..."

Staring at him, I tightened my hold on his warm hand. Damn, it was big and strong, like him. His dick must be—

"You are so right. How did you know?" Axel, now standing behind me, planted his hand on my shoulder.

I blinked, then freed a choked giggle. "No, uh, he's just joking. It's all a big joke. Here, you drink half that shot, and I'll drink the rest, okay?" I released Jeremy's hand, picked up the shot and downed half of it, the burn rattling down my throat. I flinched and fought off a gag. "Here you go." I handed it to her.

"Cheers." She drank the rest down, then slapped the glass to the table. "I'm going to be up front and center watching you play tonight." She pointed two fingers at her eyes, then at mine.

Who the hell was this girl? Definitely a wild child. "Yeah, okay."

Jeremy scoffed. "Fine, but me and him are going home after

the show. We've got to unpack gear and shit. You remember that, okay?" His gaze grew hard, and he pressed his lips together. "Just so we're clear, there will be no hookup tonight."

"Yeah, whatever. You aren't the boss of him." She bumped her elbow into mine. "What do *you* want?"

My gaze darted from Jeremy to her and back again. Shit, what would a straight guy say? I was failing at this.

"He's got shit to unpack. We all do. No hookups tonight." Axel cocked his head, giving her a fake smile. He slapped the back of my chair. "And now, we have a gig to play. Let's hit it, boys!"

I hopped up from my chair and followed the guys to the stage, then patted Axel on the back. "Hey, thanks for getting me out of that mess."

Axel flung the strap of his blue sparkly guitar over his shoulder. "No problem. It was pretty funny seeing you with a woman though." He offered me a wide grin. "When are you making a move on Superman?"

I blinked. "I-I'm not. Why would you say that?" Axel noticed *everything*. Had he seen what I was seeing?

Tapping my chest, he said, "Superman looks at you like he wants to jump your bones and it's pretty clear he doesn't want to share you with anyone. I think he's having a classical bisexual awakening." He curled his lips. "You can show him the way to sexual freedom, like I did for Remy." He shook his head. "Damn, that was fun."

"O-kay..." Planting my hands on my hips, I perused the bar and landed my gaze on Jeremy, standing off to the side of the stage, his arms crossed over his chest, fixating on me. Was Axel right? He was very rarely wrong when it came to things like this. But shit, what would Dad say? Fuck Dad. I stomped to my drum kit, picked up my sticks from my throne and sat down, then thumped the kick drums a few times with the foot pedals and twirled the sticks in my fingers. I was ready for this.

All the guys lined up with their instruments in front of me and Devin took to the mic, pulling it off the stand. "Welcome back to another night of...*The Black Parade.*" He quirked his lips into a smirk and the crowd whooped and cheered.

A light focused on Milo, his sequined top glinting, and he tapped the slow notes on his keyboard, sounding like a piano, rocking with each one.

Devin strutted to him and started the first verse of the song, wrapping an arm around Milo's shoulders. They swayed together.

Milo hit a button on his keys. That was my cue. I tapped out a quick beat on my snares while Silas and Axel started in with haunting guitar chords.

Walking across the stage, Devin's voice grew louder, harsher as the verse went on. As we built the song, with Caleb thumping slowly on his bass, Devin swung an arm in a circle to the beat.

Everyone rocked with the slow, strong rhythm. I hit my toms hard, changing things up along with the tempo. Devin scream-sang into his microphone, bending a knee sideways at the stage, his red hair flopping in his face.

The song came to a crescendo and I tapped out a cymbal swell, then we all stopped. I held my sticks up high, ready to pound out the next part of the song. My gaze caught on Jeremy for a split second.

Jeremy gave me a soft smile and a thumbs up.

Warmth flooded my heart. Fucking Axel. He had to confirm my suspicions right before we played and I was a goner.

I dropped my sticks, coming in with a bucket of fish, hitting patterns all over my kit in quick succession. Silas and Axel strummed a fast riff, jumping in time with the rhythm and Caleb strutted to me, thumping on his bass, rocking his head and smiling.

Devin strode from end to end of the stage, hand held out, his voice strong while he sang to the bouncing crowd. We fell into a quick, hard beat, everyone jumping and rocking back and forth.

Sweat beaded on my face and slid down the back of my shirt. I pounded the skins of my drums and looked out at the crowd. Many were singing along with Devin, some fists were pumping. My heart soared. This was where I was free. No Dad, no law firm, no bullshit. Just me and my best friends playing our hearts out.

The song slowed and I tapped out a rhythm on my snares. As the song built, I threw out round after round of quick beats followed by a series of drum fills.

Devin bent backward, lifting the mic, his hair falling off his face, and belted out the chorus over and over. Then the song picked back up in tempo and we all went balls out, Silas and Axel jumping like wild men, twisting in circles with their guitars, broad smiles on their faces.

As the song slowed, the guitar chords were left to reverb through the speakers and I tapped out a classic marching band beat on my snares, then topped it off with a bang on the kick drums.

Devin panted in front of the stage and the crowd roared, people filling in like sardines against the stage. "Now, a little Fall Out Boy for you." Devin turned around with his fist held high and as it dropped, we started up *thnks fr th mmrs*, Milo hitting his keyboards with both hands.

THE REST of the night passed quickly with me avoiding Amelia whenever possible and Jeremy hot on my heels everywhere I went. We didn't have a lot of time for much of anything between the crowd and people wanting a piece of the band, full of praise. After the last song, it was time to pack up the gear and head home. I scanned the bar for Amelia and stood from my throne. Would she show up still wanting a hookup?

Jeremy stepped onto the stage. "Amy left with some guy she was chatting up." He peered at me as if gauging my reaction.

"Oh?" I started breaking down my drum kit. "Too bad. She was hot." I stopped with my hand on a cymbal, then turned around. How would he react to that?

With a frown, he swiped at his chin. "Yeah, guess so." He hung his head and toed the floor with his sneaker. "Can I help with something?"

"Naw, I got this." Last thing I wanted was for him to fuck something up. I glanced at my throne. "Okay, you can grab the stool." I gave him a smirk.

He picked up my throne and walked it to the cart Caleb had already pushed to the stage.

"Hey, Superman, can you get these amps and shit?" Axel glanced at me, then gave Jeremy a knowing grin.

"Sure." He ambled to an amp and hefted it off a speaker cabinet.

Milo stepped to me. "So, Gabe, Axel says Jeremy might not be straight after all?" He lifted his brows.

I straightened and faced him, watching Jeremy grab a speaker cabinet. Axel had put him to work. With a shrug, I said, "Yeah, maybe."

"What are you going to do?" Narrowing his eyes, he cocked his head. "I know what *I'd* do if a guy like that was sleeping in my room." With a glint in his eyes, he lifted the corner of his mouth.

Milo had a wicked streak. It was always the quiet ones, like Milo, you had to watch out for. I huffed a chuckle. "Yeah, but he works for my *dad*."

"So? Do you really think he'd say something to your dad? Come on, Gabe." He slapped at my arm. "Do you like him?"

My pulse flickered. Did I? Yeah, sort of...yes, I fucking did. Who was I kidding? "I don't know."

With his eyes growing wide, Milo grabbed my arm and hauled me to the back of the stage. "What the hell is wrong with you? If you don't want him, can I have him then?"

I snapped my brows down. "No." Planting my hands on my hips, I flashed him a glare. "I thought there was some guy you were crushing on?"

"So? He's uh, not available...right now." He pursed his lips, then lifted his chin. "For all intents and purposes, I'm single."

"You cannot have Jeremy." Heat flared in my chest. Why was I getting so angry? At Milo of all people?

"Woah, dudes. What the hell is going on back here?" Caleb strolled to us, looking us both over. "Lover's quarrel?"

"Something like that." I flicked a glance at Caleb, then focused on Milo and shifted my weight. "Milo thinks he can hook up with my bodyguard."

"What?" Caleb barked out a laugh. "You two are fighting over Jeremy?"

I slapped my hand over Caleb's mouth and scanned the stage behind him. "Ssh. He might hear you." God, I was a hot mess. This was not me. Jeremy was fucking with my normally calm and collected personality.

Caleb chuckled underneath my palm, then grabbed my hand from his mouth. "Dude, he's pushing the cart out to the truck, relax."

I breathed in deeply. "Oh, sorry." I rubbed the back of my neck. "What am I going to do if Axel's right and the guy is questioning himself and he's sleeping in my bedroom and I..." Dropping my mouth open, I stared at Caleb. "And I like him?"

"You're going to test the waters and see what happens." Caleb turned his gaze on Milo. "Do you like him, too?"

Milo gave me a sly smile. "No, I just wanted to make Gabe see the light." He shrugged and patted my shoulder. "It worked."

"Yeah, it sure did." Damn, Milo. Tricky little bastard. "Let's get this gear packed up so I can go home and figure my shit out." I freed a heavy sigh. Now my dick was on high alert.

WE UNPACKED the last of the gear into the practice room at the band house and everyone hugged and said their goodbyes. Milo, Silas, and Cash retired to their bedrooms, leaving me alone with Jeremy. I was sure they were all leaving us alone as soon as possible on purpose. I opened the refrigerator. "Want a water?" I grabbed one for myself.

Jeremy leaned his ass against the kitchen island counter. "Yeah, sure. I think I already drank my weight in water at the bar, but what's a little more?"

I glanced at him. "Beer instead? You can't always be on duty." I set my water on the counter and plucked a beer out of the fridge, then snicked it open. "Here." I handed it to him. I wasn't going to give him time to say *no*. Maybe a beer would open him up a little.

"Thanks." He took a few gulps. "Damn, that's good." He twisted the can in his hands, gazing at it.

I stepped to him and leaned up against the counter next to him. "So, weird night, huh?" I flicked a peek at him. Maybe he'd come out and tell me what he was feeling and the real reason he freaked out and ran to the bathroom.

"Yeah, it was weird all right." He drank more beer down, then faced me, his hip resting against the counter, his gaze pinned on my mouth. After raking his teeth over his lower lip, he said, "I have to admit, I've never been around that many queer men before."

"Oh?" I sipped my water. "Did it make you uncomfortable?"

"No." He shook his head, his brows knitting. "I suppose I expected it might, but it seemed natural. Like they all behaved the way any other couple would, and it was no big deal." His gaze followed the movement of his free hand, sliding across the counter until his thumb rested against my pinky finger.

The heat of his finger tingled through my hand. Should I move my pinky, maybe tangle it in his thumb? That would be a clear sign, wouldn't it? "It probably helped that most everyone who comes to see us play knows we're a queer band." My breath caught. Shit, I forgot to say *mostly* in that sentence. I studied him. "And uh, so we don't typically get assholes giving us shit at our gigs." My pulse hammered in my chest. Had I just outed myself? "And maybe um...maybe that made you more comfortable with it?" Was I making any sense?

He brushed his thumb over my pinky finger, tilting his head. "Yeah, guess so." He drank more beer. "Your band is really good." He inched closer to me, his gaze meeting mine, then dipping to my mouth again.

Heat flared over my skin and my cock lengthened in my jeans. Holy fuck. All he had to do was look at me like that and barely touch me and I was about to implode. It was time to be direct. "Um, Jeremy, you know it's completely natural to question your sexuality at times."

He glided his hand over mine and held it. "Yeah?" His gaze

darted to our joined hands, then back to me, searching my face. "You're not moving your hand." His throat bobbed with a hard swallow. "In my mind, that means one of two things. Either you're really comfortable with guys touching you because of how your friends behave, or you're queer, too." He wrinkled his brows. "Which is it?"

Gazing deeply into his darkened, brown eyes, my heart thundered in my ears. It didn't matter anymore if he knew. "Jeremy, I'm gay." My breath hitched and quickened.

He nodded, picking my hand up off the counter. "Thought so." He kissed my knuckles, his gaze affixed to mine. "Hoped so." He parted his lips, his breath as fast as mine. "I'm not really happy you felt like you had to lie to me." He clenched his jaw for a heartbeat. "But I'm more concerned about me right now. I'm...I'm confused." His gaze locked on my mouth. "I-I want to kiss you. But I've never kissed a guy before." He wetted his lips. "Do you, do you want—"

Closing the gap, I pressed my lips to his, yanking my hand free and wrapping it around the nape of his neck, holding him in place. No more thinking.

A soft moan freed from his throat, and he hooked his arms around my waist, our hard cocks grinding through the denim of our jeans.

I glided my tongue across the seam of his lips, and he opened, our tongues tangling in a carnal dance. A spark of sensation flickered through my body. Holy hell, I wanted him. Fuck my father and this stupid situation. Jeremy was all hard flexing muscle against me, strong and unforgiving. I deserved to have him if he wanted me. And right now, it was clear he did.

EIGHT
JEREMY

I lost myself in the firm press of Gabe's lips against my own, in our scratchy stubble, the heat of it and the maleness of it. It was so different than anything I'd ever experienced. I pushed him back against the counter, my mouth slanting over his, claiming him again and again. My hips thrust of their own accord, seeking friction on my aching dick.

He freed a soft gasp and broke the kisses, then bit and nibbled down my chin, his fingers kneading up my chest to tease a nipple. "Oh, fuck." Pleasure rolled through me, pulsing my cock, and dribbling pre-cum into my underwear. I tipped my head back. He knew things about the male body I could only imagine.

As sensation swelled in my gut and my balls tightened, I pushed his head from my neck. "Stop, wait." Fuck, he was going to make me cum in my jeans, standing here in the kitchen, like a teenager. I hadn't bargained on kissing a man being that much of a turn on. Maybe it was because I'd buried it for so long.

Panting, he flicked his gaze to mine, his pupils blown and

lips red and swollen, his hair a mess. "Are you okay? Too fast?" He bit his lip.

"I'm okay. Just, yeah, maybe too fast." What the hell did I want? I studied his face. *Him.* I wanted him. "Can we go into your bedroom?" I stepped away from him.

"Oh..." He freed a choked chuckle and raked a hand through his disheveled bangs. "Of course. Guess I was too caught up in the moment." He snatched my hand and led me down the hallway into his bedroom, then shut the door behind us and faced me, placing his hands on my shoulders. "Listen. It's late and we both might not be of the right mind to be making smart decisions right now. Are you sure you want to do this?" His face was lit by the outside streetlight streaming in through the window over his bed.

I glanced at his bed. "What is it we're going to do?" He wasn't talking about fucking me in the ass, was he? *That,* I was not ready for. But more kissing? Yeah.

"Whatever you want. If you want to stop, that's fine. If you don't..." With a half smile, he bit his lower lip. "We could continue?" He focused on my mouth. "You can tell me to stop at any point and I will. I know it's your first time and I'd hate to spoil it for you." Creasing his forehead, his gaze met mine. "Just tell me what you want. I'm all yours."

My heart swooned. Oh, holy hell. Yeah, that was exactly what I'd wanted all night, for him to be *all* mine. It wasn't just a physical attraction. "Let's get on the bed and kiss some more, okay?"

"Yeah, sure." He climbed onto the bed and lay on his back, then bit at his thumbnail, watching me.

I glanced at my cot, folded up at the foot of the bed. Probably wasn't needing that tonight. Or ever? I crept over the bed to lie on top of him and propped up on my elbows, chest to chest, hip to hip, his hard, hot dick pressed to mine. My body was bigger than his. Would I crush him? But I'd been on top of women before and they weren't crushed. Why was my brain going there? I gazed down at his gorgeous face, brushing my thumb across his high cheek bone. "You're um...you're beautiful." Was that the right thing to say to a guy? I winced.

"Thanks, so are you." He gazed deeply into my eyes. "I have to admit, I never thought in a million years this would be happening."

"Yeah, me neither." I chuckled softly. I wasn't going to analyze this tonight. I'd have all day tomorrow to pick it apart if I had to. I lowered down and covered his lips in a deep kiss, sliding my tongue inside his mouth and tasting him once again. My dick twitched and I rocked my hips. I *was* going to come with him tonight, that was a given. And I couldn't wait to see him come undone.

With a soft groan, he slid his hands down my back and cupped the globes of my ass, pushing his hard cock against mine. He flicked and glided his tongue inside my mouth.

What would his tongue feel like on other parts of me? Pleasure pulsed my dick. More, I needed so much more. I broke our kisses and bit softly at his neck, then sucked on his earlobe.

Arching his head back, he gasped and shivered under me, his fingers digging into my ass. "Jeremy, oh God, can I touch you?" he asked in a deep rasp.

"Please do." I licked, sucked, and nibbled my way down his neck, burying my face in his skin and breathing him in. His musky scent shuddered through me. Again, so different from what I was used to, but so intoxicating.

"Roll to the side." He captured my mouth in a deep kiss as we shifted to our sides together, then snuck his hand to my fly and unfastened my jeans.

My breath hitched and my stomach clenched. Was he

going to jerk me off? Should I return the favor? My gaze met his, his eyelids hooded. "Can I uh...Can I?"

He gave me a swift nod, then lifted the edge of his lips. "Please do." After sliding his hand into my boxer briefs, he wrapped his fingers around my shaft and looked down, his breath growing ragged, then stroked.

Sensation wound tightly inside me and spun up my spine. "Oh, fuck." I snuck my lower lip between my teeth, watching his hand work my cock, sliding his thumb over the tip to spread a bead of pre-cum. He knew what he was doing. But of course he did, he had a dick, too. Pleasure jolted up my spine. I wasn't going to let myself think about who else he might have done this with.

He tipped his head up and crushed my lips in heated kisses, his tongue tangling with mine, soft moans floating out of him.

Slowly, I glided my hand down his chest, then to his jeans and unzipped them. Was I really going to do this? Yes, yes, I was. I slid my fingers under his silky briefs, then palmed his solid cock, my finger pads roaming the soft skin over hard flesh. It was similar, but not the same as mine, thicker at the base maybe, the head more flared. As I wrapped my hand around his dick and stroked, it jerked in my palm, and he gasped. A shudder of arousal swept over me. I broke our kisses and panted against his shoulder. Any more of that and I'd come.

"You okay? He kissed my cheek, quickening his pace over my sensitive cock.

"Yeah." I pumped his dick as quick as he pumped mine. "You close?"

"Oh God, yeah." He rocked his hips into my palm and groaned, another shudder rolling over his body. His cock jerked and pre-cum slicked my palm.

Pleasure surged over me, throwing me off the edge. I

gasped. "Fuck, coming." With intense waves of sensation, my cum spurted between us and dribbled onto his fingers.

"Coming, too." He gritted his teeth a second, holding his breath, then his face tensed, and he released moan after moan, his cock pulsing in my hand. Hot ribbons of cum shot through my hand to land on my shirt.

As it all slowed, he brought his hand up to his mouth and licked my cum from his palm and fingers, then rolled to his back. "Holy, shit, I needed that."

I stared at him, then held my hand to my face. Was I supposed to lick it off, too? My girlfriends never did that. They always got some tissue for me to clean up with.

He did a double take of me. "What's uh...you freaking out?" He shifted sideways. "Jeremy?"

"No, I'm not freaking out." I flicked my tongue at a blob of cum on my finger. The bitter tang of him hung in my mouth. It wasn't terrible. My gaze met his.

He rolled his lips. "You don't have to do that. I just like to." He hooked a brow at me.

"It's um, not bad. I don't know." I licked another blob. "It's salty." Now I was being stupid. I should stop. "Can you hand me a tissue?"

"Sure." With a soft chuckle, he tugged a tissue out of a box on his nightstand. "It's an acquired taste." He wiped the cum from my fingers. "Don't push yourself. I don't want you to freak out on me. We're sort of stuck together no matter what and I don't want it to be awkward." He tossed the tissue to the floor, then pulled out a few more and handed them to me.

"I'm not going to freak out and it won't get awkward." I cleaned myself up, then threw my tissue on the floor. At least right now I didn't think that would happen. I snuck a peek at him as he wiped himself, then fastened his jeans. My heart warmed. No, I still liked him after what we did, maybe even more. That much I knew.

"Are you going to break the cot out?" He lay on his back and stared up at the ceiling, then turned his gaze on me. "I mean, you don't have to. I wouldn't mind if you...if you..."

"Can I sleep in your bed with you?" That's what he was asking, right? I cupped his cheek and leaned in. I still wanted more of him.

"Yeah, you can." He pressed a quick kiss on my lips, then shimmied off the bed. "Let's get ready for bed." He picked up the soiled tissues, then opened the door and left.

With a sigh, I rolled to my back, the rush of running water filtering in from the bathroom in the hallway. I had no idea what I was supposed to do. Were things different with guys? If he was a girl, I'd give him some space and wait until he was done. But he's a guy. Should I go in and brush my teeth with him? Fuck, I was overthinking *everything*. I planted the heel of my hand on my forehead. I didn't like him leaving right after what we'd done. Did he even like me, or was this a hookup for him? Shit. Should I ask?

He strolled into the room with a grin on his face. "Bathroom is free."

"Yeah, okay." I climbed off the bed and made my way through the hallway to clean up.

A FEW MINUTES LATER, I walked into the bedroom.

Gabe lay on top of his bed in only his white briefs, the outline of his dick on full display in the light from his nightstand.

I took a hard swallow as desire shivered up my spine. Damn, I could probably go again already. Usually, he'd have his pajama bottoms on. I guess we were now at the sleep in our underwear together level.

After closing the door, I shucked my jeans off and pulled my shirt over my head, then tossed them in the laundry basket in the corner, my dick growing hard in my boxer briefs. Fuck, my dick had found something new, and it didn't know when to stop. As I turned and walked to the bed, I clasped my hands over my groin. Would he notice? And if he did, were we going again?

With a quick smile, he threw the covers down, slid inside them, then patted the mattress next to him. "All ready?"

"Yeah." I climbed between the sheets and lay on my back, his warm body so close to mine.

"Jeremy, talk to me. You look like you're freaking out." Lying on his side, he propped his cheek in his hand and edged closer to me, placing his palm on my stomach over the covers.

"I'm not freaking out." Was I? I turned to face him. "I'm just all up in my head. My brain is going a little crazy. I don't know how to act." My gaze raked over his gorgeous face, the plump lips I'd been kissing, his light blue eyes, focused on me. "I mean, I don't know how guys act when they're together like this."

"Oh, well, let me show you." With a smirk, he leaned over me to turn off his nightstand lamp, pressed a soft kiss on my lips, then snuggled into my side, resting his head on my shoulder, and throwing an arm and a leg around me. "How's this?"

Warmth crept through my heart, and I kissed his head, then brushed my fingers over his soft curls. "This is good. Really good." It felt right. This pretty much made up for the fact that he ditched me to go clean up. I held his arm over my chest and stared into the dark of the room toward the ceiling. "Should we talk about things?"

He nudged his face into my chest, then kissed it. "What sort of things did you want to talk about?"

"I don't know, but I feel like there are things we need to discuss." I pressed my lips together. I wasn't going to ask him how he felt about me, I was not. It was too soon. "How do you feel about me?" My heart jolted. *Fuck, I'm so stupid.* I winced.

"I like you." He breathed in deeply. "How do you feel about me?" He skimmed his finger pads over my chest.

My pulse pattered through the warmth flooding my heart. "I like you, too."

His fingers stopped. "We should get some sleep. We can talk more tomorrow, okay?" He squeezed me. "I have some papers to work on, but we'll definitely talk."

I nodded. He was right. Things might look different in the morning and hopefully in a good way. I shut my eyes and drifted off, breathing in the floral scent of his shampoo.

THE NEXT MORNING, I fluttered my eyes open as a sliver of sunshine peeked through the middle of the striped curtains on the window over the bed. During the night, we'd shifted and now Gabe's warm body was pressed up against my chest and I'd wrapped myself around him from behind, my morning wood nicely lodged against his ass. I nuzzled his neck. I could get used to this, waking up with him every day. Last night, I'd wondered how I'd feel in the morning and now I had my answer. I still liked him, still wanted him, maybe even more. How I'd shut this side of myself down before Gabe, I didn't know. But I'm glad I'd finally let it out, with him.

Gabe stirred and mumbled, then turned in my hold and gazed lazily at me. "Hey, how'd you sleep?" He rubbed his eyes, then focused on me.

"I slept well. You?" My dick pressed into his hip and ached. I was ready to go again.

"Well? Seems to me you might have slept hard." With a smirk, he rolled toward me and cupped my balls, then rubbed over my shaft through my underwear.

Need coiled in my gut. I snuck my hand down and fondled his also firm cock. "Looks like we both slept hard." I curled my lips. Yeah, we were going again.

"Want to take care of that?" He focused on my lips, then came in for a hungry kiss, his tongue tangling with mine, then he rolled over top of me, our cocks slotting together, and rutted against me.

I moaned and gripped the flexing muscles of his ass. Heat flared over my skin and pleasure pulsed my dick. This was different, more intense, without clothes on.

Through heavy breaths, he said, "Let's take our briefs off. Is that okay?" He rose up on his elbows and gazed down at me, cupping my cheeks, his pupils wide inside his light blue eyes, his blond curls falling around his gorgeous face.

"Yeah, I think that's preferable." We shifted and both skimmed our underwear off. What would we do this time? Were blow jobs on the menu? Was I ready for that? I'd let him lead the way. I had a feeling he wasn't going to rush me into anything. I could trust him.

He opened up his nightstand drawer and pulled out lube, then climbed on top of me again. "Everything's better with lube." He chuckled.

"If you say so." I watched him slather the lube on his fingers, then he twisted his hips to the side and reached down to slick our cocks.

"Now, we frot." He gave me a coy grin as he claimed my mouth in desperate kisses and rocked his hips, our hot cocks gliding easily against each other.

As sensation tingled through my body, I groaned into the kisses and held him, one hand on his ass and the other on his back. Holy hell, this felt amazing.

With a moan, his body trembled, and he broke the kisses. "Fuck, I'm close already. You?" His gaze met mine and his brows tensed, then he bit his lower lip and released it.

"Almost there." I thrust harder, faster against him. Yeah, I could be right there in a second. The sweet edge of climax teased me. I wasn't sure I wanted it to end already. "Can you hold out a little longer?" I nuzzled into his neck and nibbled the soft skin.

"Yeah, but fuck, you make it hard." His rhythm faltered and he shuddered. "Oh, God. So fucking good." He held my shoulders and placed his forehead on mine, his hips rocking and dick twitching against mine.

Nope, that was it. Intense pleasure sparked up my spine and my balls drew up. "Coming, oh, fuck." I lost myself in the waves of sensation cresting over me, curling my toes, gasping with each one. My hot cum spurted between us, slicking our stomachs even more.

With a sharp cry, he thrust hard against me, held it, then rocked a few times more, his cum mixing with mine. As it slowed, he fell over me, lying his head on my shoulder, taking deep breaths. "What a way to wake up, huh?" He giggled softly.

"Yeah." I held him to my chest, both my arms wrapped around his back, then kissed his head. Memories of last night flickered through my mind. He'd been so worried about me freaking out. Was he still? "I'm not going to freak out, by the way. In case you were wondering."

"Yeah?" He circled his fingers over my shoulder, leaving a light tickle. "That's good. I was afraid you might wake up, have a *what the fuck did I do last night* moment and run from the house with all your shit."

I smiled and brushed my palm over his soft hair. "No, your dad would kill me. I have a job to do here, remember?" My breath caught. Fuck...Kevin. Having sex with his son was not in the job description. I'd only meant the job comment as a joke.

Lifting onto his elbows, his gaze met mine. "My dad cannot know about this. Okay?" His gaze darted between my eyes.

I knitted my brows. "Yeah, of course." But what was *this*? "We need to talk, Gabe. Maybe we should get cleaned up and do that first." I had so many questions and we had to figure out how to move forward and not jeopardize his safety and my... holy shit, my heart. My chest tightened. Yeah, my heart was involved now. Did he feel the same? He'd said he liked me last night, so there was that.

He placed a long, deep kiss on my lips. "Yeah, we need to talk." He brushed his thumb over my cheek. "We'll work this out, okay?"

Gazing deeply into his eyes, I said, "Yeah?" So maybe he did feel the same.

"Yeah. I haven't uh..." His gaze dipped, then found mine again, his brows wrinkling. "I haven't let myself get close like this with anyone. This isn't a hookup for me." He worried his lower lip. "I-I don't know if it's the fact that we've spent every single moment together for days now, or what, but you got to me, okay?"

I nodded, fixating on him. Softly, I said, "You got to me, too." My heart bloomed with warmth.

"Okay, then. Clean up, grab some cereal, and meet back here?" He lifted his brows. "Because I'm pretty sure the rest of the house is up and hanging out in the kitchen." He smirked. "They're going to know something happened just by looking at us and holy fuck, are we in for it."

"In for it how?" I tugged the corner of my mouth up. He was so close to his friends. It was a pretty cool thing.

"They, as in Silas especially, are going to tease the shit out of us. Well, me." He dipped his head, his shoulders shaking with a soft laugh. "God, the horn blower jokes."

"What is that about?" I tilted my head over my pillow. Finally, some answers at least on that front.

He lifted his head. "I typically hook up with guys from band and yeah, they're usually trumpet players, trombone, whatever. There are a lot of wind instruments in a band. So—"

"So, like Oliver? You hooked up with him?" My chest pinched. That's why I hadn't liked him. I had sensed it.

"Yeah, like Oliver. Silas and Axel call the guys horn blowers." He chuckled. "It's so idiotic and juvenile, but that's what they do," he said, "It's like they can't help themselves."

"I get it. Don't worry. I can handle a little razzing." I squeezed him.

He planted a quick kiss on my mouth. "Okay, let's do this." He flung the covers off us, then climbed from the bed, handed me a few tissues, and wiped himself off.

AFTER QUICK SHOWERS and getting dressed in t-shirts and sweats, I followed Gabe into the kitchen to grab a bowl of cereal. I could use a little more than that, but it's all they had in the house for breakfast food. I tagged his back. "Hey, let's go shopping and get some eggs and bacon and stuff."

"Yeah, sure." He rounded the corner and stepped into the main room.

Milo sat on the couch with a bowl of Frosted Flakes, watching a show on the television while Cash and Silas sat at the dinette, eating what was probably left over pizza.

Silas twisted in his chair. "Well, well, well. Look who's up?" He smirked at Gabe, then his smirk dropped. "Holy shit." He stood up, staring from Gabe to me as I grabbed Gabe's hand.

I was going to own this. No way around it. "Good morning, Silas, Cash." I shifted my gaze to Milo. "Milo." I ticked my head at them all.

All their gazes locked on our entwined hands and Cash clapped. "Finally. Our plan worked."

"I knew it." Gabe huffed. "You three..." He pointed at each of them, then smiled at me. "Did me a solid." He squeezed my hand.

"You two have been eye fucking each other since he broke through our door. It was bound to happen." Silas planted a hand on his thigh. "He doesn't like, play the—"

"No, I don't play any instruments." I freed a sharp chuckle, then kissed Gabe's cheek. "Let's get our breakfast and head back." We had things to talk about.

"Yeah." Gabe led me into the kitchen and poured us both Frosted Flakes. "Almost out, Silas. Do you work today?" He glanced behind him.

"Yeah. I'll get some more." Silas ate a bite of his pepperoni pizza.

"Can you pick up some bacon and eggs and stuff for toast, too?" I poured milk onto my cereal from the carton sitting on the counter. These guys needed to start having proper breakfasts around here. "I'll pay you back."

"Don't worry about it. I get a decent discount and I'll buy enough for us all to eat." He arched a brow at Cash, then flicked a finger at him. "I know."

"Good, we'll finally have something besides cold cereal or pizza for breakfast." Cash turned to Milo. "Did you hear that, Milo?"

"I did. But I like the Frosted Flakes." He spooned cereal into his mouth.

"What if I made you some cinnamon toast?" Cash wiggled his brows at Milo.

Milo twisted on the couch, his eyes twinkling. "Oh, could you?"

"I will." He tapped Silas' arm. "I'll send you a list."

"Great." Silas tore off another bite of his pizza and rolled his eyes at Cash. "You two are getting lethal and you haven't even moved in yet."

"I know, isn't it great?" Cash gave him a broad smile.

"Let's get back into the bedroom before they notice we're gone." Gabe tagged my shoulder, poured us both coffees, added some creamer, then snuck through the room with me following.

NINE
GABE

I sat on my bed with my back against the pillows and the headboard, while Jeremy sat beside me, both of us shoveling cereal into our mouths, our coffees resting on my nightstand. "So, you said we have things to talk about. Go ahead."

"Why doesn't your dad know you're gay?" He set his cereal in his lap, then leaned over me to grab his coffee and took a sip.

"Bringing out the big guns, huh?" With a shake of my head, I swallowed down my food. "When my mom found out I was gay, we decided it would be best not to tell him. He has certain...well, ideas of what the perfect son should be like, and he thinks I'm the perfect son. Being gay doesn't fit that scenario."

"But he's going to find out at some point, right? I mean, you can't hide it your whole life." He twisted his lips. "Right?"

I shrugged and ate more cereal. "Yeah, I suppose. But he's..." I set my spoon in my bowl and placed it on the nightstand, then picked up my coffee. Was it wrong to ruin Jeremy's nice-guy impression of my dad? "He's not always the guy you work with in the office. He can be very intimidating. It's easier for my mom if I stay in the closet with him." There, that was about as sugarcoated as I could make it.

"You said your mom found out. What happened?" He sipped his coffee, raising his brows.

"She caught me with a guy out in the stables. You want to know more detail than that?" I studied him. He'd seemed pretty protective of me last night and I wasn't sure it was all for the job he was supposed to be doing. At least, I hoped not.

He let out a soft huff. "No, that's enough." He pursed his lips. "Wasn't a horn blower, was it?" The edge of his lips twitched.

"It was." I pinched the bridge of my nose and chuckled. God, I had a type, didn't I? But Jeremy blew that out of the water. Maybe that was why he got under my skin so easily.

He drank more coffee. "I take it your mom was okay with it? Except the part about your dad finding out."

"Yeah, she was cool with it." I looked him over. "Tell me about your dad. What was he like?"

His eyes grew wide. "Oh, he uh, well, he was a detective. It's funny, because where I think your dad wants you to follow in his footsteps, and you don't, I *did* want to follow in my dad's footsteps. I idolized him. He was..." He hung his head and bit his lip. "He was always there for me, my rock." His voice cracked. "Fuck, sorry." He swiped at his eyes.

I snaked an arm around his shoulders and rested my fore-head on the side of his head. "No, it's okay. How long ago did you lose him?" Shit, how would I feel when my dad passed? I'd always thought I wouldn't care, but maybe I would?

"Almost two years ago." He breathed in a ragged breath. "I was actually pretty scrawny growing up. Didn't hit a good growth spurt until I was in high school. So, I used to get picked on by the bigger boys."

"Shit, you did?" I brushed my fingers over his shoulders.

Nobody dared touch me, probably because of my family's wealth and my dad's reputation.

"Yeah. My dad started me in BJJ, you know, Brazilian—"

"Jiu-Jitsu, yeah." I lifted my head from his, my heart aching for him. There was so much more to him then I'd thought. "Go on."

"Anyways, he enrolled me in classes at an academy and he did them with me. We learned together." He choked out a laugh. "Eventually I got bigger and better than him. That's when he'd said I was ready to be a man." He pressed his lips together. "I think I was about nineteen. I didn't tell him I thought I already was a man." He gave a slight shake of his head, then drank more coffee. "When I started working for your dad, there were things about him that reminded me of my dad." His gaze met mine.

I took a hard swallow. Fuck, how could I tell him the truth about the man and destroy his vision of my dad? "Yeah?"

"Yeah." He cupped my cheek, his gaze flicking between my eyes. "Gabe, he's not going to have a problem with you being gay."

I drew a deep inhale. "Let's agree to disagree on that point right now. Remember, I have my mom to think about, too." This situation was really fucked right now. "I have to ask you, is it a big problem for you to keep what we're doing a secret from him?" I worried my lower lip. Shit, were we even going to keep doing this if it was? My chest pinched. I'd had a taste of him. How could I not have more?

"Well, he might have a problem with his hired gun having sex with his son. That's the part I'm not sure about." He cocked his head and lifted the edge of his lips. "I mean, I'm getting paid to be here to protect you, not uh, what did you call it? Frot?"

I chuckled. "Yeah, a paid frotter. That's what you are." I couldn't help myself. I scratched my brow. "So, we both agree not to say anything to my dad about this, but for different reasons."

"Yeah, pretty much." He nodded, then sipped his coffee.

"So, we *are* going to continue...doing this?" I snuck a peek at him. I had to be sure we were on the same page.

"I certainly hope so." He placed a warm hand on my bare thigh. "I don't know how we could stop at this point." He gazed deeply into my eyes. "I don't want to go back to the cot."

"No, that would be, that would be completely uncalled for." I wrapped my hand around his, on my thigh, then drank some coffee. "I like sleeping with you way too much."

"Besides, if I'm in bed with you and someone does try to kidnap you, it would be even harder for them to get you." He let out a soft snort.

"Is that what the threat was?" I squeezed his hand. Would he tell me more now?

"No, that's not what the threat was. I may have fibbed a little bit earlier to get you to comply. Don't worry about it. We have it handled." He kissed my cheek. "You need to focus on your studies. Your first year is the most important. Or that's what Kevin says."

I nodded with a grin. It was weird hearing him call my dad by his first name. But he did work for him. "Yeah, okay. I'll let you worry about it. I have faith in you." I gave him a warm smile.

"So, I'd wanted to know why you lied to me about being straight, but I guess I know now." He balanced his coffee next to his thigh on the bed and picked up his cereal. "You thought I was going to be a tattle tale." He ate the last of his food.

"Yeah, I did." I nodded. "But you understand now, with the situation as it is. Right?" My gaze met his. "I'm sorry, by the way."

"Apology accepted. Don't lie to me about anything else. Okay?" His grin waned as he focused on me. "I mean it."

I widened my eyes. "I won't. I promise." We were a thing now, as Axel would say. I'd never had a thing, but I was willing to try with him. Leaning over, I placed a long kiss on his lips. "You deserve better."

"Thank you." He closed his eyes for a second, then his grin returned. "Don't worry, I'll keep you safe."

My heart bloomed with emotion. Holy shit, no one had ever said that to me and with such conviction. "I believe you."

AFTER OUR BREAKFAST TALK, I decided to get started on analyzing the cases that were due this week for my classes. Silas had gone to work, Cash had gone home, and Milo was off with a friend somewhere. Lucky him, having an intern job at a marketing company, so he had his weekends off. As I typed on my laptop at the dinette, Jeremy sat on the couch, his own laptop open on his lap.

"What are you doing?" I stopped typing and rested my cheek in my palm.

"Looking through the camera videos from the house." He clicked on a few things, peering into his laptop screen. "Hmmm..."

I rose from my chair. "Hmmm, what?" I stalked to him with my hands clasped behind my back, then stopped at the couch and peeked over his shoulder. He'd magnified an image of the front of a nondescript black sedan parked on the street. "What's that?" I pointed to his screen.

"Don't know. Maybe something, maybe nothing." He switched to a new tab on his browser and the back end of a black sedan was zoomed in. "Do you recognize this car from the neighborhood?"

Shaking my head, I said, "No. But then I probably wouldn't recognize any of the neighbor's cars anyways."

"Uh-huh." He clicked on another tab and the same car showed up.

"What kind of car is that?" I narrowed my eyes and tilted my head. "A Mercedes?" The emblem on the hood of the car gleamed in the streetlamp.

"Yeah, an S-class, I think. It's been parked in various places all around the house. Looks like there might be two guys sitting in it, but it's hard to tell with all the dark window tint. And there's never a good shot of the license plate." He clicked again, pulling up a blurry image of the car driving off at a high rate of speed. He shut his laptop. "I better call Kevin."

I rounded the couch and dropped in next to him. "Jeremy, do you really think some mobsters are staking out the house?" My pulse kicked up. "Are we in danger here? Should I tell the guys?"

"Let me call Kevin first. I don't want to do something that would give away that we know about them." He plucked his cell phone from the coffee table, then dialed and pressed the phone to his ear. "Don't make a sound. He's not going to want you to hear this conversation."

"Okay." I sank into the couch and stared ahead of me. Not only was Jeremy protecting me, he trusted me more than my father did, apparently. Now, this thing felt real.

"Hey, Kevin, it's Jeremy. I've got a visual on some suspects in a car." He inhaled deeply while my father's voice murmured through the phone. "Yeah, the car looks like some sort of black Mercedes S class. Can't see the plate." He nodded. "Uh-huh." He chanced a peek at me. "All right."

I gnawed my lower lip. What I'd give to hear both sides of

this conversation. But we couldn't risk having him on the speaker of Jeremy's phone and hearing me.

"Yeah, I'll make sure of it. Talk to you soon." He hung up the call, then tossed his phone onto the couch cushion next to him. "Well, sounds like he's seen the same type of car up at his house on the cameras there." He pressed his lips together. "I think it's time I started wearing my gun."

"Are you serious?" I dropped my jaw open. This couldn't be happening. "What should I tell the guys?"

"I don't think they're in any danger. The threats are on your family." He turned on the couch, lifting a leg between us, then grabbed my hand. "Don't worry. We'll be safe here. We have the security system and I'll keep a close eye on the cameras."

"But I need to tell Silas and Milo." My gaze searched his face. "What if these mobsters or whatever they are decide to use them to get to me?"

"I don't know." He shrugged. "Your dad was adamant about not doing anything differently. He doesn't want them to know we've noticed them."

"But why? Why aren't we calling the police?" I furrowed my brows.

He dipped his head and kissed my knuckles. "You know as well as I there's nothing the police can do right now. Sitting in a car outside a house is not a crime. The threats your father got were veiled." He squeezed my hand. "My background in criminal justice taught me that when someone says, *you better watch yourself*, it's pretty different than, *I'm coming to your house right now to kill you*." He studied me. "You get what I'm saying?"

I nodded. "Yeah, guess so." I scratched my cheek, digesting everything he'd just said. "So, you really don't know what these guys are up to."

"No, we don't." He stood up and freed my hand. "I'm going to get my gun. You can let Silas know that at least, so he's not triggered by it when he gets home." He strode off to the hallway leading to the bedrooms.

"Yeah." Holy shit. How the hell was I supposed to focus on my studying now? Damn it. I fished my cell phone out of my pocket. I had to let Silas know what was happening. Maybe he'd be happier staying with Cash.

GABE

> We're seeing some very mobster-like cars parked around the house, so Jeremy will be packing when you get home. Just a warning.

The three dots blinked at me.

SILAS

> What the fuck? Are you serious? Is it safe to even be there?

GABE

> That's what I was wondering, but Jeremy thinks it is with all the security we installed.

Warmth filled my chest. Plus, I had Jeremy here with me.

SILAS

> Okay. I'll be sticking around the house then. Just in case you both need me.

GABE

> No, you don't have to do that. Just do whatever you'd normally do. My dad doesn't want to tip off whoever this is that we're on to them.

SILAS

> Fine. I have a lady here with a stupid return.
> We'll talk later.

With a sigh, I set my phone on my lap. How would Milo take this news?

The door to the garage flung open in the kitchen and Milo sauntered in, scruffing his brown, wavy hair, his Hello Kitty t-shirt stretched across his chest and his skinny jeans hugging his narrow hips. "Oh, hey, Gabe."

"Sit down. I need to talk to you." I patted the couch cushion next to me. Yeah, I might be up all night getting the case analysis and reading done for my classes.

"Sure." He opened the refrigerator and pulled out a bottled water. "Can I get you anything?" He turned and scanned the room. "Where's Jeremy?"

"No and he's uh..." I flicked my gaze to the hallway, sensing movement.

Jeremy strolled out with his handgun holstered to his hip. "Hey, Milo." He threw a glance at me.

Milo's gaze stopped on Jeremy's hip. "Shit, what happened?" His mouth fell open.

"Come over here." I patted the couch next to me again. Hopefully he wouldn't freak out too badly.

"Okay." He stepped to the couch and sat beside me, keeping an eye on Jeremy.

Jeremy dropped in on the other side of me. "No need to worry, Milo. I'm just being cautious. I saw a suspicious vehicle in the video cameras on the house. We don't know if it's a coincidence or not, but I'm not taking any chances." He pursed his lips.

Milo twisted his bottle open, then sipped his water, his eyes round. "Okay, so can I start sleeping in your room with you guys?"

I wrapped an arm over his shoulders. "I don't think that's necessary." And at this point, I did *not* want to share a bed with Milo and Jeremy. Awkward...

"Let's think about this a minute. If someone were to break in here, the alarms would go off and they'd probably go straight into Gabe's room looking for him. Is that really where you want to be?" Jeremy's gaze met Milo's.

"Uh, guess not." He gave me a sheepish grin. "Sorry, Gabe."

"No problem. I think you and Silas are safe. And even then, we've got Jeremy here." I patted Jeremy's thigh. This was fucked up. Jeremy had training, but no real-world experience. Shit, I had to trust in him.

"What kind of a gun is that?" Milo narrowed his eyes, focusing on the gun.

Jeremy tapped the handle. "It's a Glock 22, same one law enforcement uses." He glanced at me. "I have a concealed carry holster and permit, too." He winced. "But that's not going to help us on campus."

"Let's not worry about that right now." I raked my shaky hand through my bangs, my throat tightening. Fuck, this whole thing was starting to stress me out.

"I'm sorry." Jeremy knitted his brows. "I need you to relax and get your studying done." He squeezed my thigh. "Can you do that?"

"I don't know." I blew out a ragged breath. "I'll try. Let's watch a funny show to take my mind off it. Then maybe..." I glanced at Milo, studying us.

"I'll make some popcorn. We can watch something together." With a wide grin, he jumped from the couch.

Damn, he knew just the thing to calm my nerves. I edged

into Jeremy's side. This thing with him was so new. How would it all work?

AFTER AN HOUR or so and a few episodes of Family Guy later, I was working on my case analysis with my headphones in at the dinette, while Jeremy watched television, paced to all the windows, checked the feed of our video cameras, and watched more TV.

Milo had gone into his bedroom to draw. He'd been working on some digital images on his computer for art class. The guy had an amazing set up in his room—huge, high definition monitors and drawing pads along with all the standard art supplies.

I sighed as I wrote the last bit on my contracts case analysis, then closed my laptop.

Jeremy, who'd been standing at the front window a moment ago, stepped up behind me and rubbed my shoulders. "You done?"

As the aching in my shoulders released, I moaned. "God that feels good, and yes, for today."

"How about we go out somewhere and get some dinner?" He slid out the chair next to mine and sat down, planting his forearms on the table.

"Shit, is it dinner time already?" I glanced at the clock on our stove. It was almost six. My stomach growled. "Yeah, but um...what about the mobsters?" My gaze met his.

He furrowed his brows. "What about them? We can't be holed up in here. If they're going to make a move, they'll make a move no matter where we are." He grabbed my hand, resting on the table. "I'm ready for them if they do." He lifted his chin.

"But I think they'll be less likely to do anything if we're out in public."

"Yeah, okay." I glanced around the room. "I don't know if we should leave Milo here alone." My chest tightened. This situation was a little scary.

"When does Silas get back?" He narrowed his eyes at me.

"Don't know." I slumped my shoulders. I felt like a damned prisoner.

Rapping sounded from the door.

"It's Cash." Milo waltzed from the hallway to the door and opened it.

"Hi, hun." Cash stepped inside and gave Milo a quick hug. "Don't you look adorable in that t-shirt."

"Thank you. I love the yellow jeans." Milo flicked at Cash's hip.

"Silas will be here any minute and he's hangry, so let's get some pizza ordered." Cash sashayed into the room, then stopped at Jeremy and held his fingers over his lips, his gaze darting to Jeremy's holstered gun. "Oh, Silas told me about the developments. Are you two joining us for pizza?"

Jeremy twisted his lips, then said, "No, I think Gabe and I are eating out." His gaze shifted to me. "Right?"

"Uh..." My friends all had each other and come to think of it, maybe removing me from the house was removing the threat from them. "Yeah, sure." I freed a soft breath.

"Good." Jeremy lifted from the table, taking my hand with him. "I just need to get my concealed carry holster and we'll go." He freed me and walked off down the hallway.

I chanced a peek at Cash, then Milo.

"How are you doing?" Cash squeezed my shoulder. "You've got to be at least a little scared."

"Yeah, I am. It's really freaky, to tell you the truth." I mean, how am I expected to have a normal life with this shit going on?" I scrubbed my hands over my face as my pulse quickened. Maybe getting out of here would help.

Jeremy walked out, wearing a loose t-shirt over his jeans. "All ready."

"Where is it?" I raked my gaze over his muscled body and stood up. This might be a first for me, going to dinner with someone wearing a gun. Though, this was Arizona and I'd seen people with guns all over the place, even in the damned grocery stores. There were more guns in the United States than there were people for fuck sakes.

"It's on my hip." He patted his side, slightly to the back. "Are you driving, or am I?"

"I'll drive." I strode to the kitchen and grabbed my keys off the counter. "We can decide where we want to go in the car."

TEN
JEREMY

I watched Gabe back his BMW out of the garage and into the street, did a quick scan of the cars in the neighborhood, then focused back on him. Things were messed up on multiple levels. One, he looked spooked and two, could I call going out to dinner with him a date? I mean, we'd done things together. "Are you okay?"

"Yeah. I have to be, right?" He glanced at me, then turned onto the street leading to the main boulevard. "Where do you want to go?" He rested his wrist over the top of the steering wheel.

"How about someplace in Tempe Marketplace?" The outdoor mall was always packed on a Saturday night, so it would be easy to lose someone if we were being followed. I looked at his hand, resting on his thigh. Should I take it? "Gabe, can this be uh...I mean, can we go out on a date?"

He stared at me a moment, his lips parting. "Uh, yeah, sure." His mouth curled into a soft grin. "You know, I don't date much. Well, at all. Just so you know." He snatched my hand from the center console and held it. "This will be the first real date I've had in...oh, a few years at least."

"Really?" He didn't look as spooked anymore. Bringing up the date thing was the right call. "Why haven't you dated?"

He turned the corner. "Oh, because dating leads to relationships and relationships lead to someone needing all my time and then my studies would suffer." Furrowing his brows, he threw a quick look at me. "Well, at least that's what I thought it would mean." He pulled into a parking lot. "How about The Keg? It's dark, has good food and seems like a place people go who are on dates." He chuckled and parked in a spot outside of the restaurant.

"Sure, I like that place." As he shut off the engine, I climbed out of the car and stretched. I wouldn't mention the last time I was here I *was* on a date with a woman Grant had set me up with. But that relationship had only lasted about two weeks. I couldn't get into her.

I followed Gabe through the parking lot, my gaze catching on the sway of his tight ass in his skinny jeans. I was supposed to watching for the bad guys, damn it. Shit, Grant. My heart jolted. What the hell would he think of me dating a guy? Let alone the client in this situation? What would I even say to him?

Gabe stopped and opened a heavy glass door tucked under a high metal awning and between two stone features on the building. "After you." He waved me in.

I stepped inside and perused the place, all dark woods and plush booths with low lit pendant lights falling down from the ceiling. I tapped Gabe's arm as he talked to the hostess. "Get a table where I can watch the door."

His breath caught, then he said, "How about that booth right there?" He pointed toward the center of the room.

"Certainly." She led us to the booth and handed us menus

as we slid into the bench seating. "Your server will be right with you."

Did I just ruin the mood by reminding him of the situation? I leaned over the table and the fake candle glowing in the center of it. "I'm sorry. I'm just being extra cautious, okay?"

"Yeah, I know. You take protecting me seriously." He scanned over his menu, then peeked at me from over the top.

"I do, actually." I roamed my gaze over him, his curly, messy hair, and plump lips. I'd never forgive myself if something did happen to him. And it wasn't because I was doing a job for Kevin. No, it was because I felt something for Gabe. Maybe even a lot.

"So, what are you going to order?" His attention shifted to his menu.

I looked over the dinner items. "Well, it is a steak place, so I'm going with the prime rib." I set my menu down. God, I'd love to have a glass of red wine with it, but I was perpetually on duty.

"Let's get the baked brie appetizer to share, okay?" As he placed his menu on the table, he leaned over and set his hand over mine. "Jeremy, have a beer or something. Please. You deserve it and it's Saturday night and we're on a date." He hooked a brow at me.

"Shit, okay." I blew out a breath. So much for being on duty. With a shake of my head, I grinned.

The server came by the table and took our orders, then left.

"So, what do people usually talk about on dates? I'm a little rusty." Gabe unrolled his black linen napkin and spread it out over his lap.

I had to think of something that wouldn't remind him of our situation. "I think they talk about themselves and their aspirations." That sounded stupid. But the alternatives of family and jobs wouldn't work.

Tilting his head, Gabe huffed a chuckle. "Okay, I'm a band nerd, and my aspiration is to be a good-guy lawyer."

I gave him my best smile. "Gabe, you're not a nerd. You're a drummer in a pop-punk band and I'm sure you'll use your skills in your dad's firm to better people's lives."

"So, you already know everything about me." He offered a soft grin.

The server dropped off our drinks. "The appetizer will be out shortly."

"Thanks." I cupped the bowl of my red wine glass and sipped my wine, the hint of cherries and the tang of tannin coating my throat. I moaned and shut my eyes for a moment. "Damn, that's good."

He eyed me. "Can I try it? I don't usually drink wine, only when I'm at my parents' house for dinner."

"Yeah, sure." I held my glass out to him. "I had a girlfriend who liked wine. She got me into it." Should I be talking about her with him?

"You did, huh?" He drank a bit of my wine, his brows tensing. "Yeah, that is good." He set the wine glass in front of me. "Tell me more about this girlfriend." He tented his fingers over the table, something I'd seen his father do a million times at his desk.

I studied him further. There were times I could totally tell he was Kevin's son. Did I do things like my father did, too? My heart ached. "We were together for two years while I was getting my bachelor's degree. We never moved in or anything, but we got along pretty well."

"Do you still talk to her?" He sipped his beer.

"Sometimes. We parted as friends." I brushed my fingers along the stem of my wine glass. "I see her posts on social media mostly and comment and stuff." I huffed a laugh. "She has a new boyfriend now."

"Good." Gabe tossed me a smirk and took my hand from my wine glass, wrapping our fingers together. "And that was the longest relationship you've had?" He skimmed his thumb over my knuckles.

His touch tingled up my arm. How was it that the smallest show of affection from him lit me up inside? "Yeah, that was the longest."

"How did it end? Like, why?" He rested his cheek in his hand, focusing on me.

"I don't know, really." I shrugged. "We sort of gradually went from lovers to friends, I guess. There was no one thing that ended it." I thought back to that time, about a year ago now. "We just had a chat and one thing led to another and it was clear that it was over between us. No hard feelings."

"Wow, that seems really weird. I don't think I've ever heard of people ending it so quietly before. You should have seen what Silas went through with his ex." With a sigh, he freed my hand and sat back in his seat, combing his fingers through his curly bangs. "But, he's cool with her now."

I nodded. "Yeah, I think for most people relationships end explosively." I chuckled. "I have this friend, Grant, and he's in training at the police academy right now." I sipped my wine. "When he broke up with his ex it was a mess. Like, she literally threw his shit off the balcony of their apartment." I huffed a laugh. "But, he did sort of cheat on her. He was chatting up another girl on social media and she found out."

"Oh, shit. That's not cool." Gabe pursed his lips. "I guess this conversation brings up a point." He chewed his lower lip. "Do you want to be exclusive? Or is there someone on social media you're chatting up?" He bit at his thumbnail.

I blinked. If the way I'd felt last night with him being surrounded by people hitting on him was any indication, I certainly wanted to be exclusive. But was it too soon? "I don't have anyone I'm chatting up on social media."

The server set down our appetizer. "Enjoy. I'll be back with your entrées shortly."

"Thanks." Gabe cut a section off the baked brie and spread it on a slice of toasted French bread. "So that means..." He bit into his slice and peered at me.

"What do *you* want?" I straightened my spine. Why was I even asking him that? Could I handle him chatting up Oliver or someone else right now? No, not after what we'd shared. "I-I would like to be exclusive. I mean, at least while I'm around like this."

"You mean while you're working as my bodyguard, you don't want me to be with anyone else?" He set his hand on the table, his gaze locking to mine.

"Well, yeah, we're basically living together." My pulse quickened. What was he getting at?

"Jeremy, do you want to be exclusive? Because..." With his brows wrinkling, he grabbed my hand again and softly said, "I do." His throat bobbed with a hard swallow, then his gaze met mine.

"Good." My chest bloomed with warmth. I should be more direct with him. "I don't want you seeing anyone else. Last night wasn't pleasant for me at the gig." I dipped my gaze to the plate of baked brie.

With a soft grin, he spread more brie on a slice of bread and held it across the table. "Good, then we're exclusive."

I took the bread from him and ate it, then drank more wine, a pleasant buzz filling my head.

"I've never done this before, been exclusive." He spread more brie.

"Yeah?" I twisted my lips. "I've never been with a man

before." I let a grin tease my mouth. "Guess we're both in uncharted territory." And somehow it all felt so right.

"We are." He bit into the slice of bread. "Tell me, you had to have feelings for guys before me, right? Like, I didn't somehow turn you gay." He let out a soft snort, covering his mouth with the back of his hand.

With a nod, I said, "Yeah, there was something with certain guys. I always chalked it up to admiring them though. I never let myself think about it too much."

"You ever get an eyeful of gay porn and pop a boner?" He giggled.

"Gabe. We're in a nice restaurant." With a smile, I scanned around us. A family sat to the right of us, the parents trying to keep the children seated, and another couple were completely engrossed in each other to our left.

"So? Have you?" He drank some beer. "It's a serious question. That's how I knew for sure."

My gaze slid to his. "Seriously?" I thought back. I'd never exposed myself to anything, not even some of the teen gay series my ex used to watch on Netflix. I'd just immediately leave her to it and go and study. Maybe that was my way of avoiding my feelings altogether. I grabbed a slice of bread and spread brie over it.

"Yeah." He stuffed more bread in his mouth, then wiped his fingers on his napkin. "I was probably eleven when I found it, *by accident*." He made finger quotes. "Okay, me and a friend were looking up porn on our phones and making jokes about it, but I kept being drawn to the guy, not the girl. So, I typed something in, I can't remember what, and all this stuff came up on the website with men, you know." He ticked his brows. "I popped a raging boner." Biting his lower lip, he nodded. "I had clues my whole life, but that sealed it for me." He took a few gulps of beer.

"Have you ever dated a girl? Like did you try being straight?" I ate more bread. That happened, right? Especially since he'd been hiding his sexuality from Kevin.

He puffed out a breath. "Yeah, even took a girl to prom." A smile crept over his mouth. "But she was a friend of mine and knew I was gay. When I got to the dance, I made out with this guy I'd been hooking up with."

"But your mom knew, right?" I sipped my wine. This whole thing sounded really complicated. How the hell did Kevin not at least sense his son was gay?

Gabe twisted his beer glass on the table. "Yeah, my mom knew. It was all to keep up appearances for dad." He sucked in a breath and smiled at me. "I had a great time anyways."

"Yeah, I'm sure." I slowly nodded. "My prom was just the usual. I brought a girl I'd been crushing on, we had a good time and then she moved away to go to college in California." I huffed a laugh. My dad had been alive then. He'd been so proud to see me graduate high school, like it was a huge deal. I shouldn't go there though. We should keep the conversation light.

The server set down our meals, my prime rib and Gabe's filet mignon.

Gabe cut into his steak. "So, I have to ask you. What the hell happened last night at the casino?" He ate a bite of filet, then chuckled and leaned over the table. "Axel said you were having a classic bisexual awakening."

"A what?" Was that a thing? I might have to look it up. I stared at him a moment. How to explain it? "I uh...well, I think I was getting jealous of Oliver." Heat raced up my neck and I cut a piece of prime rib, then dipped it in horseradish sauce before eating it.

His eyes widened. "Yeah? And is that why I found you in

the bathroom splashing water on your face?" He bit his lower lip. "You can tell me now. I mean, we're together."

"Yeah. I was having a moment of clarity." I stuffed a spoonful of mashed potatoes into my mouth. "*You* made me pop some boners at your show." I laughed, covering my mouth with my hand.

"I know. I felt it when you were behind me at the bar." He arched a brow and dug into his baked potato. "I didn't want to embarrass you, so I didn't say anything. But damn, I was surprised." Shaking his head, he chuckled.

"Yeah, so was I." My mind filled with the rest of the night and heat sparked in my groin. Now I wanted to get back home and be close to him again. There was too much space between us with me sitting across from him at the table. "Let's finish up and get back to the house." I drank some of my wine.

"What a great idea." He ate more steak.

AFTER GETTING HOME, we made a beeline for Gabe's bedroom, waving a quick hello to Milo, Cash and Silas, all sitting on the couch watching a movie.

Gabe shut the door behind him and stood there, a mischievous grin spreading over his face. "How open are you to trying things?" He shucked off his shirt and tossed it toward the laundry basket.

As my cock woke, I unfastened my gun holster and set it to rest against the bottom of the nightstand. "I'm pretty open." My gaze roamed down his slender, but muscular body, the wide shoulders, thick arms, then the ripple of his abs and the trail of hair leading to his dick, half-mast in his jeans. My mouth watered and my breath quickened. "Yeah, I'm open." Now that I'd had a piece of him, I wanted more.

"Good." He stepped to me and cupped my cheeks, then pressed a long, slow kiss on my lips, his tongue gliding into my mouth to flick over my own. "I want to take it slow tonight and really get to know what you like." His pupils flared and he nuzzled my neck, leaving soft bites.

A shiver raced down my spine and lodged in my balls. With a moan, I grabbed his ass and pushed my hips into his, our hot cocks rubbing through our jeans. I didn't want anything between us. "How about we get undressed, and on the bed, where we can explore?" I rasped.

He lifted his head, his gaze meeting mine. "I like how you think." He dropped his jeans and briefs, then kicked them off, his dick standing tall, almost to his navel.

Damn, I wanted to touch him, even more than last night. As desire heated my skin, I undressed and threw my clothes at the laundry hamper in the corner.

He climbed onto the bed, his round, tight ass exposed to me for a heartbeat, then flopped onto his back and wrapped an arm around his head, tucking his hand underneath the pillow. Placing a few lazy strokes on his dick, he wet his lips. "You work out a lot, huh."

"Usually, yeah. Every day." I lay down next to him on my back, fixating on the stroking of his hand over his shaft. That was not something I'd ever seen, a guy jacking himself. As pleasure pulsed through me, my cock jerked and pre-cum beaded at the tip. "Can I uh, can I take over?"

"Most certainly." With a wicked grin, he lifted his hand. "Kiss me, too."

Rolling to my side, I wrapped my fingers around his firm cock and pumped it, placing hungry kisses over his mouth.

He shuddered and arched his back, groaning against me, then fisted my dick and matched my pace, stroke for stroke.

After a few minutes of heated kisses and jacking each

other, he broke away. "Are you ready for more? Like, can I blow you?" He drew heavy breaths and bit his lower lip, his gaze raking down my body.

"Yeah. I'd never say no to a blow job." With a chuckle, I kissed the tip of his nose.

He widened his eyes, then gave me a warm smile. "You are a sweet one." He crawled over me, then licked and nibbled his way to my chest. Taking a nipple into his mouth, he flicked his tongue over it, then gave it soft bite.

"Oh, fuck." Sensation shot from my chest to my dick, and it lifted off my stomach.

With a soft chuckle, he slid his tongue along my chest to the other side and tongued my nipple, then sucked on it.

Pleasure coiled in my gut. "Fuck, that feels good." No one had ever paid this much attention to my nipples.

"You like that?" As his gaze roamed up to mine, he fluttered his tongue over the peak of my nipple.

Goosebumps broke out over my chest and a shudder rolled up my spine. I hissed. "Yeah, I do."

Curling the corner of his mouth, he said, "Imagine what my tongue is going to feel like on your dick." He sucked hard on my nipple.

"Fucking hell." I squeezed my eyes shut and arched my head back, my balls tightening as a jolt of heat pulsed my cock.

Leaving my chest, he laved his way down my abs, licking over the grooves, and dipped his tongue into my navel.

My cock ached with arousal. "Are you teasing me on purpose?" I panted, watching him, and planted my hands on his shoulders, pushing him down to where I wanted him.

"Yeah, you got me." He gave me an almost grin, his lips red and wet, his eyes so dark the blue hardly showed. "Don't worry, I'll let you do this to me if you want." He hooked a brow and focused on me as if waiting for an answer.

At this point, I'd do just about anything. "I want to." I pushed on his shoulders again. "Please, Gabe, I need that tongue of yours on my dick." Apparently, I wasn't above begging either.

"Oh, that's hot." He ran his slick tongue down my groin and nuzzled my balls, sucking one into his mouth, then the other.

I gasped as pleasure surged over me. By the time he put his mouth on me, I might be ready to blow after all this. I lifted my knees beside his shoulders.

He fisted the base of my dick, then slowly, took me into his warm mouth and to the back of his throat, then pumped, his tongue flickering over my shaft and skimming over my tip.

I held my breath a moment, fighting off the spark of sensation threatening to engulf me. Twining my fingers in his messy curls, I clutched his head. Did I want him to go faster, or slow down?

He slowed his rhythm over me, then twisted his hand and swirled his tongue on the head.

"Oh, fuck." I rocked my hips, pushing my cock deeper into him. I wanted to fuck him, to possess him. I'd never felt it so strongly before.

He swallowed over the tip of my dick and moaned, squirming his hips.

I peeked down at him as a wave of intense pleasure tingled over me, down to my toes and up my neck. "Coming. Oh my God. Holy fuck, Gabe." I groaned and gasped as each contraction pushed me deeper into sensation and sparks lit up behind my eyes. My dick pulsed and spurted cum into his lapping mouth.

As it slowed, he slid off my spent cock with a wet pop and wiped his lips with the back of his hand. "Jesus, Jeremy. I almost came getting you off." Panting, he climbed up to rest on top of me, his hot, rock-hard dick pressed to my stomach. "I don't think anyone has ever turned me on the way you do." He gazed down at me, propped up by his elbows, then brushed a lock of my bangs off my forehead.

"Same. This might be the best sex I've ever had." Grabbing the back of his head, I pulled him in for a deep kiss, tangling my tongue with his. "I'm ready to do that for you."

He offered me a lazy smirk. "Yeah? I'm ready for a Jeremy blow job for sure." He rolled onto his back and spread his legs wide, lifting his knees. "Have at it. I'm all yours."

My heart swelled with warmth. Did he have no idea what it did to me when he said he was all mine? How did I get so lucky to have this smart, gorgeous man want to be with me? With a sigh, I crawled to hover on all fours over him. "So, I'm assuming you like having your nipples played with, too?"

"I do." He gave me a quick grin. "I'm so fucking close already though, be careful."

I dropped down and took a nipple into my mouth, then teased it with my tongue, flicking and sucking. His chest was hard, not like what I was used to, but damn, it lit me up inside to make him feel good.

"Oh, fuck, Jeremy. More, give me more." He gasped and arched his back, his dick jerking and dribbling a string of pre-cum over his stomach.

I skimmed my teeth along his chest to the other nipple, then sucked it into my mouth and bit softly.

His body shivered and broke out in goosebumps as he clutched at my hair and rocked his hips as if fucking the air. "Suck me, Jeremy, please. Oh, God."

I dipped my head to the center of his abs and licked all the way down, settling between his thighs, my own cock perking up again. Damn it, I could go all night like this. I wrapped my hand around the base of his dick, like he'd done to me, then peeked up at him.

He watched me, his lower lip stuck between his teeth, his eyelids hooded. "You okay?" He slid his hands from my hair to place them on my shoulders.

"I'm okay." I flicked my tongue at the head of his dick, the heady taste of his pre-cum filling my mouth. My now solid cock twitched. Yeah, I wanted this, wanted more. I swallowed him whole, taking him deep into my mouth, then sucked and pumped while stroking him with my hand.

"Holy fuck. Yeah, that's it." He pushed on my shoulders and his thighs quivered around my head. Gasping, his fingers dug into my skin. "Fuck, oh, fuck, coming. Pull off. Coming!" His hips rocked and jerked, and his cock swelled in my mouth.

Hot cum shot into my throat and I swallowed it all down, stroking him with my tongue and lips, hollowing my cheeks. As it slowed, I licked him one last time, then freed his spent dick, my own aching and hard. As I continued to hold his cock, I looked up at him. "I didn't want to pull off." Was there a reason he'd wanted me to? Surely, he'd rather I stayed on him.

Huffing out a laugh, he rubbed his eyes. "Well damn, I'm glad you didn't, but I thought you might not like it." He focused on me. "I don't want to scare you off from giving me blow jobs."

"You're not going to scare me off." I freed his waning dick and lay over top of him, chest to chest, then brushed my knuckles over his cheek. I was caught up in his world all the way and everything felt so right, even what we'd just done. "I may be new to this, but it doesn't mean I'm not all in with you. Okay?" I kissed his lips. "I *like* you." A whole fucking lot.

He swallowed hard, his gaze searching my face. "Yeah, me, too."

ELEVEN

GABE

The next morning, I sat at the dinette, reading through my case analysis for my contracts class on my laptop one last time while Jeremy cooked a mountain of bacon and eggs for the house. We'd decided on another round of blow jobs last night and God damn, if we didn't do it again this morning. I didn't think my dick had ever been sucked so thoroughly in all my life. I glanced toward the kitchen and watched Jeremy drop bread slices into the toaster, the muscles of his bare back flexing over his pajama bottoms. Damn, the guy was built.

Milo walked out from the hallway and sniffed at the air, his pink sweats hanging low on his hips, the hint of lace peeking out over the top. "Bacon? Oh my God, that smells good." He padded to me and stopped, resting his hand on the back of my chair, the corner of his mouth raising. "Wild night, huh?"

I looked up at him, my cheeks warming. "Yeah." We were going to have to tone it down this week if I was going to keep my damn grades up.

Milo leaned over and in my ear, whispered, "It's okay, I only heard some of it from my room."

Snapping my gaze to his, I said, "Shit, you did?" Hopefully Silas didn't hear it. He'd never let me live it down.

With a shrug, Milo gave me a sly grin. "Don't worry, I don't mind. I'm happy you're getting some."

"Yeah, me, too. We'll try to keep it down." With a chuckle, I hung my head. I wasn't going to tell Jeremy about this conversation.

Jeremy twisted from the toaster. "Good morning, Milo. I've got fried eggs, bacon and toast." He smiled at Milo. "I think we have some cinnamon here somewhere."

"We do." Cash strolled into the room with Silas following, both wearing pajama bottoms, Silas' in black and Cash's a lime green.

Cash stopped at Milo and placed a hand on his back, then leaned in. "I'll make you that cinnamon toast." He kissed Milo's cheek.

"What about me?" With a huff, Silas planted his hands on his hips.

"Of course, hun. You get whatever you want." Wrapping his arms around Silas' waist, Cash pecked his lips.

Silas' face lit up. "Good."

Cash waltzed into the kitchen, grabbed some sugar and cinnamon from a cupboard, then mixed it in a bowl. "See, easy peasy." He sprinkled the mixture on a slice of buttered toast sitting on a plate. "How many want cinnamon toast?"

We all raised our hands.

"Oh, everyone?" Cash chuckled. "Great. Guess this was a good idea." With a smug grin, he went to work making more.

"Okay, the eggs and bacon are done." Jeremy brought a stack of plates down from the cupboard and set them up next to platters filled with bacon and fried eggs. "Come and get it." With a broad smile, his gaze met mine.

Everyone filled their plates with food, poured orange juice

and coffee, then sat down around the table, me at the head with Jeremy next to me, then Milo on my other side and Cash and Silas squeezed in at the other end.

"So, it's nearing the end of the school year. Are you ready for your finals?" Jeremy ate a forkful of egg.

I huffed a laugh. "God, no. Is anyone?" I bit into a slice of bacon. I really had to focus on my cases this week. "My whole grade is based off the damn final in pretty much all of my classes."

Silas stared at me, his jaw dropping open. "Are you shitting me? What about all that writing you've been doing? Doesn't that count?"

"Nope. That's all for me to use to understand the material. Well, pretty much. I do have a legal writing class." I rested my cheek in my hand, my elbow propped on the table, then pushed my egg around on my plate. "I'm going to need to study this week. I hope you don't get bored, Jeremy."

"Maybe I can help you study?" He grabbed my hand and held it, then kissed my knuckles. "It'd be good for me, too, since I plan to start up in the fall."

"Yeah, being in a study group hasn't worked out so well for me. I find I focus better on my own." I gazed into his gorgeous dark eyes. Maybe with him, studying would be different. Or, I'd lose all focus and want to suck his dick instead. Fuck, I was in trouble no matter how I looked at it. "Yeah, let's see how it goes."

"Don't worry, we'll figure it out. I should probably see if there's any research work your dad needs me to do from here." He squeezed my hand. "I won't get bored. Not with you around." He let a grin creep over his lips.

LATER THAT AFTERNOON, I was left alone in the house with Jeremy, forcing myself to review my cases yet again at the dinette. I glanced at Jeremy, sitting on the couch with his laptop open in his lap. Was he looking at security footage again? It *was* his job. "See anything?"

With a frown, he twisted around sideways on the couch, knitting his brows. "No, I didn't see anything." He pursed his lips.

"What's wrong?" I rose from my chair and stretched. I could use a break, and something was definitely bothering him. After rounding the couch, I dropped in next to him.

He huffed softly and hung his head. "I'm having sort of a moral dilemma, I guess."

"What? Why?" I hooked an arm over his shoulders and leaned in. "Talk to me."

"I was so, I don't know, wrapped up in my confusion, wanting you and trying to figure out if you were queer, that I never stopped to think about if being together was right given our status." He turned into me, resting his head on my shoulder.

My heart pinched. "What do you mean by that?" This was coming out of nowhere. What the hell happened? Was he freaking out now that we were giving each other some space and he had time to think?

"Well, you're the principal, the person I'm supposed to be guarding. Me having an affair with you is sort of like having an affair with your boss. You're not supposed to do it." He puffed out a breath. "But here I am, breaking rule number one on my first time out."

"I'm not your boss. My father is. So, technically, he's the client." I kissed his head. Fuck, was he going to want to stop what we were doing? An ache filtered through my chest.

"I know, but me having feelings for you could compromise—"

"There's nothing to compromise. Nothing's going to happen." I held him closer. I couldn't stop this, not now. Now I knew how Caleb felt when he and Eric were dating in secret because Eric had become his professor. They couldn't stop seeing each other, and I had no idea how I could stop my feelings for Jeremy. My chest squeezed. Ultimately, it was up to him. "What do you want to do?"

"I-I don't know." He lifted his head and flicked his gaze between my eyes. "It's wrong on so many levels, but I can't...I don't want...I'm falling for you, Gabe." He cupped my cheek. "What am I supposed to do?"

My heart fluttered with warmth. *He's falling for me...*I swallowed hard. "You want to be a lawyer, not a bodyguard, right?" I studied him. I had to reason him out of whatever this was.

"Yeah, I do. Being a bodyguard was supposed to be a side gig, so I could pay off my student loans faster." He worried his lower lip. "Guess that worked out." He focused on me. "Your dad paid off my student loans for this job."

"He did?" I widened my eyes. I wasn't going to ask him how much. That would be rude. But damn, why was Dad willing to fork out so much money for this? Were we in that much danger?

He nodded. "He knows I was waiting to go to law school after I paid off my undergraduate loans. I think this was his way of helping me out, so I could get a position as a lawyer in the firm faster."

"Oh, yeah, that makes sense." Dad never did anything that didn't benefit him in some way.

With a huff, he said, "So, see? Your dad can be a really good guy." He twined his fingers in mine, over my thigh. "But if he finds out about us, I might lose my job." His breath hitched. "It was my dream to work as a lawyer with Kevin, for his firm. He's taught me so much." He bit his lip. "I'm letting him down."

"You're not letting anyone down and he's not going to find out about us." I squeezed his hand, then kissed the back of it. "Jeremy, don't worry about that. We're safe here."

"But what if he does find out?" His gaze found mine. "He might remove his recommendation of me for law school."

"I won't let him. If he does something like that, I'll..." What would I do? Heat swarmed my chest. Shit, I'd never thought Dad would ever find out about me until he was no longer in a position of power over me. "I'd disown him." My pulse quickened. Holy hell, the shit storm this would cause in my family. The bullshit he'd put Mom through. "It won't happen."

He rocked once, his throat dipping with a long swallow. "Well, there's no way I can hold back now anyways."

My gaze snapped to his. "Yeah?" Warmth bloomed in my heart. I hadn't lost him, not yet. I hugged him into my chest, then kissed the side of his head. One thing was certain from this conversation and how much pain it caused me. "For the record, I'm falling for you, too."

Raising his head, he gazed deeply into my eyes. "You are?"

"I am. We'll figure this out, okay?" I forced a quick smile at him. "Let's just see how things play out. For all we know, this threat thing could be over tomorrow, and you'll go back to working at the firm and we can date like a normal couple."

"Yeah, it's nice living here with you and everything, but damn." He shook his head and choked out a laugh. "It makes everything so much more intense."

"Where *do* you live?" Funny, I had no idea. I freed his shoulders, but kept my hold on his hand.

"I have an apartment up in Scottsdale. It's a one bedroom." He relaxed his shoulders.

I nodded, then narrowed my eyes. "How far up north are you?" The firm and my parents' house was at least thirty miles from here. It would suck to have him living so far away from me.

"I'm right off Hayden and Thomas." He quirked the corner of his mouth. "Don't worry, I live closer to you than to the firm." He kissed my cheek.

"You read my mind." I gave him my best smile. "It'll be nice when this threat BS is over." Though I'd probably already miss him not being around all the time. I'd already gotten used to him.

"Yeah, then maybe I can introduce you to my mom." He brushed his thumb over the back of my hand. "You already know my sister."

My heart pattered in my chest. "Are you saying you want to come out to them?" He hadn't said anything to Simone Friday night, right?

"Yeah, I do. I don't think they'd have a problem with it. Well, I know Simone wouldn't." His gaze snapped to mine. "You know, my mom works at the casino, too."

"She does?" I wrinkled my forehead. "Where? Simone never mentioned her." Had I seen her there and I didn't know it?

"She works in the spa as a massage therapist." He slowly nodded. "She's great at it. When I go see her, she always insists that she gets the knots out of my shoulders and back." A soft grin teased his lips.

"Damn, I could use some of that." I rolled my head, stretching the tightness in my neck from studying.

"She's shown me some techniques." He smirked at me. "I could maybe...give you a massage tonight?" His smirk grew. "In bed?"

"Oh, hell yeah." I slid my arm out from around his shoulders. Obviously, he was feeling better about things, especially if he was talking about coming out. "So, but you don't think your mom will have a problem with you being bi?"

"I don't think so. One of her best friends is a lesbian. A married lesbian. They met in massage school." He sank back into the couch, raking his fingers through his dark bangs. "Maybe I could meet your mom and brother sometime?" He scoffed a chuckle. "I've already met your dad."

"Yeah..." I pursed my lips. How would this work? Mom had said I should be dating. "Maybe we could meet them for dinner somewhere, but it would be hard not to invite my dad and...shit, I don't know." I huffed a sigh. Why did my family have to be so complicated?

He patted my thigh. "Don't worry about it. We have time to figure this all out. Right now, you need to study." He pressed a quick kiss on my lips. "And I'm going to see if we have anything here I can cook for dinner besides frozen pizza." He stood up.

"There might be some frozen hamburger in the freezer." I hopped off the couch. Yeah, I was really going to miss not having him around when this was over.

He strolled into the kitchen and pulled out a tube of hamburger from the freezer. "Do we have taco shells and stuff?"

"I'm pretty sure we do. We can always text Silas to bring what we need home from work." I stepped to the dinette and sat in my chair. Having Silas work at a Target with a grocery section was so damn convenient.

"Yeah, please do." He set the hamburger in the sink.

―――――

FIVE DAYS HAD PASSED since Jeremy's freak out over having an affair with me while being my bodyguard and we'd fallen into a nice routine, including evening massages followed by blow jobs and him making me and the guys home-cooked meals. Things seemed to have settled down on the threat front and dad had given him some work to do from the band house. My studying and classwork were finally back on track and it was the weekend again, a Friday night without a gig.

I sat on the couch next to Jeremy, my legs sprawled out over his lap while I sat sideways in the corner, watching the evening news. "What do you want to do tonight?"

He drew a deep inhale. "I don't know, grab some dinner at a sports bar maybe?" He rubbed my bare feet, kneading into the sole.

His touch tingled through my foot and up my leg. "Oh, damn, that feels good." Nothing like a good foot rub. I raked my teeth over my lower lip and let out a soft moan.

"You keep making noises like that and we might be ordering in." With a chuckle, he pulled on each of my toes.

Silas strode out from the hallway. "You two need to get out of here. You've been hogging the TV and the couch every night. It's my turn to make out on the couch with Cash."

"Hey, no dicks out in the main room." I flapped my index finger at Silas and huffed a laugh.

"Yeah, yeah." With a scoff, he opened the front door and Cash walked in, threw his arms around Silas' shoulders, and planted a hard kiss on his mouth. "Hi, hun."

"You know what? I think he's right. Let's get dressed and get out of here." Jeremy pushed my legs off his lap and stood up. "Hey, Cash. Nice to see you." He walked to Cash and gave him a swift hug, patting him on the back.

I climbed off the couch and pulled my t-shirt over my sweats. He was right, we'd been in the house all week except for school. "Hey, Cash." I greeted him with a side hug.

"Hi, Gabe. Are you both going to watch a movie with us

and get takeout?" He kissed Silas' knuckles, beaming at him, then focused on us.

"No, they're going out." Silas gave me a thin-lipped smile. "Aren't you." He patted me on the back.

"Yes, we're going out." I yanked on Jeremy's hand and tugged him into the hallway. "Where do you want to go?"

"How about a movie date?" He followed me into my bedroom.

I stopped and faced him. "A date, huh?" I couldn't remember the last time I'd been in a theater. "You know what? That sounds fun." I squeezed his hand. "In fact, I'll even wear something nice for it." I let a soft grin curl my lips.

"Okay, then. Me, too." He pressed a kiss on my cheek. "Let's get out of here."

I PARKED at the Tempe Marketplace outdoor mall and climbed out of the car, then tucked my deep blue button down into my tan trousers and met Jeremy on the other side of the car as evening descended on the parking lot and the tall lights started to glow. The setting sun threw hues of orange against the blue sky. "You look gorgeous tonight." I roamed my gaze over his tight white shirt, showing off all his muscles, then down to his jeans, hugging him in all the right places, especially his ass.

"Yeah? Thanks." As he dipped his head, his cheeks pinked.

"It was kind of nice you left the firearm at home for our second date." Snatching his hand, I strolled with him through the parking lot.

"Well, I haven't seen those black cars around the house except for that one time and your dad hasn't heard anything more either." He tugged on our hands, bumping his shoulder to mine.

"Maybe this thing is finally over." An ache wrapped around my heart. Maybe he'd also be leaving the house soon, too, then. I didn't really want him to go.

As we approached the last car in the row, a bang cracked through the air. Screaming and shouts followed.

"Fuck, get down." Jeremy threw me behind the car, my face hitting the pavement, and he fell over me, splayed out.

My heart jolted and I fought to breathe. "What, what is it?" Trembling rolled through my body. Was this it? Were the assholes here to get me? I tried to lift my head. My gaze caught tennis shoes running over the asphalt.

"Stay down." His body covered me from head to toe.

My chest pinched and my eyes popped open. Holy fuck. Jeremy was willing to die for me. I swallowed hard, my heart swelling with emotion. He was prepared to take a bullet for me. The corners of my eyes stung. I couldn't let that happen. I fucking loved him too much. Oh God, I did. *I love him.* I shoved up and he fell to the side.

"What are you doing?" He crouched down next to me behind the car, his gaze darting over me, his brows furrowing. "Are you okay? I didn't crush you, did I?"

I sat on my ass with my knees drawn up, then brushed the dirt from my hands. "No, I'm not going to let you die for me." I scanned the area around him, looking for a black Mercedes sedan. Where were those bastards?

"What?" He winced, then stared at me.

A security guard in a dark blue uniform stepped to us with a walkie talkie in his hand. "You two okay? Looks like a car backfired." Something unintelligible squawked through his walkie talkie.

"Oh, shit." Jeremy covered a grin with the back of his hand. "Guess I overreacted." A choked laugh snuck out of him. His attention drew to the guard. "Yeah, we're fine. Thanks." He stood up, then held a hand down to me. "Sorry." His cheeks reddened.

"Are you serious?" Grabbing his hand, I let him pull me up, then swiped the dirt off my ass.

"Have a good night." The guard walked off. "Nothing to see here folks, just a car backfiring." He waved his hands at people, huddled by cars.

I stared at Jeremy. I knew he was here to protect me, but holy fuck. "You really thought we were getting shot at, didn't you."

With a tight grin, he hung his head. "Yeah, I did." He tugged on my hand. "Come on, let's go see what fast food restaurant catches our eye."

I walked with him to the sidewalk. "What were you trying to do? Cover me, so you'd get shot instead?"

He halted in front of a trendy clothing store and huffed. "Yeah, that's what I was doing. It's what I'm supposed to do as your bodyguard." His gaze searched my face and in a soft voice, he said, "Even if I wasn't getting paid, it's what I'd do."

My heart fluttered and a lump grew in my throat. "Y-you could have uh, you could have died." What were we both trying to say here?

"But I didn't, and it was just a stupid car backfiring." He huffed a laugh. "Guess all this stuff with the black Mercedes and the threats got to me." He tugged on my hand. "Come on. Let's go." He hauled me into the section of the mall where multiple fast-food restaurants were lined up on each side of the walkway. "What do you want? Our movie starts in a half hour, if you want to see the funny one."

"I definitely want to see the funny one. How about some Mexican?" I pointed to a Taco Bell, tucked between a pizza and a hamburger place. I was tired of both of the others.

"Sure." We strolled to the Taco Bell and ordered some

dinner and sodas, then sat down at a metal patio table, under some tall palms and beside a long wall fountain. I wasn't going to let him off that easy with his answers about the car backfiring.

I unwrapped a taco and bit into it, the spicy meat and cool lettuce filling my mouth, then watched him eat the end off his burrito. I was going to be direct. "I don't want you taking a bullet for me." I sipped from the straw in my soda.

"What?" He peered at me. "Gabe, covering you in case of a threat like that is what I'm supposed to do."

My chest heated. Were we about to have an argument over this? "But I don't want you to. What if you get shot?"

Shrugging a shoulder, he said, "Then I get shot." Under his breath, he said, "Better me than you."

"What is that supposed to mean?" I glared at him. Did he think I was so weak, I couldn't handle getting shot? "My friend Axel got shot and he was okay." Well, after a lot of therapy, both physical and mental, but fuck if I was going to bring it up right now.

He dropped his mouth open and set his burrito down. "There is no way I'm going to stand by and let you get shot." He shook his head. "No fucking way, Gabe."

I ate more of my taco, thinking on what he'd said. "So, every time there's a *threat* you're going to man handle me to the ground or some shit?"

"I am." With a curt nod, he bit into his burrito, then sipped some soda. "And you can't stop me."

"Oh yes, I can. What if I run away?" I squeezed some hot sauce onto a new taco. I sounded like a spoiled child, but I didn't care.

"I'll run after you, catch you, and then manhandle you." His gaze hardened on mine. "You won't get away. I'm not going to let anything happen to you."

"Even at the expense of letting something happen to you?" I scoffed, looking him up and down. "Why the hell would you do that?"

"Because I couldn't stand it if you got hurt." He stared me down, his brows lowering. Stabbing the table with his finger, he said, "Do you have any idea what it would do to me if something happened to you?"

I huffed out a breath and leaned forward. "Do you have any idea what I'd go through if something happened to *you*?"

We glared at each other, breathing hard and fast. Finally, he said, "I don't want another person I love to die. Okay?" He blinked, widened his eyes, then covered his mouth with his fingers. "Shit, I didn't mean to say that out loud." He stared at me.

My heart bloomed with emotion. "Did you just...did you mean..." Did he just tell me he loved me?

After puffing out a long breath, he said, "Shit, yeah." He scanned the table and shifted in his seat, then scratched at the back of his neck. "It all happened so fast, and in the moment, I don't know, it hit me. My feelings for you just knocked me in the face." With a wince, his attention drew to me.

I jumped from my chair, then stepped to him and crouched down, wrapping my arms around his shoulders, burying my face in his neck. My heartbeat pounded in my ears. "I love you, too, Jeremy. It was the same for me." My eyes stung. *Don't fucking cry like a baby.* "I've never said that to anyone before."

He hooked his arms around me and kissed the side of my head. "I love you, too, Gabe. That's why I can't let anything happen to you. I don't care about the job your dad hired me for. I'd do it anyways." He squeezed me and nuzzled into my hair. "I can't lose you."

"I can't lose you, either." I sniffled and released him, then rubbed my eyes. "Fuck, you got to me." I huffed a chuckle and straightened.

He stood up from his chair, his gaze softening as it locked to mine. "You got to me, too. Hell, I've never had such an intense, what is it, two weeks? With someone." Cupping my cheeks, he pressed a long kiss to my mouth. "I never thought on the first day, I'd be here, totally in love with you."

I gave him a coy grin. "Yeah, well, I definitely knew I was going to have a hard time lusting after you." I drew a deep inhale. "I almost lost my mind trying to figure out how to keep you from finding out I was gay and telling my dad."

"I was never going to out you to your dad." He tapped the tip of my nose and smiled. "Can we finish eating now and go and see the movie?"

"Yeah, that sounds good." I dropped into my chair and picked up my taco, then glanced at him, taking a bite of his burrito and smiling at me. Holy hell, I never had a chance against him. "So, I guess we're boyfriends now?" I bit into my taco.

"Boyfriends?" He swallowed down his food. "Yeah, I guess I assumed we were already. You know, when we had the whole exclusive discussion."

"Oh." I nodded. "Okay." Shit, I had a boyfriend. My first one. Mom would be happy, if only I could tell her. That, I'd have to think about.

AFTER THE MOVIE, we drove home, hands entwined on the center console of my BMW. As I turned onto our street, my gaze caught on a black Mercedes S class, parked in front of the neighbor's house. "Shit."

Jeremy pursed his lips, fixating on the car. "Gabe, drive

around the block. I'm going to see if I can get a picture of the license plate on the back bumper. It was hard to tell, but I didn't see anyone in the car."

"Yeah, sure." I stepped on the gas and drove around the block, past where Axel and Remy lived with Axel's brother, Leo, then past a park with colorful playground equipment all lit up, and finally, turned onto my street again. The black Mercedes was gone. "Fuck." I pulled to the side of the road where the car had been.

"Fuck is right. They saw us and left." He sucked in a deep breath, then let it out slowly. "They're messing with us, I'm sure of it. I'll bet your dad has or will be hearing from them again."

"You think? Why are they only here on the weekends?" I scanned the street that fed into this one. No taillights, either. "Think they've got day jobs and can only fuck with us on their time off?" I snickered.

"No idea. But you guys are all out of the house on the weekends when you have gigs. Maybe they figure it's a good time to scope the place out and see if they can find a hole in the security system?" He perused the area around the houses, leaning forward in his seat and looking out the window.

A shiver worked up my spine. "Shit, Jeremy, now you're scaring me." I rubbed the goosebumps rising on my arms.

"Come here." He grabbed the back of my neck and pulled me close, then planted a kiss on my forehead. "If they're smart, they should know the name of your band by now and know when you have gigs. It's not hard to find out from your social media accounts." He freed me and gave me a warm grin.

"Yeah, that's true." Another shiver rolled down my spine. This whole situation was unnerving.

TWELVE

JEREMY

P oor Gabe looked spooked. I didn't blame him. The threats were real, and we were being staked out. That much was clear. What they wanted, I didn't know. "Let's go inside. Maybe there's some footage on the cameras that'll be useful."

After he parked in the garage, I climbed out of the car and followed him into the kitchen.

Cash and Silas were tangled in each other on the couch.

"No dicks out, I assume?" With a smirk, Gabe stepped to them and placed his hands on the back of the couch.

Silas turned his head, resting on a throw pillow in the corner of the couch. "No, we got that out of the way early. Don't mind the stains." He curled the edge of his lips.

"You stop that." With a giggle, Cash snuggled into Silas' side and slapped at his chest.

"Uh-huh." Sighing, Gabe grabbed my hand and led me to the other end of the sectional, then dropped in, pulling me down next to him. "Apparently our mobsters were hanging out on the street when we got home."

"Shit, what?" Silas moved Cash off him, then sat up with

Cash doing the same. He furrowed his brows. "Are you sure that's what they are?"

"We don't know for sure, but it's looking likely that the threats are coming from the mob." I grabbed Gabe's hand and held it over his thigh. I probably wasn't supposed to be confirming this information, but they needed to know. "Did you notice anything strange while you've been here?"

With rounded eyes, Cash shook his head and said, "No, not a thing. But then, we were either, um, busy or watching a movie." His cheeks flushed.

Busy...did that mean they'd had sex? As in the kind of sex men had together? I glanced at Gabe and heat flared in my groin. I had to keep my mind on the topic at hand. I'd been thinking about what anal sex would be like all damn week during all of our blow job sessions. I drew a deep inhale. "Okay, so I'm not sure what's going on. Last time that car was here, you all had a gig. I wonder if they thought everyone would be out again?"

"Let's look at the footage and see what we can." Gabe swallowed hard.

"Okay." I jumped up to grab my laptop from the dinette, then settled into the couch next to Gabe again. It would be much easier to zoom in on my computer than on my phone. I started it up and opened the app to the cameras, then scrolled through them until I caught a video of the black Mercedes pulling up to the curb next door. I pointed at the screen. "There they are. Looks like they got here around eight."

"It's about ten now, so they were here for two hours?" Silas straightened and slid his arm over Cash's shoulders, then drew him into his side.

"Yeah." I zoomed in on the car, but again, I couldn't see into the tinted windows and there was no plate on the front bumper. "Shit, I can't see a thing."

"Fast forward it. They were there for two hours. I can't believe they'd never get *out* of the damn car." Gabe leaned into me, the floral scent of his shampoo wafting over me. I could think of so many better things we could be doing right now... but this was my job. "Okay." I set the video on fast forward and after around thirty minutes of footage, the passenger door opened and a man in a dark suit crouched down from the seat, then scrambled across the neighbor's yard and behind a tall bush.

"Did you see that?" Gabe inched closer beside me and jabbed a finger at the screen. "The dude was actually hiding in the damn bushes. If that isn't suspicious, I don't know what the hell is."

"Let me see that." Silas twisted my laptop to face him, then tapped on the keys. His brows snapped up. "Holy shit." He tucked Cash closer into his side. "What the hell is he doing?"

I turned my laptop back to me and the video went black. "Wait a minute. What happened?" I searched the other videos, but there was nothing on them. I opened up the footage we'd been watching and fast forwarded about another half hour, then the camera showed the yard again and the car on the street. "The camera either malfunctioned or was tampered with." I pursed my lips, my chest tightening. This was getting serious. They didn't care if we knew they were here now.

"Our friend, Remy installed the cameras. Maybe he can come by and check on them tomorrow." Gabe slumped against my side and rested his cheek on my shoulder. "Remy knows his shit. He's been doing security systems for a few years now. He installs systems in a bunch of high-end homes."

I nodded, biting at my thumbnail. I should call Kevin. He needed to know about this. And I should keep my gun close tonight. "I'm calling your dad." I stood up and paced into the room.

"Seriously?" Gabe's gaze chased me.

Raking my bangs off my forehead, I stopped and faced him. "He needs to know. It's what I'm here for, remember?"

"Fuck, yeah." Gabe frowned.

"Come here." Silas held out his arm and Gabe edged into him, on the other side from Cash. "Don't worry, we're not going to let anything happen to you." He furrowed his brows and threw a look at Jeremy. "You got more than one gun lying around here? I know how to shoot."

My pulse spiked. It wasn't a bad idea, but were we really going to prepare for a shootout with the mob? This was out of control. "I-I don't, actually. I do have a knife."

"Shit, I have a knife." Silas scoffed. "I even have a shillelagh under my bed."

"You do?" Cash's gaze grew even wider as he scanned Silas' face.

"Yeah. I am Irish, you know." He did a double take of Cash. "You knew that, right?"

"No, we never discussed it." Cash kissed his cheek. "I learn something new about you all the time, my little leprechaun."

"Okay, that's not going to stick." Silas tutted at Cash.

"What the hell is a shillelagh?" Gabe stared at Silas. "I knew about the knife. You're always using it for shit at our gigs." Under his breath, he said, "Never thought you'd use it to fend off a gangster."

"A shillelagh is a heavy wooden club you can use as a weapon. Mine was passed down from my grandpa O'Hearn, who emigrated here from Ireland." With a quick tick of his head, he smirked. "And yes, I know how to use it."

"I'm not surprised." I chuckled. Silas might be useful in this case, but I certainly didn't want him getting hurt, or any of them for that matter. "Let me call Kevin and see what he wants us to do." I slid my phone out of the back pocket of my jeans, dialed Kevin's number and held the phone to my ear.

The call rang once, then clicked. "Hello? Jeremy? Everything all right there?"

"For now, yes." I strode into the hallway, into Gabe's bedroom and shut the door, then flicked on the nightstand lamp. I had to keep Gabe from getting more upset than he already was. He had to get through those finals with as little distraction as possible. "We were out uh..." Shit, what should I tell him we were doing? A movie might look weird. "Getting food and when we came back, the black Mercedes sedan we'd seen on the cameras last weekend was parked outside the neighbor's house."

"We've got footage of a similar vehicle at my home as well." He huffed. "So, they're back."

"That's not all." I paced in front of Gabe's bed, the same one we both slept in now. Shit, this was weird talking to Kevin right next to where Gabe and I...He was now my boyfriend's father *and* my employer. "I reviewed the camera footage from earlier in the evening and it looks like they arrived around eight PM, waited about a half hour, then ran for a bush at the neighbor's house. Shortly after that, our camera went out."

"Wait, what do you mean it went out?" His breath caught.

"The camera went black. It was like that for about fifteen minutes, then came back on." I stopped my pacing and planted my hand on my hip. Would he want to call the police at this point? It might be time.

"The same thing has been happening here. Our cameras have been going dark at various times." He breathed in deeply. "Get the camera checked. We have to rule out a malfunction."

"And if it's tampering, do we call in the cops?" I glanced at the door. Surely Kevin wouldn't want his son in danger like this.

"Not yet. We don't have enough to go on. We can't prove anything. But if this continues, I may put a call in to the FBI. I have a friend there," he said. "We're winning the case, by the way. It's looking like the court is going to find TRS Waste fully at fault. There are going to be some serious fines to pay."

"Good news." I tipped my head back, then glanced out the windows, the drapes open. Shit, we should start closing these as soon as the sun went down. I'd warn the guys about it when I saw them. I snapped them shut. "What do you want me to do?"

"Hold steady for now. See if the cameras were tampered with and let me know," he said.

"Yeah, sure." I set my hand on the doorknob. "Talk to you soon. Bye."

"Bye." The call hung up.

I strolled out into the main room and fell into the couch, next to Gabe, sitting by himself.

"Well?" Gabe shimmied to my side and snatched my hand. "What did he say?"

"He uh..." I looked Gabe over. I didn't want him to worry too much. "He said they're winning the case, so it might be over soon." I wasn't going to tell him about the things going on at his parents' house. "We need to have Remy check on the cameras tomorrow, okay?"

"Yeah, sure, I'll text him now." He plucked his cell phone from the coffee table and tapped the screen. "There." The phone buzzed in his hands. "Looks like he can come over in the morning."

"Good." I perused the room. "Where did Cash and Silas go?"

"They went to bed." He kissed the back of my hand. "Maybe we should, too, huh?" He wagged his brows at me. "It might help get my mind off all this shit."

My cock woke. "Yeah? Okay." Would he want to do more

than we'd already done? I felt like I was ready. After the confessions at the mall, I was all in.

"Let's go." As he lifted up, he pulled me from the couch and led me into his bedroom, then closed the door.

"Gabe, can we talk for a minute?" I climbed onto the bed, then lay down on my back against the pillows and the headboard. I had no idea how to start with this whole thing and I was pretty sure he'd been taking things slow on my account.

"Yeah, sure." He crawled up next to me and lay down with his head facing me. "What's up?"

"I think I'm ready for more." I rolled to my side and placed my hand on his flat stomach, then snuck my fingers under his t-shirt and skimmed them over the ripples of his abs.

His breath caught. "More, as in sex?" His pupils flared and his dick bulged under his zipper. "Are you sure?"

"Yeah. I mean, what we've been doing is fun and all, but..." I bit my lower lip. How did guys approach this? If I was with a woman, I wasn't sure we'd be having this discussion. "I don't know what I'm doing." With a huff, I dipped my face into his neck. "Help me out here."

With a soft chuckle, he rested his cheek on my head. "I'll just start from the beginning. So, first of all, I'm on PrEP. It's an anti-viral med for HIV."

I lifted my head, my pulse quickening. "Oh, do you have it?" Shouldn't he have told me this a long time ago?

"No, I don't. I'm negative. I get tested every three months. The medicine keeps me from getting it and transmitting it." He pursed his lips. "Are you still in the mood? Sorry..."

"No, it's okay." Holy shit, this was a way different deal than being with a woman. I scratched my cheek. "Why are we talking about this?"

"Um...condoms?" He quirked his lips. "When was the last time you were tested for STDs?"

I widened my eyes. "Maybe a year ago. The last time I had a wellness exam." I thought a minute. Was he worried about me giving him something? "I haven't had many partners since then."

"But you've had some." He peered at me. "I'm sorry, I'm not trying to make you feel uncomfortable, but we should probably use condoms."

"Yeah, okay." My heart pattered in my chest. Did that mean we were going to have sex? "Who's um...do you catch or pitch?" Was that the right way to put it?

He giggled and kissed my cheek. "You mean do I top or bottom?" He snuck his lower lip between his teeth, his gaze raking over me. "I usually top, but I'm not opposed to bottoming with you." His grin waned. "Would you be more comfortable with that?"

"I-I don't know. I suppose." Warmth rushed up my neck. I really should have thought this through better and maybe Googled some things before I brought this up.

He skimmed his fingers under my shirt and up my chest, leaving a shiver, then brushed his finger pads over a nipple. "How about if we stop talking and see where things go? If you want to try something, just tell me."

I nodded, my gaze fixating on his plump lips, then pressed my mouth to his.

As he rolled me on top of him, a soft moan crept out of him and he slid his tongue against mine, slanting his mouth and claiming me, his hands slapping to my ass, his hard cock rubbing over mine through our jeans.

With a groan I lost myself in the sensation coiling in my gut, the feel of his hard body below mine. This was way better than talking. I cupped his cheeks and gazed deeply into his blue, hooded eyes, my chest warming with emotion. We loved each other and all the other bullshit didn't matter.

After a few minutes of kissing and rubbing on each other, I rose up onto my knees and shucked my shirt off. "Let's get undressed." I wanted skin on skin. Sitting to the side, I slid my jeans and boxer briefs off while he did the same. I snuck a peek at his slender frame, the curve of his thick cock rising up at the top of his thighs. It should have felt weird to be with a guy at some point, but it never did. Not with him. And getting to know him even more intimately would feel just right, too.

I lay to the side of him, my head propped up on an elbow in my palm, then admired him, trailing my finger down the center groove of his abs.

His stomach clenched and his breath snagged as his gaze flicked to mine. "Fuck, want to touch me down there?" He lifted his knees.

Biting my lip, I nodded. I knew what he meant. "Can I have some lube?"

With his brow ticking, he raised a corner of his mouth. "Of course." He slid out his nightstand drawer, grabbed the lube and opened the cap.

As I held out my hand, he squirted some out. "I really like having my dick sucked and my ass played with at the same time." His pupils grew and his cock pulsed off his stomach.

I had my marching orders. "Okay." As my balls ached with need, I crept between his legs and fisted his dick, then slathered his crevice with the lube, my finger finding his hole, circling it.

He hissed, tipping his head back. "Harder." Pre-cum beaded on his tip.

With a shiver racing up my spine, I dropped over his thick cock, pumped it with my mouth and rubbed over his hole, over and over.

"Oh, fuck, more, I need more." He gasped and rocked his hips, thrusting his dick to the back of my throat.

I dropped my hips and rubbed off on the bed, easing the

ache in my balls. Why had I never tried this before? Holy hell, it was getting me hot.

"Put it in, Jeremy. Slide your finger in." He dipped his head and gazed at me, tensing his brows.

I pulled off him with a wet pop, stroking his shaft with my hand, then snuck my finger into his hole. Oh my God, he was tight. What would it feel like to have my cock in there? Pleasure shuddered over me, and I halted the rocking of my hips. Just the thought of it might make me come.

"Fuck me with your finger, Jeremy." He clutched my shoulders, his fingers digging in. "Come on, I'm dying here."

"Yeah, okay," I gritted out. I could do this. I pumped my finger in and out and circled.

He shuddered and his thighs quivered around my head. "You got it, right there." He twined his fingers in my hair. "Add another finger...fuck, add two more if you want. Stretch me right out." His face tensed and he panted.

I pushed a second finger in and stroked his insides, then ran my tongue up and down his shaft, licking the pre-cum dribbling from the tip. Gabe was coming undone right in front of me. If I so much as touched my dick on the bed, I might go off.

"Fuck me, Jeremy. I need it." He groaned and shuddered again. "Condoms are in the nightstand." He flung his arm out to the side and ripped the drawer open.

I jumped up, grabbed a condom, then unwrapped it and sat on my tucked legs as I unrolled it. I wasn't going to think too much about this. He'd tell me what he wanted. I just had to follow his lead. I slathered more lube over the condom.

He tucked his knees into his armpits, exposing his puckered entrance to me. "Fill me up, but go slow, okay? Your dick is as big as the rest of you." His eyes widened and he licked his lips, focusing on my hard cock.

With a chuckle, I crept over him, hovering on a straight

arm, and lined myself up to him. "Let me know if you need me to stop." Tension knotted in my gut. I had to calm myself down, damn it. I breathed in deeply, then let it out. Slowly, I worked my cock inside of him, the tight heat of him threatening to overwhelm me. "Jesus, Gabe, this feels so damn good," I rasped.

Gasping, he wrapped his ankles around my hips. "You feel fucking awesome." He gazed deeply into my eyes, his pupils blown, and brows tensed. "Kiss me."

I dropped down onto my elbows, my dick buried up to my balls in him, then placed hungry kisses over his mouth, devouring him. If I moved, I might lose it.

With a deep moan, he rolled his hips and his ass clenched around me. "Fuck me, Jeremy. Do it. I'm ready."

I rocked my hips, my cock slipping out, leaving the tip in, then thrust back into him, again and again. Sensation heated my skin and curled my toes. Dropping my forehead to his, I bit my lower lip and groaned.

"That's it...faster, fuck me hard and fast." He squeezed his thighs around my hips and slapped his hands to my ass, digging his fingers into my flesh. "God, I need it, need you."

I pumped short, quick thrusts into him, then claimed his mouth in needy kisses, sweat beading up on my back.

Slanting his mouth over mine, he deepened the kisses and met my pace with his hips.

As the seconds turned to minutes, pleasure surged at the base of my spine and tingled out through my limbs. I broke the kisses, then stopped. I was almost there, but I didn't want it to end. "Look at me, Gabe." I brushed a wet lock of curly hair off his forehead. We were so close now, so connected in the most intimate way. "I love you."

He blinked, then as his eyes grew glossy, he took a hard swallow and met my gaze. "I love you, too." He brushed the back of his fingers down my cheek. "So much." He inhaled deeply.

"Are you close?" I inched out of him, then back in, a hot knot of sensation shuddering through me.

"Yeah." He lifted his head to place a deep kiss on my lips. "Come for me, Jeremy. Fill me up."

"Oh, fuck." I rocked my hips, thrusting deep inside him and my climax surged over me, pulsing pleasure through every nerve ending. With sharp gasps, my cock spurted into the condom.

"Coming, so fucking hard." He pumped his dick between us, his face tensing, and painted our chests with his release, crying out.

As it slowed, I fell over him and panted. We had to lose the condoms. "What do I have to do to go bareback with you?"

"Shit, you're asking that already?" He chuckled and skimmed his finger pads up and down my back. "Get tested."

"I'll get tested tomorrow then." I smirked against his shoulder, then kissed it and lifted my head. "Seriously, that was intense." As my dick waned, I pulled out.

"Tomorrow, huh? My ass is that good?" He freed a soft snort, then pecked my cheek. "Let's clean up and cuddle."

"Cuddle?" I gave him a lazy grin, my heart warming. "Yeah, that sounds perfect."

AFTER WE HAD both cleaned up, we lay in bed under the covers, him tucked into my side with his leg wrapped over both of mine, his spent dick resting against my hip.

"You really want to get tested?" With his cheek pressed against my chest, he circled his fingers around my nipple.

"Yeah, why wouldn't I?" I hugged him tighter to me, my

chest warming. Was it possible that after what we'd done, I'd fallen even more in love with him? "It's probably a good idea anyways. I mean, I do use condoms with um...you know, women, but you never know."

He nodded, and lay there for a few moments wearing a slight frown, then lifted his head, his gaze searching my face. "Different topic. What do you think is going to happen? What do you think these mob guys want?"

I puffed out a breath. How much could I tell him when I didn't even know the whole story? "I really don't know. Like I said, the threats to your father haven't been very clear. I think they know what they're doing."

"But what form have the threats come in as? A letter? A phone call? A fucking email?" He furrowed his brows.

Shit, I'd never even thought to ask that. "Don't know. Kevin hasn't specified anything like that." I brushed a curl off his forehead. "Look, my job is to make sure nothing happens to you and through all this, you're able to do well on your finals. So, focus on studying and leave the rest to me and your dad. Okay?"

He pressed his lips into a hard line. "I'll do my best. This week is going to suck. I'm going to have to study as much as possible."

"Then let's go to sleep, so you're well rested." I reached to the lamp on the nightstand and flicked off the light, then pulled him into my chest and kissed his head. "Love you."

"Love you, too." He kissed my chest, then settled in.

THE NEXT DAY, Gabe studied at the dinette, pouring over a book, and typing on his laptop with his headphones on. We were waiting for Remy to come over and take a look at the cameras to see if they'd malfunctioned or were tampered with last night. I'd decided I had to do something physical. All this sitting around was killing me. I hadn't worked out since I'd been here. I jumped off the couch, then strolled into an open area of the main room and did some push-ups, two handed first, then one handed.

Milo walked out of the hallway from the bedrooms, did a double take of me and stopped. "Shit, you're strong enough to do that?"

I sat on my haunches and chuckled, then scratched my cheek. "Yeah, guess I still am. I haven't been to the gym for a while."

"I've never been able to do that. I'd just fall flat on my face." He walked off into the kitchen and took some bread out of the cupboard, then some lunchmeat and condiments from the refrigerator. "Can I make you a sandwich?" He twisted to look at me.

"Naw, that's okay. Let me see if Gabe wants one, though." I finished out my set of push-ups, jumped up and walked to Gabe, then tapped his shoulder. "Hey."

Gabe's blue-eyed gaze met mine and he pulled a headphone from his ear. "Yeah?"

"Milo's making sandwiches, you want one?" I stepped behind him and kneaded my fingers into the muscles by his neck.

"Oh, fuck." Closing his eyes, Gabe moaned and hung his head.

"Take it into the bedroom. Jesus, fuck." Striding into the room, Silas scoffed, his red Target t-shirt stretched over his chest.

"Stop it." Gabe chuckled. "I can't help it if my man has great hands." His gaze raked over me. "And great uh—"

"Nope. Stop." Silas snatched a bottled water from the refrigerator.

"You going to work?" Milo squirted mustard on a slice of bread sitting on a plate.

Silas huffed out a breath, tipping his head back. "Yes, I'm going to work. Why is it you or someone else in this house always asks me that when it's plain to see I'm wearing my work shit?" He smirked at Milo. "Is there any other time you see me dressed like this?"

Milo shrugged. "Guess not."

"Silas, why are you being so damn ornery today?" Gabe asked as I worked on the muscles closer to his shoulders. "Isn't Cash putting out?" He snickered.

Silas sipped his water, lifting a brow. "Cash always puts out." His smirk faded. "Guess I'm just a little on edge with all this mobster shit." He flashed his eyes at Milo, then side hugged him. "Sorry, man."

I halted my rubbing on a knot at the top of Gabe's shoulder blade. "Don't worry, Silas. We've got this." My phone buzzed on the coffee table. "Shit." I ran to the table and picked it up, the screen reading, *Kevin Johnson.* "It's Gabe's dad. I'll be right back." As I pressed the phone to my ear, I strode down the hallway and into Gabe's bedroom, then shut the door. "Hello, this is Jeremy."

"Jeremy, are you someplace we can talk?" Kevin asked.

"Yes. What's up?" I glanced out the window of Gabe's bedroom, the curtains drawn open, and into the front yard. No black cars in sight.

"We've had a breach at the law firm. One of the admins opened a phishing email that gave some hackers access to our servers. We don't know if it's related to the mobsters from Philly and the case we're working on, but it sure is coinciden-tal." He huffed out a breath.

"Shit, really? I had no idea mobsters were into cyber-crimes." I paced by the bed, raking my fingers through my hair. There was a hell of a lot of information they could have taken. "Is any money missing from accounts? Or do you think they were looking for case material?"

"No money is missing, and we've secured all our assets. I don't know what the hell they were looking for," he said. "Anything new on your end?"

I shook my head. "No. We're waiting on Gabe's friend to come and take a look at the cameras for tampering, but we haven't had any visitors since we came home last night."

"Good. Let me know what you find out." He sucked in a breath. "You can text me. I'll be at a function this evening for ASU with my wife. We're getting ready to donate again this next year to the college of law."

My chest tightened. "You are? That's great." His donations along with his recommendation of me when I'd applied to law school last year, were probably what helped me get my deferral. That and me working at his firm in the meantime. I owed him so much. I rubbed the heel of my hand over my chest.

"So, I guess that begs the question. Now that your loans are paid off, will you be starting up school in the fall?" he asked.

"I plan to, yes." My heart jolted. Shit, I had to get on that. I was already late in picking my fall courses. Maybe I could do it today and Gabe could help. He already knew who the better professors were.

"Okay, well, you know how much I appreciate you, your dedication and hard work. We'll accommodate you any way you need." The smile in his voice filtered through the phone. "When you graduate, I'd love to have you as an associate."

"Thank you, Kevin. I'd love that, too. You've already helped me so much." My chest tightened further. Would he still be saying that if he knew what was going on between Gabe and me?

"How is Gabe doing?" he asked.

We were both thinking about Gabe. "He's doing well. He's studying today and probably all day tomorrow. He's focusing on his finals." Shit, he only had a few more weeks until they started.

"Okay, well, make sure he's not distracted. I don't see any reason to bother him with this hacker situation. It might not be related at all," he said, then huffed. "Text me later."

"I sure will." I inhaled deeply. What was I going to tell Gabe? He knew I was talking to his dad. He knows his dad wouldn't call without a good reason.

"Okay then, talk to you soon." He hung up the call.

"Fuck." I scratched my forehead. This thing was getting messy.

THIRTEEN
GABE

I watched the hallway, twisted in my chair, my headphones lying next to my laptop. Why was dad calling? Something had to have happened. I tapped the back of my chair with my index finger. Silas had left for work and had wanted an update as soon as I had one.

"Do you want mayo or mustard on your turkey and cheddar sandwich?" Milo sucked mustard off a finger.

"Mayo, please." I pursed my lips. Where the hell was Jeremy? Something had happened, I could feel it in my gut.

Jeremy strode into the room, his gaze finding mine.

"Well?" I stood up and walked to him. "What did he say?"

Milo turned from the kitchen counter with wide eyes. "Something happened again, didn't it."

Flicking his gaze from Milo to me, Jeremy said, "Shit, yeah. I'm not supposed to tell you though. Your dad's not sure if it's related or not." He grabbed my hand and led me to the couch. "So, take this with a grain of salt."

"Come on, Milo. You should hear this, too." I dropped in

next to Jeremy while Milo sank into the other end of the sectional.

Jeremy breathed in deeply. "Some hackers broke into the company through a phishing email that an admin opened and clicked on by mistake." He choked out a chuckle. "It's probably not related to the case he's been working on. It's probably pure coincidence." His lips quirked. "He said they've already secured all their assets and no money has been stolen."

"Maybe they weren't looking for money. Maybe they were looking for files on the case that started this whole situation." I studied him. Was he downplaying it for my benefit?

Milo played with the strings on his pink sweats. "What is the case about that's bringing mobsters to our house? Was it a murder or something?"

"No, nothing like that." Jeremy patted Milo's thigh. "Desert Solar hired a contractor in an attempt to dispose of some toxic manufacturing waste for a cheaper rate. Well, the rate was cheap because the contractor, TRS Waste, basically dumped it out in the desert. The company has ties to a mob out of Philly, or so Kevin thinks."

"Shit, this has to do with the drinking water problems out in Gila Bend, doesn't it? I saw that on the local news. People were getting sick." My chest heated. What assholes these guys had to be to pull something like that. At some point, this might end up being a high-profile case on the news, too. So far, Desert Solar had probably found a way to keep it quiet. They did have some deep pockets and far reaches into the local government.

"Wow, that's terrible." Milo's gaze met mine. "But your dad's law firm will put them in jail, right?"

"No, the prosecutor for the state would do that." I shook my head, twisting my lips. Maybe I should be a prosecutor if I could get out of dad's law firm? My gaze met Jeremy's. He'd probably work at the firm someday. Might we be working together at some point?

"It sounds like the EPA and the feds are trying to figure out who's at fault and there are some hefty fines involved. Kevin's law firm is fighting to make sure Desert Solar isn't held liable." Jeremy slowly nodded his head, twining his fingers in mine. "This is all strictly confidential. So, it doesn't leave this room." He looked at Milo, then me.

"Okay. I understand." Milo jumped up from the couch, then strolled into the kitchen. "All this excitement is making me hungry." He plated the two sandwiches he'd been working on. "Sure you don't want one, Jeremy?" He turned from the counter with the plates in his hand.

"You know what? Yeah, I'd like one, too. Turkey and cheddar with mustard." He squeezed my hand, then kissed my knuckles. "When do you think Remy will be here to take a look at the cameras?"

"If I know him? Soon. I'm sure Axel had some bedroom activities he wanted to engage in before he let him go." I chortled. That was an understatement. The two of them probably had more sex than any of us.

Jeremy leaned in close, then whispered, "Maybe we should be doing more of that?" He waggled his brows at me.

My cock woke. "Hell yeah. Let me get these cases down and I'll take you up on that." The sex we'd had last night was amazing. Hopefully he'd want more and maybe, just maybe, he'd let me top.

AN HOUR LATER, knocking sounded on the door, then it swung open. "Hello, hello. Remy's security service is here." Axel pranced into the room with Remy following, and looked around, hefting up his black skinny jeans.

I peered up from my book. Axel always had to make an entrance. "Hey, good to see you."

Jeremy and Milo stood from the couch. They'd been watching a baseball game on the television and Jeremy had been trying to get Milo to understand it. Little did he know what a lost cause that was.

Remy met Jeremy at the couch, then shook his hand. "Can you show me the video?"

Axel sauntered into the kitchen, perused the contents of our refrigerator, then pulled out a beer. "Anyone else want one?" He snicked it open.

"I'm studying, so no." I straightened. I wasn't going to be able to focus while they were here, so I might as well take a break.

Milo stalked into the kitchen. "I'll take one. "

Axel handed the beer he'd just opened to Milo, then grabbed another one for himself. "Good, I don't want to be the only one drinking." He hooked a brow at me. "Gabe, do you ever relax?"

"Not when finals are coming up." I shifted my attention to Jeremy and Remy, now seated next to each other on the couch with Jeremy's laptop open on the coffee table.

I stood up and stepped behind them, placing my hands on the back of the sofa.

Jeremy pointed to his screen. "See here? This is where the video goes dark."

"Let me see something." Remy pulled the laptop into his lap, then zoomed in and slowly scrolled through each microsecond of footage. He went forward and back a few times. "Look, you can see the camera going dark from one side, like somebody put something over it. I don't think it malfunctioned. I think someone covered it on purpose."

A shiver raced up my spine. "Why would they do something like that?"

"Good thing Silas isn't here. Isn't that when he was home alone with Cash watching a movie?" He snickered. "What if the mobsters looked in the windows and saw Cash and Silas fucking on the couch?"

"What?" Jeremy twisted his head, his brows snapping up.

With a shoulder shrug, Milo said, "It happens."

Axel barked out a laugh. "Oh my God, and Caleb used to give *me* shit about doing things with Remy on that couch. Wait until he hears this."

"Let's not focus on who's doing what on the damn couch." I straightened and planted my hands on my hips. "Do we have any leather cleaner around here?" Now I wasn't sure I wanted to sit on the thing.

Busting out a giggle, Axel covered his mouth. "I think there's some in the laundry room."

"Good." I knew what I was doing later. I focused on the laptop still in Remy's lap. "So, is there any way to get around having these guys cover our cameras?"

"We can install some cameras inside the windows that look out, but the range won't be as far." Remy twisted to gaze at me, then pursed his lips. "How long has this been going on, Gabe?"

"Uh..." I brushed my hand down the back of my head. "A while, like it started back when Silas was having problems with his ex." Might as well tell them the truth now.

Axel dropped his mouth open. "Is that why you were so eager to install and pay for all this shit?" He sipped his beer, then stepped closer to me. "Or did your dad pay for it?"

"It's the same thing, isn't it?" I rubbed the back of my neck. I hated for people to think I was an entitled rich kid, but I sort of was. "Anyways, let's get some cameras inside the windows, too. Do you think you can do that today?"

"Yeah, sure." Remy gave the laptop back to Jeremy. "You only want the cameras to point outside, right?" He smirked at me.

A shudder rolled down my spine as I glanced at the couch. "Yeah, we don't need footage of Silas and Cash fucking on the couch." I loved those guys, but damn. I didn't need to see that.

Axel snorted. "That would be hilarious to show him, though, wouldn't it? Maybe we could turn the cameras around when he's home alone with—"

"No, Axel." Remy held up his palm to Axel. "There are privacy laws."

With scoff, Axel rolled his eyes, then drank his beer. "It's not like Silas would take us to court." He rubbed his chin. "But, we could turn the cameras on the room and prank him. I bet we could get a viral TikTok video out of it."

Jeremy furrowed his brows and glanced at me.

He probably thought we were all nuts at this point. I patted his shoulder. "No, we're not doing that. When this is over, we can take all this shit down." I pursed my lips. When would it be over? Court cases could drag on forever.

"Anyways, I'll run to Home Depot and pick up some more cameras, then come back here and add them to the system." Remy stood up, then walked to Axel. "Is that okay, lover boy?" He kissed Axel's cheek.

"When you say it like that, it is." Axel hugged Remy into his side. "I'll let you borrow my life partner for the afternoon. I have some studying to do, too. Finals aren't going to take themselves."

"You're going to study after drinking beer?" Milo tsked.

"I'll take a nap first. One beer doesn't get to me very much."

He twisted his lips. "Now a shot of tequila? That's something else."

"No tequila, Axel." Remy flashed his eyes at him, then shook his head. "We don't need a repeat of Mexico."

Jeremy flicked his gaze to mine. "What happened in Mexico?"

"My dad has a mansion on the beach in Rocky Point, and we stayed there for a few days. Axel got pretty drunk and that's where Caleb met Eric." Okay, it was a four-day drunk fest really, but Jeremy didn't need to know that. We'd all had a lot of steam to blow off.

Milo snickered. "Axel was shitfaced."

"I was recovering emotionally and physically from being shot." Axel's face grew slack, and his attention drew to Jeremy. "Don't get shot, either of you." He huffed. "These are mobsters you're dealing with, right?"

I stared at Jeremy. We'd thought we were being shot at last night. And Jeremy had...Shit, he'd shielded me. He'd put his life on the line for me. My heart stung. "Nobody's getting shot, Axel." And if it did happen, I wasn't going to let Jeremy get hurt. I couldn't live with myself if that happened.

"Good. Just...be careful." Axel gave me a pointed look, then sucked in a deep breath. "Anyways, we got a gig this weekend at the Yucca Tap House on Saturday night. I checked the work calendar and we're all free, so I took it." He sipped more beer.

"Great." I flicked my gaze to Jeremy. Would he think a gig there would be too dangerous? Playing a gig was how I decompressed from all this shit. "It is okay, isn't it?"

Jeremy shrugged a shoulder. "Let's see how this week plays out." His attention drew to Axel. "You can cancel if things pick up around here, right?"

I looked him up and down. "Are you serious?" I shifted my stance. "But I thought we were supposed to act normal."

"Gabe." He grabbed my hand. "I was thinking if we catch these thugs peeking in our windows, maybe it would be a good idea to head up to your parents' house for a while."

I blinked a few times. "What? Oh, hell no." I shook my head with a scoff. How the hell would we hide what we had if we stayed there?

"Just think about it, okay? You'd probably be safer there." Jeremy pursed his lips. "I don't want anything to happen to you." He squeezed my hand.

Axel wagged a finger at me. "Listen to him, Gabe." He pressed his lips together. "None of us want anything happening to either of you."

Slumping my shoulders, I said, "Shit, I'll think about it." I wasn't going to be able to fight them all, so I'd give in for now.

"Anyways, I'll leave you in the hands of my very capable lover boy and we'll see how things go this week." He gulped down the rest of his beer, kissed Remy's cheek, then hugged each of us and left.

Jeremy's gaze wound to Remy. "He's quite the whirlwind, isn't he."

With a chortle and a shake of his head, Remy said, "Yeah, that's one way to put it. A lovable whirlwind."

THE DAY WOUND DOWN and Remy had installed the new cameras, Cash and Silas were out on a date and Milo was at last studying for his own finals in his room. We'd ordered some delivery pizza for dinner and my eyes were blurry from reading cases. "Hey." I pulled my headphones out of my ears and shut my laptop, then faced Jeremy, watching television on the couch.

"You done?" He twisted to me, resting a bent arm on the back of the cushions.

"I am." I gave him a teasing smile and toyed with the edge of my laptop. "Want to um...go into my bedroom maybe?" He had said he wanted to—

"Yes. Thought you'd never ask." He hopped from the couch, rounded the end of it, then snatched my hand. "Let's go." Tugging me out of my chair, he led me down the hallway and into my room.

My gaze caught on the darkness outside the window over the side of my bed. "Shut the curtains." A shiver sparked over my skin. I didn't like the idea of having mobsters outside our house. "Do you think these guys might be looking in our windows?"

He tossed the curtains closed. "I don't know. I can't imagine why they'd want to do something like that, but we should be more careful just in case." Turning to me, he creased his brows. "Try not to think about it, okay?" He stepped to me and wrapped his arms around my shoulders, then held me to his chest and kissed my head. "I really don't want you thinking too much about it. You need to be focused on school. I've got this, okay?"

I nodded against his shoulder, his musky scent filling my senses. I wanted to be lost in him. It was so easy to let him take care of everything. Being in his strong arms was the safest I'd ever felt. Hooking my arms around his waist, I breathed him in and nuzzled his neck. "Love you."

"God, I love you so much, Gabe." He skimmed his hand down the back of my hair, then kissed his way down my cheek to claim my mouth with hungry kisses. "Need you," he rasped, his hardening cock brushing mine under our jeans.

I slipped my tongue between his lips and slanted my mouth over his, taking him again and again, grinding my dick on his.

Moaning, sensation coiled in my gut and my skin flashed with heat. Would he be open to more tonight?

With a deep groan, he nibbled down my neck and unfastened my jeans, then worked my cock out and gave it lazy strokes. "You're so hard for me." He bit at the soft flesh of my neck, then pinched a nipple.

I gasped and tipped my head back, my fingers digging into the round globes of his ass. "We need to lose these clothes, damn it."

"We do." With faster strokes over my shaft, he bent down and sucked my nipple through the fabric of my t-shirt, then softly bit it, peeking up at me.

I hissed and thrust into his hand, a spark of pleasure bursting through me. "Fuck, yeah." He'd learned quickly what I liked. But I wanted skin on skin. I pushed him away from me. "Get undressed. Now." I tore my shirt off and shimmied out of my briefs and jeans while he did the same, then climbed onto the bed and under the covers. For some reason, even with the curtains closed, I couldn't shake the sense that the mobsters could be out there, right now, watching the house. Fuck, quit thinking about it. I raked my gaze over Jeremy's tall, muscular body as he stepped to the bed.

His hard cock bobbed as he walked, then he flung his dark bangs off his forehead and bit his lip. "I want to try things..."

"Good." I flipped the covers down for him, my mouth watering. I wanted him bad, wanted to suck that big cock of his and do so, so much more.

He crept in next to me, then pulled me over him, our hot dicks pressed together. "I want to know what it's like, you know..." His cheeks flushed and he looked away for a heartbeat, then focused on me. With his pupils widening, he said, "Play with my ass."

I ticked my brows up. "Yeah?" My dick pulsed against his

and his twitched in return. No mistaking that. "I was sort of hoping you might want to try that." Could he be any more perfect for me? I rubbed the tip of my nose over his and grinned softly.

"While you're sitting there studying, I seem to have a lot of time to myself to think." His cheeks reddened further.

"And you're sitting there thinking about anal?" With a soft chuckle I dipped my head, then focused on him. "You know I'm never going to get any studying done now." I planted a kiss on his lips. "And you thought the mob was going to distract me."

"Oops." He chuckled softly. "Yeah, maybe I should have kept my mouth shut."

With a shake of my head, I said, "Oh, no, no, no. See, I need to know these things." I placed a kiss on his lips, then his cheek, then nibbled down his neck and worked my way to his chest, pulling the covers down with me. "First, I'm going to play with some other parts of you though." Because fuck, was he a sight to behold. I flicked my tongue over his nipple, then the other and gave it a soft bite.

He arched his back and gasped. "Oh, fuck, Gabe. Keep going." He pressed on my shoulders.

As a grin quirked my lips, I licked down the grooves of his abs, nibbling along the way, until his firm cock nudged my cheek. Creeping between his legs, I fisted the base of his dick and fluttered my tongue over the flared head, lapping up a bead of pre-cum, the salty taste of him shivering desire through my body. "God, you taste good, Jeremy."

"Yeah?" He tilted his head over the pillow, his dark gaze fixated on me, his fingers tangled in my hair.

"Yeah." All at once, I swallowed him whole and pumped my mouth over him.

"Oh, fuck!" He shuddered and lifted his knees, his thighs quivering, his abs clenching.

I stayed on him, milking him with my mouth, twisting my fist around the base of his cock. I wanted to make him feel so fucking good. As saliva trickled from my mouth to his balls, I slicked my fingers in it and teased a ball, then the other, all while stroking him with my tongue.

He groaned, over and over and pulled at my hair. "Do it, Gabe. I want to feel it."

While working his solid dick with my mouth, I slid my fingers into his crevice and circled his hole.

He whimpered and his ass clenched around me.

Leaving his cock with a wet pop, I said, "Relax for me, Jeremy." If we were going to do this right, I should probably get the lube.

"Okay." His face tensed. "It's just so...feels so good."

"Yeah, it does." Didn't I know it. I reached over him into my nightstand drawer, then grabbed the lube. Sitting up on tucked legs, I slicked my fingers. "You do want penetration, right?" I'd assumed, but I knew better than to assume.

"I think so?" He watched me with dark, wide eyes. "Just your finger, right?"

"Yep." I chuckled. "I don't want to scare you right off the bat." With a soft smile, I came down again, fisting the base of his dick, then flicked the head with my tongue. "Relax for me. I'll go in slow. If you want me to stop, just say so."

He nodded and raked his teeth over his lower lip. "I'm ready."

Stroking his firm cock with my mouth, I dipped my fingers to his hole, circled, then pressed.

He let out a long, slow breath and relaxed.

I slipped my finger inside while pumping his dick with my mouth, licking up the underside.

With a groan, he clutched my hair and panted, his thighs trembling. "Yeah, do it. Feels good."

Stroking his insides slowly, I curled my finger just so and stayed on him, tipping my head to watch his reaction.

His brows wrinkled, then his abs clenched. "Oh, fuck, yeah, right there." He pulled my hair. "Go faster."

While bobbing my head over his cock, I worked my finger inside him, rubbing over his prostate. My dick ached with need and a thread of pre-cum dribbled from my tip. Fuck, it was hot watching him get off like this. I snuck a second finger inside him, and his ass tightened around me. "Too much?" I halted my fingers and flicked my gaze to his.

With his mouth dropped open, he shook his head. "N-no, just needed a minute." He rocked his hips. "Go."

I stroked his insides while pumping his cock. A shiver of desire rushed up my spine. After this, would he let me fuck him? I could only hope. He seemed to be enjoying it so far.

"Gabe, holy shit." He shuddered and his ass clenched. "Coming, oh fuck." As his dick pulsed in my mouth and spurted hot cum down my throat, his hole spasmed over my fingers. He threw his head back and let out a whimpering cry.

My cock jerked between my legs and grew harder. God damn, I was so close. After swallowing the last of his cum, I freed him and sat up, then stroked my aching cock. As I fell over the edge, sensation surged inside me in harsh waves and I dropped over him on a straight arm, painting his chest with my release, gasping as each contraction shuddered through me. As it slowed, I panted over him. "Oh fuck, that was intense."

He swiped a blob of my cum from his chest, then licked it off his finger. "Yeah, looks like it was." With a soft grin, he ruffled my hair. "Guess you like playing with my ass."

Letting out a soft chuckle, I fell onto him, between his legs, and he wrapped his arms around me, our still half-hard cocks pressing together. "Yeah, I do." Would he let me fuck him? Was now a good time to ask? "You seemed to like it, too. Didn't you?" I tipped my head up to gaze into his face.

"I did." He curled the edge of his mouth. "It wasn't until we had sex and I saw how much you liked it that I'd even considered it." He squeezed me and kissed my head. "You're pretty good at that."

"I've had some practice." Maybe that wasn't a great thing to admit. I twisted my lips. How could I ask him what I wanted to know? "But watching you get off on it...well, that was really hot."

"Yeah?" He chewed the side of his lower lip and peeked at me. "You said you usually like to top."

I slowly raised my head. Was he about to offer to bottom? "Yes, I do." My gaze searched his face, his tensing brows. He was thinking about it. "Would you uh, like to explore it some more maybe?"

"Yeah, I think so." He sucked in a quick breath. "I never thought I'd consider something like that, but the time I've spent here with you and your friends has given me a whole new perspective on life." He creased his brows. "Is that weird?"

I shook my head. "No, that's not weird. It makes perfect sense." I set my chin on his chest, keeping my gaze on his. "If we'd met under different circumstances, I wonder if we'd have gotten together?" Probably not. A faint ache crept through my chest.

"Maybe, but I'm sure it would have taken me a lot longer to figure out my feelings for you." He brushed his knuckles down my cheek. "I'm glad I met you, like this, under these circumstances. I'm glad this chance was given to me."

I kissed his chest. "Me, too." I had my answer. He was open to bottoming for me. I just had to give him time. I glanced at my drawn curtains. I had indeed lost myself in him. For a good half hour, I'd totally forgotten about the assholes that could be lurking around outside. "I hate to say this, but my curiosity is killing me. Let's clean up and check the cameras."

"You sure?" He peered down at me, his brows wrinkling.

I huffed a breath. "Yeah, is that weird?" I lifted onto an elbow and looked down on him, his lips still red and dark hair mussed over the pillow.

"No, not really. If we can get a face we can ID, it would help a lot, I think." He raked his hand through his hair. "It would be nice to take some action against these guys, and the sooner the better."

"Agreed." I kissed his chest, then peeled off him. "Quick shower?"

"Absolutely." He climbed off my bed.

After cleaning up, we both dressed in pajama bottoms and ambled into the main room, then Jeremy grabbed his laptop from the coffee table. "Let's see if we've got anything."

I glanced at the clock over the stovetop. It was after midnight already and Silas wasn't back. "Guess Silas must be staying at Cash's tonight."

"Maybe." Jeremy dropped into the center of the sofa, opened his laptop, and booted it up.

"Want a drink? Water or a beer maybe?" I sauntered into the kitchen and opened the refrigerator, perusing our options. I didn't want to hover over him while he checked the video feeds. "We also have orange juice."

"I'll take a water. I gotta rehydrate after that session in your bedroom." He waggled his brows at me, then clicked the mousepad on his computer.

"Yeah, good idea." After snatching out two bottled waters, I stalked to the couch and fell in next to him. "So, see anything?"

Peering at his screen, he shook his head. "No, not a thing." He stopped on a video, then zoomed in on a rabbit eating the grass on the front lawn. "I hope they didn't come by when Remy was here and saw him putting new cameras in." With a sigh, he closed the lid on his laptop. "Let's give it a few days." Winding his arm around my shoulders, he pulled me into his side.

I twisted open a bottled water and handed it to him, then opened my own and took a sip. "What if they saw them and they don't come back?"

He shrugged a shoulder. "Don't know. Maybe we can quit worrying?" He rested his head against mine. "I sure wish I knew what they were up to."

"Yeah, I wish they'd make a move one way or the other. I'm starting to get the heebie-jeebies from this shit." I snuggled into his side, his body warming mine.

He kissed my head. "Anyways, there's nothing to see, so let's go to bed."

Yawning, I nodded. "Yeah, I'm tired." Maybe there'd be something on the cameras in the morning. Now that we had a chance of getting a face shot, I wanted them to come around.

FOURTEEN
JEREMY

The next morning, I'd made a hearty breakfast of bacon and eggs with hash browns for the house, then Cash and Silas had offered to clean it up. I was itching to get back to the video feed. I couldn't believe the thugs might have seen what Remy was doing here yesterday. I sat on the couch, eyeing my laptop and chewing my thumbnail. Should I look, or was it too soon to be starting this?

Gabe sat at the kitchen table with Milo, both nursing a second cup of coffee. Gabe asked, "So, how late were you two out?" He glanced toward Silas and Cash, washing dishes in the sink.

"I don't know, one?" Silas handed a frying pan to Cash.

Wiping the pan with a towel, Cash stepped toward Gabe. "I got Silas to go to the gay bar with me." A wide smile swept over his lips.

"Shit, you did?" Gabe straightened in his chair, a smirk playing over his mouth.

"Why didn't you tell me? I would have joined you." Milo sipped his coffee.

"It wasn't a planned thing, okay? Cash sort of tricked me into it." Silas scoffed and shook his head.

"Oh? And how did he trick you?" Gabe planted his elbows on the table and held his coffee cup to his lips.

I focused on Gabe. What would it be like to go to a gay bar with him? Last time I'd gone with my girlfriend, I hadn't quite felt like I'd belonged. Something inside me had wanted to belong though. Would Gabe want to go?

"He promised me a blow job if I went and then we had too much fun and he fell asleep on me." Silas grabbed a dish rag off the counter and flicked it at Cash's ass.

"You got your blow job this morning and then some." Cash flashed his eyes at Silas and scoffed.

"Yeah, well..." Silas returned to the sink. "I had a boner all night."

"Silas, you sound like Axel right now." Gabe chortled.

With a glare and pointing his finger at Gabe, Silas said, "Don't you dare say that."

I watched them banter, my heart warming. These guys were so close, closer than I'd ever been to a friend. Even Grant. It was so cool to see. What would Grant say when I told him? I pursed my lips. I didn't have to say anything to him right away. I picked up my laptop and started it up.

Gabe stood from his chair, then dropped in next to me. "What're you doing?" He sipped his coffee.

I huffed a sigh. "I'm looking at the video feeds from last night." I clicked on the app, then opened the videos and started one. Cash's Mini pulled up to the curb and Silas stepped out of the car, stumbled, then righted himself, grabbing the top of the door.

"Oh shit." Gabe chuckled. "Silas, I think you were too shit faced to have enjoyed any blow job from Cash last night."

"What?" Silas jogged to the couch and leaned over my shoulder, peering at my laptop screen.

Biting my smile, I rewound the footage. "There, you look like you almost fell getting out of the car."

"Oh, fuck." Silas let out a soft snort. "The curb jumped out at me. Didn't you see it?" He pointed at the screen.

Cash waltzed up behind Silas, covering his giggle with his hand. "Hun, you were pretty happy last night." He kissed Silas' cheek. "Let's go and finish these dishes."

"Yeah." Silas followed Cash into the kitchen.

I clicked on a few more videos and didn't see anything of interest. I closed the laptop. "Nothing."

Gabe's phone buzzed on the table and Milo picked it up. "Gabe, your mom is texting you."

"Yeah?" He reached his hand back behind him and Milo slapped the phone into it. Tapping his phone, Gabe said, "Oh, shit." He dropped his mouth open.

"What?" I rested my hand on his thigh, my pulse quickening. Had something bad happened at his parents' house?

His throat dipped with a hard swallow. "My mom wants us to come up there for dinner tonight." He lifted his brows.

I blinked a few times. "Us?" Was he sure the invite was for me, too?

He held his phone to my face, and I peered at the message.

MOM

Can you come up for dinner tonight? With all that's going on, I thought it would be nice to have the family together. You can invite the young man your father hired to be your bodyguard. Your father thinks very highly of him, and I'd like to meet him.

I stared at the screen, rereading it. Kevin thought so well of me he'd even told his wife about me? "Um..." My gaze snapped to Gabe's.

"Holy shit, what are you going to do?" Milo held his coffee cup in his hands and straightened his spine.

"Not go." Pursing his lips, Gabe snuck a peek at me. "I can always say I have too much studying."

I scratched my forehead. How did I feel about this? I did sort of want to meet the rest of his family. "What if we just go?" I squeezed Gabe's thigh.

His gaze met mine. "Are you going to be able to hide what we have while we're there?"

Shrugging a shoulder, I said, "Yeah, sure." How hard could it be? I just wouldn't touch him. I could do that. "It sounds like your mom really wants to see you. She's probably worried with all the mafia stuff that's going on."

Gabe twisted his lips and stared at his hands, turning the coffee cup in his lap. "Yeah, guess so. My mom doesn't deserve to worry." He sighed. "I'll tell her we'll come up for dinner."

"Have you thought about coming out, Jeremy?" Milo gave my shoulder a squeeze, then released it.

"I have." I snapped my gaze to Gabe, now frowning. "I'll do it as soon as Gabe is ready for me to." I twined my fingers in his and rested them over his thigh. I didn't want to put any pressure on him to do the same, knowing how his family dynamic worked.

Gabe worried his lower lip. "I'm ready. If you're ready to do that, then don't let my fucked up situation stop you." Leaning over, he pressed a soft kiss on my cheek.

"I'd like to come out to my mom and sister first. My friend Grant, well, I'm not sure how he'll take it." I slid my fingers along the edge of my laptop. Grant wasn't a homophobe, was he? I had no idea. I looked around me at Cash and Silas finishing up the dishes, then at Milo, still sitting at the table eating the last bite of his cinnamon toast. If I lost Grant as a friend but gained all these guys, would it really be all that bad? "I'm ready." Now I had to find the time. It needed to be in person.

THAT EVENING, I sat in Gabe's BMW as he drove it to a rounded drive in front of a sprawling, Tuscan-style mansion in North Scottsdale. The property was flat, but there were still mountain views all around us and a long front lawn gave way to desert landscaping around the sides of the home. My gaze roamed over the tall columns lining the covered portico. "Damn, this place is huge."

Gabe stopped the car and shut off the engine. "Yeah, my dad wouldn't live in anything less." With a sigh, he stepped out of the car.

I climbed out and followed him to the tall, double-front doors of the home, enjoying the way his tan slacks hugged his tight ass, then grabbed his arm at the entrance, stopping him. "Hey." He'd been quiet the whole ride up and I was sure his nerves were getting the best of him.

He faced me. "What?"

"It'll be okay. We can do this." I grabbed his hand and lifted it to my mouth.

He ripped his hand away. "Jeremy, there are cameras." He pointed to a camera in the upper corner of the portico.

"Shit, sorry." With a huff, I hung my head. I had to do better. No wonder he was worried. I straightened my shoulders. "That was stupid of me."

Wrinkling his forehead, he said, "It's okay. You're not used to hiding who you are." He patted my upper arm, then opened the door and stepped inside.

As I followed him in, I took in a long hallway with more columns. On one side of us, a living room with marble floors and silk tufted couches in creams sat between marble and gold tables along with a white baby grand piano. Large windows rose up, showing off the mountain views beyond a stable painted in white. Under my breath, I said, "Jesus..."

"Yeah, I know." Gabe gave a soft chuckle. "Bet you really think I'm entitled now."

"Gabe..." I pursed my lips, reaching for him and stopping. It was going to be harder than I'd thought to hide what was going on between us.

"Oh, Gabe, you're here." A woman rounded the corner at the end of the hallway, her cropped curls almost as light as Gabe's and her eyes just as blue. She held a glass of red wine and walked toward us, her flowered dress billowing around her legs.

"Mrs. Johnson? Nice to meet you. I'm Jeremy." I held out my hand as she approached.

She shook my hand with a light grip, smiling at me. "Oh, you're the young man I've heard so much about. Kevin is waiting for you in his study."

Gabe glanced at me. "Just him?"

"Yes, dear. I think he has some business to discuss with Jeremy before dinner." She hooked her arm in Gabe's. "Come and join me in the kitchen. You can help set the table for me." She motioned to a closed door in the hallway. "The study's right in there. Go on in."

"Sure, okay." I stepped toward the closed door and gave it a quick knock, then watched Gabe leave with his mother. This was not at all how I expected things to go. But they had no idea of our status.

"Come in." Kevin's voice filtered through the door.

I stepped inside and shut the door behind me. "Hi, Kevin,

you wanted to see me?" I scanned the room. The inside was dark with wood bookshelves and paneling lining the walls and similar furniture to what he had at the law office.

"Have a seat." He stood up and held out his hand to one of two leather wing chairs opposite his imposing desk.

As I sat down, I cleared my throat. "Is there an update on the case?" My pulse raced. How would he react if he knew what was going on between me and Gabe? Could he really be as volatile as Gabe made him out to be?

"Not too much, really. But I did want to let you know that we think the email phishing incident wasn't a coincidence." He dropped into his desk chair and folded his hands over the desk. "We think the mobsters were indeed looking for something. Maybe some dirt on the firm." He lifted the edge of his lips. "Which they won't find." He studied me. "Right?"

I jiggled my leg, then stopped and fidgeted with the hem of my button-down shirt. "Of course not." Did he somehow know what was going on between me and Gabe? Maybe that was why he invited me in here alone? I'd never lied about anything to anyone. I wasn't used to being in this position. Sweat beaded in my hairline. I tugged at the neck of my shirt.

"How are things going between you and my son?" He narrowed his eyes at me.

"F-fine. We're uh, we've become friends...um, sort of." I darted my gaze to the window. I needed to get out of here.

"Friends, huh?" With a smirk, he leaned back in his chair and hardened his gaze.

I focused on him. I had to maintain eye contact, or he'd surely know something was up. He was a damn good lawyer and always saw through people bullshitting him. "Yes, I'm helping him go over his cases for his final exams. I figure it not only helps him, but will help me as well when I start up classes in the fall." There, he'd like to hear that.

"Good. So have you enrolled?" His gaze softened.

"Not yet, but I'll probably enroll this week." I inhaled a long breath, letting it calm me. Now I'd have to keep my word and sign up.

"Let me know if there are any classes you need that are already full. I'll pull some strings and get you in." Narrowing his eyes, he raked his gaze over me. "I know you're signing up a little late."

"Yes, thank you." I rolled my lips, glancing over the books on the shelves, the classics in leather bound volumes. "Uh, Gabe is going to let me know the best professors, so..."

Knocking sounded on the door.

"Who is it?" Kevin stood up.

Gabe opened the door and stepped inside. "Your son. You do remember me, right, Dad?" With a glance at me, he said, "You seem to have stolen my bodyguard and Mom says it's time for dinner."

"Yes, well." Kevin walked around the end of the desk. "We had business to discuss."

As I stood up, Kevin patted my back. "You're doing a fine job."

"Thank you." I followed him and Gabe out of the room, down the hallway and into a dining room with a long table, with seating for twelve. Paintings of landscapes hung on the walls inside ornate, gold frames and a set of crystal candlesticks held glowing tapered candles. The table was set with white china, and platters of steak, salmon, roasted potatoes, and asparagus. "Wow, this looks really good."

"Thank you, Jeremy. Have a seat beside Gabe, there." She sat opposite Gabe toward the head of the table and held out her hand.

A young man, with curls like Gabe's but darker, was seated

beside her. That must be his younger brother, Aiden. "Hi." I held my hand out to him.

The young man stood up. "Hi, you must be Jeremy. I'm Aiden." He ran his blue-eyed gaze over me, then shook my hand with a wide smile.

"Nice to meet you." After releasing his hand, I dropped in next to Gabe, then unfolded my napkin and placed it in my lap. I didn't think I'd ever been to a family dinner as formal as this.

Gabe, arching a brow, glanced at me. "So, everything okay? I mean, since Dad won't tell *me* anything." He placed a steak on his plate and passed the platter to me.

"Gabe, I tell you what you need to know." His father, now seated at the head of the table, shook his head. "This case is confidential, and you don't work at the firm. Jeremy does." He stabbed a piece of salmon with his fork and dropped it on his plate.

"Are we arguing already?" With a quick chuckle, Aiden scooped potatoes onto his plate.

"We're not arguing." Kevin flashed a glare at Aiden, then drew a deep breath. "Are you ready for your finals, Aiden? It appears your brother is." He sipped from a glass of red wine resting at the top of his place setting.

"Ready as I'm going to be." Aiden piled salmon and asparagus onto his plate. "Even though you're making me drive all the way to school every day." He flashed his eyes at Gabe. "Dude, you got off easy."

"Driving into Tempe is not as far as central Phoenix." Gabe snuck a glance at me. "Besides, Jeremy here is very capable at keeping me safe." He looked around the table. "Which reminds me, where are the other bodyguards?"

"They're around. They've been covering the grounds as well." Kevin cut into his steak. "Your mother was concerned about the horses." As he peeked at her, the edge of his mouth lifted. "She might even be more worried about her horses than she is about you." He ate a bite of steak.

"Oh, Kevin. You stop that." With a soft giggle, she tapped his forearm. "Anyways, I'm glad you boys could come up for dinner. This whole thing has been so unnerving." She shivered, then drank some wine.

I watched Gabe for a moment, eating his dinner and paying no attention to me whatsoever. It was like I *was* only a body-guard and an employee at his father's firm. It was uncanny how he could become someone different here. I wasn't sure I liked it.

"So, Jeremy, you must be bored to death, having to hang with my nerdy brother all day." Aiden sipped some water from a goblet, a grin playing over his lips.

With a scoff, Gabe gave Aiden a wry smile. "He's working, Aiden. Something you know nothing about."

I met Aiden's gaze. "I am doing some work from Gabe's house and I'm helping him study for his finals." I plucked a potato off my plate with a fork and ate it.

"Oh, that's right. You're going to be a lawyer, too." Aiden nodded and cut into his salmon. "Gabe will probably be your boss someday." He chuckled and shoveled salmon into his mouth.

"If he is, that's all right with me." I turned my attention to Gabe and his gaze snapped to mine, then held it for a moment, softening. Finally, we had a connection.

"So, Jeremy, do you have a girlfriend or a wife at home waiting on you through all this?" Mrs, Johnson held her wine glass up over her plate, focused on me.

My heart stuttered. Had she noticed our connection? She did know Gabe was gay. "Uh, no, not at the moment." I cut a bite of steak.

"Maybe Jeremy doesn't like girls." Aiden let out a soft snort and swirled the water in his goblet.

"Aiden." Kevin glared at his son. "Don't make accusations like that." He turned his attention on me. "Sorry about that, Jeremy. Aiden is my troublemaker."

"Would it be so bad?" Gabe slowly lifted his gaze from his plate and shrugged a shoulder. "Surely you're okay with queer people working at the firm, right, Dad?"

Kevin dropped his mouth open, staring at Gabe.

Holy shit, what was Gabe doing? My pulse kicked and I pressed my knee to Gabe's under the table. I had been the one to tell him his father wouldn't care, though.

"Of course, queer people can work at the firm. We're an equal opportunity employer as defined by law and embrace diversity." Kevin furrowed his brows. "Why are you even bringing this up?"

"I suppose one of the partners is queer then?" Gabe lifted his chin, his gaze locked on his father.

My chest tightened and I cleared my throat. Had my comments started this? Or maybe Gabe was finally testing the waters with Kevin now that we were together? This was awkward as fuck. "Gabe, um..."

"No, let him answer." Holding his hand up, Gabe glanced at his mother, then Aiden.

"Come on, Dad. Who's the troublemaker now?" With a snicker, Aiden shifted in his seat, his eyes twinkling.

Mrs. Johnson watched the exchange, sipping her wine.

"Well, no, uh, not that I'm aware of." Tapping the table in front of Gabe's plate, Kevin said, "That doesn't mean anything. It's not like we've turned down a queer person for a position." He sucked in a breath. "Why in the hell are you bringing this up?"

Gabe snuck a peek at me, then focused on Kevin. "I don't know." He pushed potatoes around on his plate. "Must be one of the cases I'm studying. Has me thinking." He pressed his lips together. "Sorry."

Warmth touched my thigh, and I ducked my hand under the table to twine my pinky finger around his. He *had* been testing the waters. Did he get the answer he was looking for?

With a sigh, Gabe left my hand to cut a bite of salmon. "Anyways, how are the horses, Mom?" He ate the forkful of salmon.

"Oh, they're great. We're going to have a new foal running around by this time next year." She ticked her brows at Gabe.

Aiden rolled his eyes.

FIFTEEN
GABE

"What the hell was that all about at dinner?" Mom huffed at the sink next to me and handed me a platter to dry while Jeremy enjoyed an amaretto with Dad on the back patio now that dinner was over. I'd insisted on helping Mom do dishes while Aiden had skipped out to study. One bodyguard stood at each end of the patio, all dressed in black. What a weird thing to see along with a weirder night. It was amazing how much we *didn't* talk about what was going on.

"I don't know. Nothing." I glanced at Jeremy and Dad through the sliding glass doors, sitting on our resin wicker patio chairs at a glass table, laughing. They sure were getting along all right. Maybe Jeremy had been right about Dad?

"Nothing?" She turned to face me and dried her hands on a towel. "Gabe, is something going on I don't know about?" She darted a glance toward the patio. "He can't hear us."

Should I tell her? I let my gaze search her face, my pulse ramping up. No, I couldn't. "Jeremy knows about me."

"Okay, and?" Her brows dipped. "I take it he's not going to tell your father."

"No, he's not." I blew a lock of hair off my forehead. "Mom..." Shit, *should* I tell her? She's the one who wanted me to start dating.

"What is it?" She grabbed my hand, studying me.

I glanced at our hands. I shouldn't say anything without letting Jeremy know first. It wasn't right to out him to her before he'd even come out to his own family. "Do you think maybe Dad would be okay with me being gay after all?" I bit my lower lip.

"Oh, honey." She squeezed my hand, then released it and shook her head. "No, not now. Not yet." Turning to the sink, she washed a new platter. "I think once you're out of school and established in the firm, then maybe—"

"But Jeremy thinks he'd be fine with it and look at them." I lifted my chin in their direction. What I'd give to be able to hang out with Dad like that. How the hell did Jeremy do it? All this time I'd spent hating the man. But maybe Dad was just showing his charming side with Jeremy being an employee and all.

She drew a deep inhale. "So, Jeremy put you up to this?" She handed the new platter to me, and I dried it.

"No, he didn't put me up to anything. It's just when I explained to him about my situation with Dad, he thought it was unfounded." And I hadn't exactly gotten a good answer out of Dad either way.

"Please, wait a few more years." She faced me and touched my cheek, her gaze meeting mine. "Believe me, it's better this way."

"Yeah, okay." I set the platter into a bottom cupboard. No way I could argue with her.

Jeremy opened the sliding door to the patio. "You ready to go?" He stepped to me with his empty glass in his hand.

Dad followed Jeremy in and leaned against the kitchen

island, crossing his arms over his chest. "You do have classes in the morning, right?"

"I do." I threw a glance at Mom. "You all right to finish up?"

"Of course. You two get moving. It's a long drive." She kissed my cheek and patted my shoulder.

"Okay, let's head out." I tagged Jeremy's chest.

AFTER SAYING our goodbyes to everyone and leaving in my BMW, I drove along the highway heading down to the band house in Tempe. I couldn't wait to get home to my friends. I watched the freeway lights dance along the pavement and over the hood of my car. "So, what were you and my dad chatting about?"

Jeremy grabbed my hand from the steering wheel and kissed my knuckles, then rested our hands on the center console. "Actually, your dad was telling me funny stories about when you were a kid."

"What?" Widening my eyes, I stared at him for a second. "No fucking way." A grin tugged at my lips.

"Yes fucking way. He told me you used to sit at his desk in your diapers with one of your shoes held to your cheek, like you were taking a very important call from a client." He let out a soft snort.

"Oh, fuck." As heat rushed up my neck, I dipped my head. I'd forgotten all about that.

"Apparently, at one time, you wanted to be just like him." As his smile dropped, he squeezed my hand. "Just like how I was with my dad. It seems we had that in common, at least when we were little."

"Yeah, guess so." I inhaled deeply, speeding up the car as

my chest ached.

"When did it go bad for you, Gabe?" He pursed his lips, raking his gaze over me. "Because he sure talks highly of you."

The ache deepened. "I, I don't know. I suppose it was probably when I realized I was gay." The corners of my eyes stung. Fuck, this was bringing out shit I'd kept buried. With my voice wavering, I said, "I mean, how are you supposed to tell—" My breath caught. Fuck, don't break down.

"Gabe. It's okay." Leaning over, he snuck his arm around my shoulders and kissed my cheek, then rested his forehead on the side of my hair. "I'm here and if you want to come out to him, I'll be right there with you. Together, we can do this."

"Thanks." I clenched my jaw as the road blurred. Swiping my eyes, I took deep, calming breaths. Maybe with Jeremy's help, there was hope. He'd found a way to get through to Dad that I'd never had.

After pulling off the freeway and driving toward the band house, I slowly turned the corner on our street. "Should I go around the block and see if the thugs are anywhere close by?" I peered down the street. So far, no black Mercedes.

"Yeah, why don't you." He sank into his seat and looked out his window.

As I drove, I inspected every car along the street and in driveways. "Looks like Axel and Remy are home." We passed their bungalow and the windows glowed with light, much like ours, but smaller, and Axel's Jeep gleamed in the streetlight.

"Yeah? That's where they live, huh?" He pointed out the window at the house.

"It is. Axel's brother, Leo, lives there, too." Funny, we hadn't seen him around lately. Jeremy had yet to meet him. I drove past the park with the colorful playground in it and then up our drive and into the garage, next to Silas' sedan. "Guess the mobsters aren't around tonight." I shut off the engine and climbed out of the car, then met Jeremy at the door to the kitchen.

"Looks like Silas is home at least." Jeremy opened the door and held it for me as I stepped inside.

"I am." Silas sat at the dinette with his laptop open. "How did it go?" He leaned back in his chair and spread his legs out. "Milo is home, too."

Milo turned from the couch, an episode of Family Guy droning on the television. He waved at us. "Hey, guys."

I set my keys on the kitchen island and sighed. "It went fine. Food was good." Opening the refrigerator door, I asked, "Want a water, Jeremy?" We should probably head off to bed, but would I even sleep right now? I wasn't sure what to make of the evening, and now I was starting to question Mom's motivation for keeping me closeted with Dad. Was it really necessary?

"Sure." Jeremy walked to the table and dropped in next to Silas. "Anything interesting happen around here?'

"Nope, it's been quiet." Silas peered at me, then leaned in toward Jeremy, jabbing his thumb in my direction. "Is he okay?"

Jeremy glanced at me. "I think he's processing some things."

"I am." I handed an opened water bottle to Jeremy, then sipped my own.

"What are you processing, Gabe?" Milo shut off the television, then ambled to me, wrapping an arm around my waist, and resting his head on my shoulder. "Talk to us."

Draping an arm around Milo, I brushed my cheek over his brown hair. "I'm starting to question the way I've viewed my dad all these years." My gaze drew to Jeremy's and I puffed out a breath. "Fuck, maybe I was a little jealous of how well Jeremy got along with my dad tonight. I've never been able to just sit on the patio with him and chat like he did."

"Gabe..." Jeremy rose, then snuck his arm over my shoulders and kissed my cheek. "You can have that, too. I know he was really strict with you when you were young. But maybe things are different now that you're older. Maybe he's mellowed out."

Peeking up at me, Milo freed me. "People do change. It might be time to let him in a little and see."

"Yeah, look at how much Mia and her mom's relationship has changed with therapy. Maybe you and your dad should look into it." Silas studied me.

"Maybe..." I edged into Jeremy's side, and he hugged me to his strong chest. "I have some thinking to do anyways." After finals and this ridiculous mobster thing, I'd make an attempt to mend our relationship. "Want to go to bed?" I snuck a glance at Jeremy. I could lose myself in him for a little while. That always made things better.

"Yeah." He quirked the edge of his mouth.

AFTER GETTING READY FOR BED, I climbed between my sheets in only my briefs, my dick waking. What would Jeremy let me do with him tonight? Every time was an adventure.

Jeremy closed the door behind him and stepped to me, his half-hard cock tenting his boxer briefs.

I raised the corner of my lips. Yeah, he was on the same page as me. I opened the covers for him.

He slipped into bed to lie on his back, his arm held high. "Come here."

"Gladly." I shimmied in beside him, his arm wrapping around me. As I rested my head on his chest, I toyed with his nipple, my dick hardening against his thigh. "What do you want to do tonight?"

"After the day you've had, I'd like to give you whatever you need." He kissed the top of my head. "What do you need from me, Gabe?"

Warmth swept through my chest. "How about we take our underwear off first?" I skimmed my briefs down my legs and kicked them into the bottom of the sheets while he did the same. Rolling over top of him, I slotted our hot dicks between us and rocked my hips. Tension knotted inside my gut. "How's this?"

"Mmm, good." Wrapping his hand around the nape of my neck, he pulled our lips together and gave me heated kisses, his tongue slipping through to dance along mine.

As we kissed and rubbed on each other, soft moans worked out of me and everything else disappeared. It was only me and him right now and the heat of our bodies gliding together.

He groaned and tilted his head back. "Oh, fuck, Gabe." His body shuddered. "I can't get enough of you."

"Yeah? Me, neither. No amount of you is enough." I nibbled down his chin and bit at the soft flesh of his neck, then fluttered my tongue over the peak of his nipple.

His cock twitched against mine. "Lube?"

"Yeah." I teased the other nipple with my tongue and sucked hard, rocking my sensitive dick against his.

He grabbed the lube from the nightstand and handed it to me. "Fuck me tonight."

Halting all motion, I snapped my gaze to his. "Are you serious?" My cock pulsed and dribbled pre-cum down my shaft. Holy fuck was that a turn on.

"Yeah, I'm serious. But use a condom. I'm uh...haven't had time to get tested yet." He bit the side of his lower lip.

"Okay. But if you want to stop at any time, just say—"

Pressing his palm to my mouth, he said, "I know. I'm not

going to want to stop." He gave me a soft grin. "I'm ready for this. Been thinking about it."

I nodded, then swallowed hard. How the hell had I gotten so lucky? "Hand me a condom from the drawer then."

After grabbing the condom, he set it on the bed beside me and lifted his knees exposing his perfect hole to me. "Have at it."

"Damn." I sat on my tucked legs and lubed up my fingers, my cock jutting up between my thighs. I didn't think I'd ever been this hard before. Sex with someone you loved was so much more intense. I'd really been missing out by just having hookups. Peeking up at him, I circled his entrance with my slick fingers and dipped one inside.

He hissed and shut his eyes, then raked his teeth over his lower lip.

"You okay?" I worked my finger inside him, rubbing over his prostate.

Goosebumps broke out over his thighs, and he moaned. "Fuck yeah, I'm all right. Keep that up."

As I pumped my finger inside him, I fisted the base of his solid cock and dropped my mouth over him, sucking and flicking my tongue at the head.

He twined his fingers into my hair and made needy little noises.

My balls ached as desire heated my skin. If I touched myself now, I'd come, and it would be all be over with way too soon. I added a second finger and stretched him while pumping over his swollen cock with my lips.

His toes curled and his hips jerked as his dick pulsed in my mouth. "Holy fuck, more."

Adding a third finger, I slipped off his cock with a wet pop, then licked the flared head, panting. "You ready?" God, I was so fucking ready for this.

"Yeah. Do it," he gritted out, then pulled his knees into his armpits.

As my gaze took in the sight of him all sprawled out and open to me, I swooned and pre-cum beaded at my tip. "Okay, I'll go in slow." Quickly, I rolled the condom over me and slathered on more lube, then lined up my dick to his hole, propping myself on a straight arm. "Going in."

His ass clenched, then released. "Go, please, I want to feel you."

I nudged my cockhead in and stopped, then snuck a peek up at him. "You okay?"

With his brows tensed, he gave me a quick nod and bit his lip.

I slowly pushed deeper and stopped, his tight heat enveloping me in pleasure. "Fuck, you feel good." I took deep breaths, struggling to keep the sensations rushing my body in check.

"I'm good. It burns, but in a good way. More." He cupped my cheek and his gaze found mine, his pupils blown, and eyelids hooded.

I admired him for a heartbeat. He was getting off on this as much as I was. I pushed in a little more. "Almost there." As my balls rested against his ass, I hovered over him on my elbows. I wanted him close. "You okay?"

He winced, then said, "Yeah, I'm okay. It's weird, but good, you know?" He hooked his ankles around my waist.

"Yeah, I know." With a slow grin, I pressed my lips to his and pulled out, then pushed back in. Sensation sparked up my spine.

Grabbing the back of my neck, he held me close, slanting his mouth over mine and tangling our tongues. Small moans rumbled in his chest.

With faster thrusts of my hips, I placed hungry kisses over

his lips, then down his chin and bit at an earlobe, his breath puffing against my cheek. Tension knotted inside me, and my balls drew up.

Gasping, he grabbed my back and dug his fingers into my skin. "Faster Gabe. I don't know what's happening, but it feels really good," he gritted out. "Oh, God." He panted and groaned, arching his head back. "Fuck me harder."

As pleasure jolted through me, I quickened my pace and held onto his shoulders, nuzzling into his neck. "You close?" Release teetered on the edge and heat flared over me.

"I-I think so." He reached between us and stroked his swollen cock. "Fuck, coming." Hot cum spurted onto my chest.

That was all I needed. "Fuck yeah." Pleasure surged over me in harsh contractions and I lost myself to it, every nerve ending firing at once as I filled the condom inside him. As it slowed, I panted over his chest. We needed to lose the condoms. I'd always used them, but with him, it was a barrier I wasn't willing to have between us.

He held me tight and kissed my hair. "I love you, Gabe. Probably even more now."

Warmth flooded my insides and I lifted to gaze deeply into his eyes. "Yeah? I love you, too. So, anal wasn't terrible?" I raised the edge of my mouth.

"It was great once I got used to it." He rubbed the tip of his nose on mine. "Now I know what I've been missing all my life. We'll have to do that again."

"We do." My spent dick slipped from him. "Shit, have to clean up. Be right back." I met his gaze for a heartbeat.

"Go, I'll wait here." He unwrapped his arms and legs from me.

AFTER WE'D both cleaned up, I lay snuggled into his side in bed, attempting to see his profile in the ambient light in the room. How do I broach the subject of getting rid of the condoms? We were definitely in a committed relationship now and he'd said he wanted to get tested. "So..."

"So I want to come out to my family this week." He held me tighter into his side.

My heart fluttered. Committed for sure. "Yeah?" I brushed my finger pads over his chest, enjoying the hard muscle under his skin. "You said you didn't think they'd have a problem with it, right?"

"You know Simone. She's not going to care." He let out a soft breath. "My mom's pretty open minded. She won't care either." He nuzzled into the side of my head. "I want them to know about you, about us. I want them to know how happy I am."

My chest pinched. Could I do the same with my family? I owed him that. But not until after all this bullshit settled down. Maybe I could spin it in a way so they wouldn't know we were together while he was my bodyguard. I had to figure this out. "I want my family to know about us, too. But I need time."

His breath snagged. "Do you mean you want to come out to your dad?"

"It does. But not until this is over." I kissed his chest. "I was thinking it would be better if they didn't know this started while you were guarding me." I pursed my lips, thinking it through. "Maybe we could make them think we became good friends during this time, but then started dating after? Then you don't have to worry about it affecting your job." I lifted my head to study his face. "What do you think?"

He nodded and twisted his lips. "Yeah, that works."

With a sigh, I said, "I'm just thinking out loud here." I owed him so much. He was willing to risk it all for me.

"I'm going to make the time to get tested this week, too." He hugged me closer. "I can't imagine how much better having sex will be without a condom." A low chuckle rolled through his chest. "Maybe I can and damn, that sounds good."

As a smile ghosted across my lips, I said, "I was thinking the same thing. I'm glad you brought it up." I skimmed my hand down to the grooves of his abs, my cock waking. "You know, I've always used condoms. I've never been close enough to a guy to make this kind of commitment."

"Yeah?" He tilted his head over his pillow to peek down at me. "You've never gone bareback?"

"No, I never have." As my dick swelled against his hip, I slid my leg across both of his. "It kind of turns me on."

"I see that." With a chuckle, he shifted to face me. "I'll be your first, same as you've been my first." His smile faded. "I have a feeling you'll also be my last." His gaze darted between my eyes. "I'm serious, Gabe. What we have is like nothing I've ever experienced. I've never felt so strongly for someone before." His throat bobbed with a swallow.

I parted my lips, gazing deeply into his eyes, my heart aching with emotion. "Same for me." Would he be my last? It sure felt like it right now. I cupped his cheek. Something had definitely changed for us tonight. "You have me. All of me. I don't think I'll ever love like this again."

With a faint smile, he gave me a long, deep kiss. In a whisper, he said, "Good. We have a big week ahead of us. Let's get some sleep."

As he rolled to his back, I snuggled into his side and closed my eyes.

SIXTEEN
JEREMY

It was Wednesday afternoon, and I was perusing the video camera footage on my laptop once again, while sitting on the leather sectional while Gabe studied. I'd had to find a way to keep my mind off the testing I'd had done. I'd never been so serious about a person in my life. Was it the fact that we'd been inseparable from each other for weeks now? I glanced at him, sitting at the dinette, his headphones stuffed into his ears while he read from a book.

Yeah, this was not a normal situation to be in. We only left each other's sides to use the restroom. With a slight grin, I pushed *play* on a new video, my mind continuing to wander. What would it be like when this was over, and I had to go back to my lonely apartment? An ache wound through my chest. I couldn't fathom not being here every day, with Gabe and his friends, fully immersed in their lives. I wasn't sure I could fathom going back to being surrounded by straight people again and working at the law firm office. Funny, but most people would surely get sick of each other by now. Not me and Gabe. My feelings for him only grew stronger.

My phone buzzed next to my thigh. I startled and gasped. "Shit." After answering, I held it to my ear. "Hello?"

"Jeremy Sweet?" A male voice asked.

"Yes, this is he." My heart thumped in my ears. It had to be the clinic with my test results. I snuck a glance at Gabe.

Gabe flicked his gaze to mine, tensed his brows, then pulled an AirPod from his ear. "Is that the clinic?"

I nodded. He was probably as nervous about this as I was. It was big step for us to take.

"This is Doctor Brady. I'm pleased to let you know your test results came back negative," the man said.

"Oh, thank God." My shoulders relaxed and I rushed out a breath. "Thank you."

"Do you have any questions?" Doctor Brady asked.

"No, I'm good." A wide smile spread over my lips. I couldn't wait to get Gabe back in bed.

Gabe stalked toward me and squeezed my shoulder. "Well?"

"Let us know if you need anything else. Have a great day, Jeremy."

"Thank you, doctor." I hung up the phone and set it on the coffee table. "The tests were negative." My dick twitched behind my zipper. I didn't want to push it, but damn, I wanted him.

A broad smile broke out over Gabe's face, and he leaned over, then planted a hard kiss on my lips. "We're going bareback." He giggled. "Damn, I'd take you into my bed right now, but I have to go through this fucking case."

I tossed a glance at his book, my hardening cock waning. His studying had to come first. "Don't worry, we have time." I thought a moment. "Maybe I'll call Simone and tell her about us now." I'd have to tell Mom in person, but I had to stay by Gabe's side for now. I still had a job to do.

"Are you sure?" He rounded the couch and dropped in next to me.

"I'm sure. This'll be pretty easy." I plucked my phone off the coffee table. No time like the present and she probably wasn't at work yet. I dialed her number, then held the phone to my ear.

The phone rang a few times, then clicked. "Hey, Jeremy. To what do I owe this unexpected call? Everything all right?"

With a glance at Gabe, who was fixated on me, I said, "Yes, everything is all right. In fact, it's more than all right." I wound an arm around Gabe's shoulders and drew him into my side. "I have something to tell you."

"Okay," she said. "Should I be sitting down for this?"

"Maybe." The corner of my lips tugged up. "Come to think of it, yeah, you might want to sit down." My pulse sped up a notch. How exactly do I put this?

"I'm sitting." She breathed in deeply, then in a low voice, said, "Are you sure you're okay?"

"I'm fine. I've uh..." I glanced at Gabe, his gorgeous face so close to mine. "I've figured something out about myself and I uh..." Shit, this wasn't as easy as I'd thought.

"You're gay?" She giggled. "Or bisexual?"

"Shit, how'd you know?" A full-on smile spread over my lips.

"Duh, the way you were behaving with Gabe at the bar a few weeks ago? You didn't think I'd notice, did you." She scoffed a laugh. "I asked another bartender about Gabe and she confirmed to me that he's gay. So, I put two and two together." She tsked. "Why were you trying to lie to me about him?"

"What is she saying?" Gabe lifted his brows and focused on me.

"She's saying...oh, shit. Simone, can I put you on speaker?

Gabe's right here." I dropped the phone from my ear, then faced Gabe. "She already figured it out."

Gabe parted his lips. "What? How?"

"Hold on." I held the phone to my ear. "I'm going to put you on speaker, okay?" This was too confusing juggling between the two of them.

"Yes, please do," she said.

I tapped the speaker button. "Okay, like I said, Gabe's right here."

"Hi, Gabe. So, you're dating my brother, huh?" She huffed a chuckle.

Leaning in closer to the phone, Gabe said, "I am, but it's more than that." He glanced at me. "I love your brother."

My heart swelled with warmth. Holy shit, I wasn't expecting that. "And I uh, I love him, too."

"God, I hope so. I'd hate for it to be one-sided." She huffed. "That's sweet though." She sucked in a breath. "Jeremy, when did you figure this out? Have you been with guys before?"

"No, I've never been with a guy." I curled a lock of Gabe's hair around my finger. How to explain this to her? "I think I've had feelings for guys, but never really examined them too much, you know?"

"Yeah, I get it. I suppose I'm kind of like that, too." She sighed. "Maybe if the right girl came along, I might try it out."

"Well, Gabe was the right guy. I mean..." Through a laugh, I said, "We've spent every second together for weeks because I'm his bodyguard right now and we haven't gotten on each other's nerves yet."

"Speak for yourself." Gabe smirked at me. "No, your brother is something special, Simone."

"Don't I know it," she said. "Don't break his heart, Gabe, or it won't be the mafia you have to worry about."

Gabe snuggled into my side and gave me a warm grin. "Don't you worry about that."

"Have you told Mom yet?" she asked.

"No. I wanted it to be in person and right now, I have to stay by Gabe's side." I winced. "I think she'll take it okay, but I think having him there might be a little awkward." Turning to Gabe, I mouthed *sorry*. I should have mentioned that before, damn it.

In a whisper, he said, "It's okay." He planted a quick kiss on my cheek.

"So, how do you think Mom will take it?" I stared at the phone. I probably should have FaceTimed for this conversation, so I could see her expression.

"I think she'll be cool with it. She does have a lesbian friend, you know."

"Yeah, I know." I pursed my lips. Now that I was opening this door, I wanted it all the way open. How could I tell my mom and not leave Gabe unprotected?

"You know what..." Her breath caught. "Mom works a shift at the spa on Sunday. What if we all meet up in the nicer restaurant in the casino and I hang out with Gabe at the slots while you talk to her? Then if everything's all right, she can meet him."

My gaze snapped to Gabe's. "What do you think?"

He nodded. "Yeah, that's cool with me." A soft grin played over his lips. "I'd like to meet your mom."

"Great, then I'll set it up. I'll just tell her, her kids miss her and want to see her and she'll move mountains to be sure she can be there." She freed a soft giggle.

With an eyeroll, I said, "Yeah, you know Mom. She never passes up an opportunity to see us both." My chest warmed. This could work and having all my favorite people in one place for my coming out? Priceless.

"Okay, so I'll set it up and text you later this week," she said.

"Sounds good." I squeezed Gabe's shoulders. God, how I loved this man. "Talk to you soon, Simone."

"Yep, later, bye." She hung up the call.

"Well, that seemed easy." Gabe slumped his shoulders and picked at a loose thread on the hem of his t-shirt. "Maybe I can call Aiden and tell him." He shrugged. "I suppose I should have done that before we had dinner with my family."

I rested my forehead against his hair. "It's okay, Gabe. The situation with your family and what they're going through right now is totally different. It can wait." I didn't want him feeling bad about this.

"Yeah, guess so." With a quick breath, he lifted his head and gave me a flash of a grin. "You know the faster I get through this case, the faster we can get into my bedroom." He hooked a brow at me.

"Oh, shit yeah. I almost forgot." My dick twitched in my jeans. How would it feel to be that close to him? "Who's going to um...bottom?"

Gabe tapped his fingers to his lips. "Good question." His breath snagged and his eyes widened. "How about we both do? You can fuck me, then I'll fuck you. Or vice versa." He waggled his brows at me.

I dropped my mouth open, possibilities rushing through my brain. "You can do that?"

"Of course." He brushed a soft kiss over my lips. "We can do whatever we want."

"We sure can." I slapped his back. "Hurry up and get that case study done."

A few hours later, I lay naked in Gabe's bed, watching him undress in the glow from his nightstand lamp, my dick already hard as a rock. It had been agony waiting for him to finish his studies, knowing what we were about to do. No amount of boring camera video could keep my mind off it.

Now naked, Gabe climbed up into the bed with a towel in his hand. "It could get a little messy and I don't feel like changing sheets or sleeping in the wet spot tonight." He smirked.

"Yeah, good idea." I flung my arm out over the pillow next to my own and he snuggled into my side, resting his head on my shoulder.

"You know, Jeremy, it just occurred to me how trusting of a guy you are." He brushed his finger pads up and down my chest, leaving a light tickle. His hard, hot cock pressed against my thigh.

Heat sparked low in my belly and my balls ached. I'd never wanted anyone more, but what the hell was he talking about? "Trusting? Why?"

"Because I told you about my status and you just accepted it. A lot of guys would probably want proof." He slowly rocked his hips, rubbing his dick on me.

I fought to think straight. "B-but we love each other. You wouldn't lie to me about that." It never even occurred to me to check for the meds in his medicine cabinet. Yeah, I was a trusting guy all right.

"Even if I didn't love you, I'd never lie to someone about something so important. But..." He rushed out a breath. "I don't know, guess my mind is going in weird places because I can't believe how close we've become." He lifted onto an elbow and propped his cheek in his palm. "I can't believe I'm about to do this with you and how incredibly safe and loved I feel." His eyes grew glassy. "I wasn't sure I'd ever find love like this.

Maybe I wasn't sure I deserved it. I don't know." He shook his head, then locked his gaze on mine. "This is more than bare-back, Jeremy. This is the two of us taking our love to a new level." He cupped my cheek, then pressed a long, deep kiss on my lips.

Emotion threatened to overwhelm me, and my eyes stung. As the kiss broke, I sniffled and placed my palm on his cheek, then swiped my thumb over the wetness under his eye. "I love you more and more each day, Gabe." I gave him a lazy grin. "This is only the beginning, you know."

"Yeah, I know." He rolled over top of me and rocked his hips, our hot cocks slotting together. "This is going to be so good, so perfect." Slanting his mouth over mine, he placed needy kisses over my lips while rutting into me for a few good, long minutes.

Sensation flared over my skin, and I slapped my hands to his ass, then lifted my knees and broke the kisses. "Fuck me first, Gabe." I couldn't wait to see him come undone inside me.

With a sly smile, he said, "Yeah?" He rose up, set the towel beneath us, and grabbed the lube from the nightstand. "I think maybe we should prep both of us first. Then in the heat of the moment, you won't impale me." He let out a soft snort.

"Whatever you want." I gave him a quick kiss on his cheek, then let him slide off me.

While lying on my side, he squirted lube on his fingers, then handed it to me. "Let's sixty-nine." He crawled over me and in a circle, putting his knees on either side of my head, then fisted my cock and licked the tip.

"Fuck." Pleasure pulsed up my spine and I shuddered. "Not too much of that, okay?" I didn't want to be too close, or I might come before it was my turn to top.

"Yeah, okay." He snuck his finger to my hole and circled, then twisted his head. "Go ahead, play with my ass, too."

I lubed up my fingers, then nudged one inside. As his finger entered me, my ass clenched with a burn, then relaxed.

His cock twitched and dribbled a thread of pre-cum onto my chest. "Do it, Jeremy." He laved one of my balls and pumped his finger inside me, then found my prostate.

A jolt of heat sparked up my spine, and I arched my back with a throaty moan. "Yeah, that's it." As I stroked his dick with one hand, I snuck a slick finger into his entrance with the other.

"Oh, fuck." He squirmed his hips over me, then slid a second finger in. "You all right?" He sucked the head of my cock into his mouth.

My stomach muscles clenched as pleasure-pain washed over me. I breathed through it and relaxed. He was going much faster this time, but now I knew what to expect. "Yeah, I'm okay." I pushed two fingers into him and pumped, angling them just so.

He groaned and freed my aching dick, then bit at my inner thigh, his fingers stroking my insides.

My thighs quivered around his head. "You want more?" Could I fit a third finger inside him?

"Yeah, Oh God, yes." He pushed his ass at me as more pre-cum dripped from his tip.

As I stretched his hole, he stretched mine and once again took my cock into his mouth, flicking his tongue over the head.

Need flared up my spine and I gasped. The edge of climax was within reach. "Gabe, I'm ready." I stopped stroking his swollen cock and slid my finger out of his hole.

He swiveled around and pushed my knees up to my armpits. "I'm so fucking close, but I'm going to make this last." His darkened gaze met mine and he raked his teeth over his bottom lip. "At least I'm going to try." The edge of his mouth curled, then waned. Sitting on tucked legs, he slathered lube on himself, then lined up his dick to my hole and nudged it inside.

"Oh, holy hell." He squeezed his eyes shut for a moment and hissed.

The burn morphed into an intense desire, and I grabbed his hips. Without the condom, it was already better than last time. "Gabe." I squeezed my fingers into his skin. "Look at me."

He slowly opened his eyes and as his gaze met mine, it softened. "Fuck, I love you, Jeremy." He bent over me on a straight arm and worked his dick another inch inside me.

My heart bloomed with warmth. "Love you, more." I guided his hips closer and his cock all the way into me, the rawness of him filling me up, body and soul.

With a gasp, he dropped onto his elbows and nuzzled my cheek, then in a soft voice, said, "No way, I love you more."

I wiggled my hips, stirring his dick inside me. "I need you to move, Gabe." Wrapping my arms around his shoulders, I hooked my ankles around his hips. I wanted to feel his love in a primal way.

"Yeah, okay." He slowly pulled out, then pushed back, letting out deep moans. "Holy hell, this feels good." He quickened the pace and claimed my lips with his own, sliding his tongue inside my mouth.

I flicked my tongue against his and rocked my hips in time with his thrusts, little bursts of sensation sparking up my spine with each one. We continued on for a few moments, fully connected, tension growing in my gut.

As his body shuddered, goosebumps rose on his skin. He broke the kisses. "I'm close. You ready?" He lifted his head to gaze down on me.

"Yeah, ready." I locked my gaze on his as his brows tensed, and his mouth dropped open.

With a raspy moan, he quivered over me and thrust hard, then held his hips to mine.

The heat of his release filled me. My cock jerked and my balls ached. If it touched anything, I'd go off.

"Oh, fuck, oh fuck, oh fuck." He pulled out and thrust a few more times, then exhaled. "God, that was good." His dazed eyes focused on me. "I'm rolling over. Just put it in." With a smirk, he fell to his back and lifted his knees.

My body trembled as I climbed over him and nudged my dick to his hole. "You sure you're ready?" I certainly didn't want to hurt him.

"Hell yeah." He wrapped his legs around my hips and pulled me into him. "Come here." He waved his fingers at me.

With a soft grin, I slowly pressed my cock inside him, the heat of him enveloping me in pure pleasure. I nearly swooned as my balls hit his ass and I hovered over him. "Holy shit, this is good."

"Right?" He cupped my cheeks. "Go, and look at me."

"Okay." Fixating on him, his gorgeous blue eyes, still dark with lust, I thrust my hips. Sensation surged over me in a torrent and my balls drew up. Panting, I slowed my pace and dropped to my elbows. I had to slow this down before I lost it. Pressing my lips to his, I lost myself in hungry kisses. As his hot cum slid out of me and down my thighs, his face caught up in ecstasy flashed through my mind. A wave of pleasure tossed me over the edge and a shudder rolled through my body. My toes curled and I gasped as my cum spurted deep inside him. "Oh fuck, Gabe." I held him tightly and rode it out, the best orgasm of my life.

As it slowed, I panted and relaxed over him. "Wow, that was, that was..." I squeezed his shoulders, then kissed the side of his head. "The best."

"It was." He unwrapped his legs from my hips as my waning dick slipped from him. "I'm glad no one is home right now."

I nodded against his shoulder, caught up in a post-climax haze. "Yeah? Why?"

"Because I think we were both pretty loud when we came. If Silas were home, I'd never hear the end of it." A chuckle rumbled his chest.

"Silas can kiss my ass." I huffed a laugh. These guys teased the hell out of each other, but it was always with love. My heart ached. I really didn't want to leave this house. It was like some other world I was being allowed to see and somehow, I fit better in it than any other place I'd ever been. "Gabe?"

"Yeah?" He brushed his hand up and down my back.

"What if..." Did I dare ask it? My pulse quickened. "What if I moved in here with you?" Biting my lip, I lifted my head, my gaze meeting his. Was it too soon to ask? Probably, but I didn't care right now.

He knitted his brows. "Like, with all your shit?" His hand stopped on my shoulder blade.

"Well, yeah." I sucked my upper lip into my mouth and released it, thinking. "I have a pretty nice black leather sectional and you—"

"Yes." He gave me quick nod. "Oh, hell yes. Our old sofa needs to go to Goodwill or the trash. I'm not sure which."

The corner of my mouth quirked. "So, you're saying you'd let me move in with you because I have a nice sofa?" I kissed the tip of his nose.

"Yeah, and you have a great ass, and well, a great everything. You *are* Superman, you know." He skimmed his finger pads over my shoulder and up and down my arm, his gaze chasing his fingers. "I have to talk to the guys first, but I'm sure they won't mind. They're pretty used to you being around already and saving on rent with more people in the house is always a good thing. Especially when you start up law school."

He snapped his gaze to mine. "We could carpool to class and study together and—"

"You've got it all figured out." I placed my palm on his cheek and brushed my thumb over it. "Have you thought about this already?"

"Maybe..." He lifted his brows. "I wasn't looking forward to a cold, empty bed. That's for sure." He twisted his lips. "And besides, you cook a damn good breakfast and make sure we all eat right." With a soft chuckle, he said, "I don't see a problem with it at all."

My heart soared. I could stay here with him and his friends and be a part of whatever this thing was they all had. It was like I'd found a new family. "Thank you, Gabe. You have no idea how happy this makes me."

"Oh, I think I do. It feels right to me, too." He squirmed under me. "I think we should probably clean up. I'm leaking."

"Yeah, me, too." I glanced at the closed door of his room and thought about logistics. "So, I have a lease, but it's up in a month."

"Don't renew it. Let's do this." Flinging his arms around me, he squeezed me to his chest. "I'm too used to you always being here. It would be like ripping a scab off a wound to have you go back to your place."

"Yeah, I feel the same." I placed a long, deep kiss over his lips, then climbed off him. More cum dribbled down my leg. "Shit, I'll use the bathroom first." I scrambled into the hallway bathroom and shut the door. As I wet a washcloth from under the sink, I gazed at my reflection in the mirror. I was not the same person who entered this house a month ago. No, I was someone completely new. I was Gabe's Superman.

SEVENTEEN
GABE

After unloading all of our gear onto the stage at the Yucca Tap Room and setting up my drum kit, I ambled off the stage toward Jeremy, sitting at two tables pulled together. This place was a hoot with all the dark wood paneling and rustic décor. It reminded me a little bit of a biker bar, but a nicer one where the rich Scottsdale boomers came on their Harleys. As I dropped into a chair next to Jeremy, I roamed my gaze over the bar centering the place, the string of lights twinkling under the overhang and the rows of colorful liquor bottles lit up from below.

"Got you a beer." He slid a beer to me on the table. "You finishing setting up before the other guys tonight, that's a first." He leaned in and pecked my cheek.

I glanced toward the stage, all the guys were still plugging in amps and mics, tuning their guitars, and setting volume levels. "Yeah, sometimes I have it a little easier." I drank a sip of beer, the cool bubbles sliding down my throat. It had been a long week of studying and it was good to get out of the damn house. "This is tasting pretty good."

"I'll bet." He looked toward the stage. "So, did you talk to anyone about our living arrangement when this is over?"

"You mean the fact that you're staying on and not leaving... ever?" With a chuckle, I bumped his shoulder with mine. It was such a peaceful feeling to know he'd be by my side no matter what. I'd never had that before. Well, not along with the kind of love we shared. "I did. I talked to Milo and Silas while you were showering this morning. They have no problem with it." I drank more beer down. "You do know Cash is moving in after Silas graduates in May, right?"

"I think I heard something about that." He draped his arm around my shoulders. "It's going to be like one, big happy family in that house." He sipped from a soda water.

"You got that right." I edged into his side, his warmth surrounding me. "Silas has plans to start up a business helping animal rescues with their finances, so he's happy to have cheaper rent, too."

"When does Milo graduate?" He snuck a peek at the stage.

"Not until next year. He's the youngest of us all at twenty-two." I ran my finger over the lip of my glass. "He started college out of high school, but then took a year off to see if he could make it as an artist and did some of the craft fairs around the state."

"Yeah?" Jeremy arched a brow. "What happened?"

"He became the stereotypical starving artist." I let my gaze find Milo as he adjusted a setting on his keys. "I guess the old farts that go to those shows aren't into the amazing art he does. He said they were all looking for flowers and cactus, or old trucks and shit out in a field. You know the vanilla stuff you can find at places like Target."

"Hey, I have a few pieces from Target. It's not all bad." He let a smirk tease his lips, then it waned. "What sort of art does he do?"

"One of these times we'll have to go in his room and look at it. It's hard to describe, like comic book characters or anime or something, but realistically drawn and just...amazing." My heart ached for Milo. Would he really be happy doing graphic artwork for some company's social media posts? Only time would tell.

Jeremy's gaze caught on something by the door. "Look, the wives are here." He pointed at Brandon, Remy, Eric, and Cash strolling in together.

"Damn, at some point, you'll be joining them and not watching over me while I set up." I snuck a peek at him. I had a wife. *I have a fucking wife.* How the hell did this happen to me?

As the wives surrounded us, we stood and greeted each one with a hug, then we all sat down, and the other band members joined us.

"Shit, we might need to start putting three tables together." Axel kissed Remy on the cheek, then sat in the chair beside him on my left.

"The only single guy now is you, Milo." Caleb twined his fingers in Eric's over the table, then sipped from a beer.

"Yeah, well, hopefully I'll be next." Milo glanced at Cash, sitting next to him.

"Oh, hun, you'll definitely be next. I know there's someone wonderful out there for you." Cash hugged him from the side, then kissed his cheek.

"Let's order some food. I'm starving." Silas looked around the table and flagged down a waitress. "What song are we starting off with tonight?"

"Black Parade?" Devin, clinging to Brandon's side, his blue eyes lined in dark eyeliner, brushed a lock of red hair off his forehead. "It seemed to go over well at the casino, and we haven't played it here yet."

"Sounds good." Axel nodded, then drank his beer. "It's kind of sucked that with finals coming up, we haven't had much time to practice."

"I'm sure you'll all sound great." Jeremy gave each of them a broad smile.

Yeah, he fitted right in. My heart warmed and as I cupped his cheek. I gave him a long, deep kiss. As it broke, I whispered in his ear, "Love you."

"Love you, too." He turned his smile on me.

As the ending of *I'm Not Okay* by My Chemical Romance approached, I smiled so hard my cheeks hurt, banging my drums with abandon, and watching Silas and Axel twirl with their guitars, playing off each other, while Devin scream sang the chorus. The crowd went wild for us, jumping to the beat, and the bar was so full, they'd had to cut people off at the door and turn them away.

Devin gave me the tell-tale flash of his eyes for the last go through and as everyone onstage hopped in unison, I banged hard on my drums and rolled my kickdrums, then halted.

The crowd roared and clapped, and men pumped their fists.

"Holy shit." Silas flipped his dirty blond hair over his head and panted.

Devin set the mic in the stand, then said, "That's it for now. We'll be back after a much-needed break. Again, we are Knot Me." He stepped off the stage into Brandon's protective embrace.

Jeremy appeared on my right. "Hey, this place is nuts. I know we haven't seen or heard anything from our mobsters this week, but I don't want you going out in that crowd." He tapped his side. "I'm packing, just in case."

"What?" I stared at him. Shit, he was my lover, but he was still my bodyguard. I'd almost, *almost* forgotten.

"I brought it in the trunk of your car and put it on while you guys were playing. The bar allows guns. There's not a sign saying—"

"Yeah, shit, I know. As long there's not a sign saying you can't, and you're not drinking, it's totally legal." I looked around us, pressing my lips together. Some of the firearm laws in this state made no sense, but right now, I wasn't going to question it. "Have you seen anyone suspicious?"

"No. I did take a quick look around the parking lot, and I didn't see any of those black Mercedes." He huffed a sigh. "Who knows, maybe they finally gave up?"

"What are you two doing back here?" Milo strolled to us, eyeing me, then Jeremy.

"I don't want Gabe out in that crowd. Is there someplace else he can hang out between sets?" He set his hand on my shoulder.

"Jeremy, I could really use a piss." I stood up and wrapped an arm around his waist, wedging myself into his side. He was so big, I could probably hide behind him.

"This place doesn't have a green room, so I don't know of any place you can go. Maybe out to Gabe's car in the parking lot?" He wrinkled his forehead.

With a scowl, Jeremy said, "Yeah, okay. I'll take you to the restroom, then let's go out to the parking lot." He grabbed my hand and led me off the stage, then pushed through the crowd and into the men's room.

A few men were already using the urinals and one was waiting for the only stall in the place.

"Fuck." Jeremy tightened his hold on my hand, then leaned in and whispered, "Piss in the parking lot?"

"What? No." I tsked. "Let's just wait." He was really on edge for some reason. Was there something he wasn't telling me?

One of the men at the urinal finished up and stepped to the sinks. "Hey, nice set, man. You guys are awesome." He tossed me a grin.

"Thanks." I lifted my chin at him, then did my business.

Jeremy leaned against the wall and crossed his arms over his chest, then eyed everyone who came in.

As I washed up at the sink, my gaze caught on an older, heavyset man with short, almost black hair, wearing nicer pants and a black, button-down shirt. He didn't look like one of our regulars.

Jeremy bumped off the wall and stepped to my side, grabbing my elbow. Under his breath, he said, "Let's go." He peered at the man I'd noticed and hustled me out.

As we reached the back door and flung it open, I asked, "Did you see that guy?" I stopped at the back wall of the building, next to the dumpsters. The night was warm, now that we were well into May. A full moon glowed overhead in a cloudless sky.

"I did. Let's take a walk around the parking lot." He stepped away from me, but I pulled him back.

"Wait. It's hot out here and I could really use a beer, or a water or something." This sucked. Why did we have to see the guy in the bathroom? Maybe he worked for the bar, and we were overreacting?

He faced me. "Gabe, I've got a weird feeling right now. I can't put my finger on it, but...I don't know." He dipped his gaze to the pavement, then focused on me. "How bad would it be if we left right now?"

"What? The guys can't finish the gig without me. I'm the *drummer*. I'm not like Silas or Axel who could probably fake it if the other one couldn't play." I scoffed. Definitely overreacting.

The back door swung open, and Jeremy shoved me behind him, lifting his shirt and setting his hand on his holstered gun, his stance wide and knees bent.

Axel and Caleb walked out. "Whoa, dude, what's up?" Axel held his hands up in surrender.

Ducking for a heartbeat, Caleb shook his head. "Fuck, you scared the shit out of me." He puffed out a breath, then planted his hands on his hips.

"Sorry. Guess I'm a bit jittery." Jeremy straightened and combed his fingers through his long, straight bangs.

"Milo said you didn't want Gabe out in the crowd, and you'd headed out here. What's up?" Caleb scanned the parking lot, then faced Jeremy.

Stepping out from behind Jeremy, I said, "We think we saw...*someone*, in the bathroom. I don't know." I pursed my lips. "It could have been anyone, really. Just a guy." I crept my gaze to meet Jeremy's. I didn't want to tell him outright I thought he was overreacting.

Jeremy shifted his stance. "Something just feels off. What would happen if you didn't play—"

My phone buzzed in my back pocket, along with Jeremy's. "Fuck." I whipped it out. A red notification blazed across my screen. "The fucking alarms went off at the house." I cut my gaze to Jeremy's, the same red alarm lighting up his phone.

"Holy shit." Axel sided into Jeremy and peered at his phone. "Someone broke in?"

"Looks like it." Caleb's eyes grew wide.

The back door flung open, and Silas, Milo and Devin all ran out. "Shit, what's going on?" Silas asked.

225

My phone lit up and *No Caller ID* scrolled across it. I answered the phone and put it on speaker, then held the phone between us all, huddled together. "Hello?"

"This is Tempe PD. We have an alarm at the residence of twelve-thirty-two East Broadmor Drive. We have officers enroute. Is anyone home or is this a false alarm?" a woman asked.

My pulse raced and my hand trembled. "Uh, no one is home, and I don't think it's a false alarm."

Jeremy draped an arm around my waist and tugged me into his side. "How long before the officers get there?"

"It should only be a few minutes, sir," she said.

"What do we do?" Milo gazed at me with wide eyes. "If we can't finish the last set, we might have a riot in the bar."

I rubbed my forehead. "Fuck, I don't know."

"I can play drums." Axel ticked his head. "How hard can it be?"

With a glare, I said, "No fucking way. You don't have a clue how to play drums." I scoffed, my attention drawing to the phone.

Silas flicked Axel in the head. "What's wrong with you?"

"Ow." Axel rubbed his head. "It was worth a shot." He snickered.

"Okay the officers are on site," the woman said over the phone. "They're not seeing anything yet."

"Shit, the video." Jeremy left my side to open up the camera app on his phone.

"We uh, we might have videos. We have cameras all over the house." I glanced at Axel, then returned to my phone.

"Someone tried to break in through the sliding door in the back yard. But it's dark and it looks like they might be wearing face masks." Jeremy shoved his phone over mine and held it there.

I watched while two masked men in black took a crowbar to our back door. As the alarm went off, they scrambled and ran off. "What the fuck?"

"The officers aren't finding anything. Do you want them to enter the house?" the woman asked.

Dropping my mouth open, I stared at Silas, then Milo. If it was obvious the attempt to get in failed, did it matter now? "No, that won't be necessary. According to our camera footage, it looks like they never got in." Besides, I didn't need them breaking our door down for nothing.

"Okay, I'll ask the officers to stand down. Is there anything else you'd like for us do?" she asked.

"No, thank you." My heart beat in my throat. Should we not play the last set and go home?

"Good night." She ended the call.

"Gabe." Jeremy creased his brows. "What do you want to do?"

I looked at each of my bandmates in turn, dropping my phone to my side. "I-I don't know. They didn't get inside the house, right? Just jiggled the door enough to set off the sensors on the alarm?" So, the house was probably still secure. With all the band gear here, there wasn't anything of value left in the house anyways if we were getting robbed.

"Yeah, it looks like that's what happened." Jeremy held me tighter to his side. "If the mobsters are at the house, then maybe they're not here."

"Or, maybe they're at the house because they know we're here, and more of them are here, staking us out." Caleb narrowed his eyes at me.

"Or, maybe it's some idiots looking to rob us and not the mobsters at all." I huffed out a laugh. "Fuck, I don't know. Let's just play this last set and get home." I was done with this night and very done with the situation dad's case had put us all in.

"Okay. Let's do it." Axel held up his palm and everyone took turns slapping it. We all filed inside to finish up the gig.

As we pulled up to the band house, I peered out of my windshield at it, all dark and ominous looking. Jeremy's car was parked across the street. A knot formed in the pit of my stomach and my nerves frayed. "This is creepy, Jeremy."

"I know." He squeezed my forearm. "But we'll all be here with you."

The headlights from Axel's Jeep flickered inside the car and in my rearview mirror from behind us. I drove up the driveway and into the garage. We had gear to unpack, and Remy was going to check all the sensors and cameras on the security system to see if anything had been tampered with. Thank God for my friends and for Jeremy. As I parked my car, I said. "I'm so glad you're here." My gaze flicked to his.

His gaze softened. "Me, too." Leaning over, he pressed a soft kiss to my cheek. "I think the excitement is over for tonight, so try and relax, okay?"

"Yeah." I climbed out of the car, then strolled into the driveway where Axel had parked along with Caleb in his Tacoma. "Let's check out the house first, then grab the stuff."

Remy stepped out of Axel's Jeep and strode to Jeremy, then tagged his arm. "Come on, you and me."

"Sounds good." Jeremy unholstered his gun and held it in his hand as he stalked to the door with Remy close behind.

I watched the two of them enter the house, Jeremy holding his gun in front of him. "This is so fucked. I'm sorry, guys." I exhaled and hung my head.

"For what?" Milo wrapped an arm around my waist and side-hugged me. "It's not your fault this is happening."

"Yeah, you can't be held responsible for this." With a frown, Axel patted my shoulder.

"Let's just hope the cameras were right and they didn't get in and nothing was stolen." Caleb looked up and down the street, his hands planted on his hips.

"I suppose." I huffed a sigh. "I just don't understand what these people want." My gaze found Caleb's. "Do you think they're just trying to scare us? Scare my dad?" And if they were, they didn't know my dad *at all*.

Jeremy stepped into the garage from inside the house and waved at us. "Start bringing in the gear, it's all clear."

"Okay guys, let's get to work." Axel opened the tailgate of his Jeep, then ducked inside for his guitar case.

After grabbing my throne from the back of Caleb's truck, I met Jeremy in the garage. "So...nothing?" I raised my brows. It didn't make any sense.

He shrugged his shoulders. "Honestly? I'm starting to think this was an unrelated event. It's not like robberies never happen around here." Jeremy glanced at the trucks in the driveway. "Let's get unpacked and go to bed. I texted your dad a little bit ago, but haven't heard from him. He's probably sleeping already."

"Yeah, okay." I ambled to the tailgate of Caleb's truck and grabbed one of my snares as exhaustion took hold of me. It was going to feel great to be in Jeremy's arms tonight.

AFTER GETTING everything unpacked and set up in the practice room, we all sat on the sectional in the main room with me tucked into Jeremy's side at one end.

Remy strolled out of the hallway leading to the bedrooms, then blew a lock of his curly brown hair off his forehead. "I don't know. The alarm system looks good. It's fully functional and I didn't see any weird videos where the cameras could have been covered."

"We didn't find anything missing, either." Silas crept his arm over Cash's shoulders and pulled him close.

Jeremy's phone buzzed on the coffee table. "Shit, it's Gabe's dad." He stood up from the couch and paced toward the hallway. "Hello?" He nodded. "Yeah, some guys tripped the alarm on the house down here."

We all watched Jeremy turn and come back.

"No, nothing was stolen, and it doesn't appear they got into the house." He stopped and gazed at me. "He had a show tonight with the band, so no one was here." He pursed his lips. "I did see someone suspicious at their show, but...I don't know." He blew out a breath, and stepped toward the front windows. "Yeah, Okay. Talk to you later." He dropped the phone to his side.

"Well? What did he say?" I stood up. God, I hated not knowing what Dad was telling him, hearing the tone of his voice.

Jeremy faced me. "He said to wait it out. There's still no movement at your family's house. It's like these guys disappeared."

"Well, that's it. Time for bed." Axel stood up and walked to Remy. "Note that I said *bed* and not sleep." Grabbing Remy's hand, he gave him a coy smile.

"Anything you want, lover boy." Remy planted a hard kiss on Axel's lips. "See you all soon." He waved as he rushed Axel out the front door.

Milo shook his head. "Even at almost three in the morning, they're going at it." With a sigh, he stood up and stretched. "Goodnight all."

"Goodnight." I twined my fingers in Jeremy's hand and led

him to my bedroom. "I'm exhausted." Both mentally and physically at this point.

Jeremy shut the door behind us. "Cuddle?" He released my hand and shimmied his shirt off his head.

"Hell yes." After we undressed, we crawled into bed, him wrapping around me from behind, his arm hugging my chest. I kissed his knuckles. "This has got to end, right?"

"Yes, it will end, and you and I will still be here, just like this." He pressed a soft kiss to the back of my shoulder.

I shut my eyes and shifted closer into his front.

EIGHTEEN
JEREMY

Buzzing filled my head, over and over, then another set of buzzing and back to the first set. I dragged my eyes open to sunshine streaming through the sides of the curtains on Gabe's window. "What the hell is that?"

More buzzing.

"I don't know." Gabe, still snuggled in my arms, nodded into his pillow. "Maybe a phone? Is it yours?"

My eyes popped open. "Shit, yeah." The buzzing stopped, then started up again. I jumped up to sitting in the bed, wiped the sleep from my eyes, then focused on my phone. *Kevin Johnson* scrolled across the screen. "Shit, it's your dad. Maybe something happened." I lurched for the phone, grabbed it, then fumbled with it and caught it again. "Fuck." As I shook my head, I hit the green answer button and glanced at Gabe, blinking at me, and rubbing his eyes. "Hello?"

"Jeremy." Kevin huffed, then in a low growl, he said, "I need to see you and Gabe at once."

"O-kay..." I scrubbed my chin. I'd never heard him talk to me like this before. "Is everything all right?"

"No it's not all—" A clang rang out in the background. "Fuck! Just get up here."

Gabe slid up to sit against the pillows on his headboard. "Jeremy? Is someone hurt?"

"Is anyone hurt?" Furrowing my brows, I raked my gaze over Gabe, his curly blond hair a disheveled mop on his head. Something bad had happened. Why couldn't he tell me over the phone?

"No, no one is hurt." He growled. "Get up here, now." Kevin ended the call.

Gabe stared at me. "What's going on, Jeremy? Talk to me." He worried his lower lip.

"I, I don't know. He seemed...angry?" My chest tightened. Something must have happened with the case. It was the weekend, so the mobsters must be to blame and not the court. "He wants us up at your family home as soon as possible." I glanced at the time on my phone. "Shit, it's only eight." After the adrenaline of that call wore off, I was going to be damned tired.

"Why though?" His eyes widened. "Do you think we're in danger?" Sitting forward, he grabbed my bicep. "I have my fucking finals this week. I have to study. I can't just waste a bunch of time driving up there."

"Gabe, he was pretty adamant that we go up there now. Let's get dressed and get going. Maybe whatever this is won't take very long, and we'll be back down here by noon." I climbed out of bed and raked my fingers through my bangs, looking around the floor for my discarded clothes. Did we have time to shower? "I'm going to hit the shower really quick."

Gabe stood up next to me. "I'll go with you." He kissed my cheek. "Although I'd love to start the day sucking your cock in the shower, the Great Kevin Johnson awaits our presence. So, we better get a move on." He let out a soft snort.

At least he was finding humor in this. I slid my boxer briefs up my legs. But then, he didn't hear the tone in his dad's voice. My pulse kicked. What were we in for?

AFTER A RECORD-BREAKING QUICK SHOWER, Gabe drove us in his BMW up to his family's home in North Scottsdale and pulled into the rounded drive only an hour after the phone call. Gabe had sped the whole way up and neither one of us had said a word about the call, only commenting on the beautiful morning. As Gabe stopped the car, nausea balled in my gut. If I'd had an uneasy feeling at the bar last night, this was one-hundred times worse.

We climbed out of the car and approached the front door of the house, under the giant portico.

Gabe grabbed the handle, then looked at me. "Jeremy, whatever we're about to face, we do this together. Right?" He snuck his lower lip between his teeth.

"Absolutely." I squeezed his free hand, and it trembled in my grasp. "I'm not leaving your side." He was feeling the unease as much as me.

"Let's do this." He pushed the door open.

Mrs. Johnson stood in the front room in a long, flowing robe with a coffee cup held up to her chest. "Oh, Gabe, honey." Her gaze darted to mine. "Jeremy. My God." She strode to us and squeezed Gabe's hand, then my own. "I wondered when you were up here for dinner the other—"

"Stop it, Jessica." Kevin tramped down the hallway wearing running shorts and an athletic shirt, his cheeks red and a grimace on his face. "Let's go in my office." He threw the door open and waited with his arm extended.

"Mom?" With a glance at me, Gabe stepped to his mother's side. "Is Aiden all right?"

Tears welled up in her eyes and she rolled her lips. "He's fine, honey." She threw a peek at Kevin, then leaned in. "He knows."

"Jessica!" Kevin stomped his sneakered foot. Pointing and leering at her, he said, "Not another word." His hard gaze focused on Gabe. "Get in here this instant."

"Gabe?" I grabbed his elbow. "Let's go." Whatever this was, I had to help him through it without giving us away. I led Gabe to his father's study and stepped inside behind him, my pulse getting faster with each step.

Kevin stood behind his desk. An open manilla envelope rested in the center of it. "Sit down." He motioned to the leather wing chairs facing the desk.

"Yeah, sure." I dropped into one while Gabe took the other and I folded my hands on my lap, then swallowed thickly, my mouth going dry.

"Dad, what is this about and why is Mom upset?" Gabe planted his hands on the arms of the chair and glared his father down.

"When were you going to tell me?" With the corners of his lips twitching, Kevin stepped around the corner of the desk and clapped his hands together, then stood over Gabe. "Answer me."

Gabe scoffed and shifted in his chair, darting his gaze up, then down to the wood floor. "I have no idea what you're talking about." He sneered. "Maybe if you weren't so cryptic—"

"You know exactly what I'm talking about!" Kevin's voice thundered in the room and his gaze hardened on Gabe.

We both jumped.

"Kevin, please. He really doesn't know. What's going on here?" I lifted my palms to him. "Is this about the case?" Why in the hell was he behaving this way? Was this the Kevin Gabe had told me about, the one who only showed himself at home?

The one who was so demanding, he'd grounded his son for not getting straight As?

"Jeremy, what has he done to you? How could you engage in such..." Kevin huffed and scrubbed his face, turning to face his desk, then picked up the envelope and slid out some photos.

Gabe's eyes grew wide. "What is that?" He jumped up and crowded into Kevin's back.

Throwing the envelope and photos to the desk, Kevin twisted around and shoved Gabe into his chair.

"Fuck." Gabe thumped into the cushions.

Heat swarmed my chest. "Mr. Johnson, I can't let you do that." I stretched to my full height and towered over Kevin, shielding Gabe. I would not let him touch Gabe like that again.

Kevin stared up at me. "Why, because I hired you to protect him?" He leered at me, tilting his head this way and that. "That's what you were hired for, Jeremy." He pointed at the photos, strewn across the desk. "I didn't hire you to have sex with my son."

My heart jolted. "Wh-what?" My gaze cut to the photos, and I pushed by him to pick one up. Me and Gabe were at Tempe Marketplace, kissing at the table we'd ate at before our movie. It was the night we'd confessed our feelings. "Where did these..."

Kevin stomped around the desk and held up photo after photo, Gabe and me holding hands at dinner, caught in what appeared to be a blow job on the sectional in the band house, kissing pretty much everywhere we'd gone. "Let me ask you something, Jeremy. Does this make you a bodyguard or the paid male prostitute that's going to be on all the conspiracy news sites by Monday morning?" He tossed the photos on the desk.

Gabe shot up to lean over his father's desk, glaring at him. "Dad, they can't do that. You're not paying Jeremy to be my—"

"How the hell can I prove it? Huh? I paid Jeremy to be

with you. They have the account information. They have proof of you having sex." He threw his hands in the air and scoffed. "They probably got the account information from the damn phishing email." He rubbed his forehead, turning his back on us. "We could all end up in court, trying to prove that the money I paid Jeremy was *not* to keep my gay son's sexual appetite under control." He spun around and stomped to Gabe. As he jabbed Gabe's chest, he said, "Why didn't you tell me you were gay? How was it I never knew about all the men you've slept with?"

"I-I didn't uh..." Gabe's eyes grew glassy, and he glanced at me.

I grabbed Gabe's hand. "He was afraid you wouldn't approve of him. It sounds like you've put tremendous pressure on him to be what you wanted him to be. He was only doing his best to make you happy."

Kevin widened his eyes. "Make me happy? By being gay and hiding it from me when his mother and brother both knew all along?" Shaking his head, he planted his hands on his hips and paced in a circle behind his desk. "Oh, I see now. It's my fault he was too much of a coward to tell me." He glared at Gabe and pointed at him. "I didn't raise you to be a coward."

"Dad..." Gabe's breath hitched. "I'm not a, a coward." He hung his head.

I hooked my arm around Gabe's shoulders and hugged him to my chest. "Kevin, what's the real problem here? The fact that Gabe's gay or that he hid it from you?" This was insane. How was this happening?

"Both!" Kevin paced another circle, his face tensing and relaxing. "I never saw this coming. Maybe if I'd have known, I could have done something to stop it." He halted, then glared at me. "I thought *you* had a girlfriend. Are you gay, too?"

"N-no, I'm bisexual. I think." I stared at him, my chest squeezing. Would he think less of me now? Did I even care?

Gabe edged closer into my hold, resting his cheek on my chest, his body trembling. In a small voice, he said, "There's no way you could have stopped me from being gay, Dad."

"What did you say?" Kevin faced us, his lips in a grim line. "Talk to me and quit hiding. We have a potentially huge problem here."

Pushing out of my hold, Gabe swiped at his eyes and planted his hands on the desk, glanced at the photos and winced, then glared at his father. "You're right. I'm done hiding. I'm gay and Jeremy is my lover. We love each other. We fell in love. First time in my damn life I've been in love. First time I've ever let myself even have a boyfriend. Why? Because of you. I was afraid and a coward, I guess. But you didn't help any." He glanced at me, then turned his attention on Kevin. "You punished me for everything. Remember that time I came home late from the marching band competition, and you punished me for it like there was something I could have done to stop it?"

Kevin blinked a few times. "I did what?"

Gabe slowly shook his head. "You know what I'm talking about. Don't pretend you don't. If you punished me that severely for shit like that, why would I tell you about being gay? What the hell sort of punishment would you have doled out for that?"

Tapping his finger on the desk, Kevin said, "Gabe, I know I was hard on you. But I had to be. You're my successor and I need you be hard, not soft. Not—"

"Gay?" Pressing his lips together, Gabe stared at Kevin.

With a scoff, Kevin shook his head. "I don't know." He hung his head. "We have a mess on our hands now though, don't we." He huffed out a breath. "Fact is, I have no evidence that I paid Jeremy for anything but—" he flashed his eyes at me "—being your prostitute."

"What uh, what does that mean?" My chest pinched. There was way more to this problem than Gabe coming out to his father.

Kevin shifted his weight. "When I went back to find any evidence of the threats against the firm, they were gone from the servers. How am I supposed to prove—"

"You didn't print that shit out? What's the first thing you've always told me, Dad?" Gabe dropped his mouth open. "Have multiple copies. Backups."

"We did, but they were all electronic." Kevin glanced at me and shook his head. "I didn't think I'd need it printed. I didn't think anyone could hack into our systems. Fuck." With his brows furrowed, he focused on me. "What the hell happened here, Jeremy? I thought the first rule of being a bodyguard was to keep things all business with the client?" He pursed his lips. "How could you be protecting him properly if—"

Slapping his hand to the desk, Gabe said, "Dad, Jeremy's a great bodyguard. He'd take a bullet for me. Almost did."

"He what?" Kevin stared at Gabe, then me. "Why didn't you tell me that?"

"It wasn't a real bullet. A car backfired and oh...shit." With an exhale, I walked to the window and gazed outside into the side yard, the rock and cactus. My mind raced. What could this mean for me? Would this somehow cause a problem with me going back to law school? "They can't actually press prostitution charges against me, right?" I wasn't even sure who *they* were.

"I don't know. If they have even more evidence than they gave to me and they present it to the police, the state might press charges," he said, "But the real problem is what those ridiculous Q-Anon fake news sites and their followers will do with this information." Kevin sank into his chair and rubbed his chin. "They want me to reveal to the court that Desert Solar knew about the dumping of the chemicals, so their company won't take all the blame. They want me to say that Desert Solar was on board with the plan in order to save money."

"That's ridiculous." Gabe scoffed, then his face went slack. "It's not true, is it?"

"No, it's not true." Kevin sucked in a deep inhale. "I don't know how to stop this train wreck you both have put me in."

"Us? Why didn't you go to the police in the first place? Why were we hiding the fact that the firm and our family was threatened by the fucking mob?" Gabe shook his head, then walked to me. "I'm sorry, Jeremy. I'll tell anyone who'll listen that you were not getting paid to have sex with me."

The room spun for a moment, and it all hit me. Fuck, my name could be dragged through the mud. I could have crazies coming out of the woodwork attacking me. I rubbed my forehead and breathed in deeply. This was too much to take, especially after not sleeping last night. "What can we do to stop this?"

Gabe paced to his father's desk. Jabbing his index finger over the photos, he said, "You need to fix this."

"Me?" With a wry grin, he held up the photo of Gabe and me making out on the couch. I didn't even remember exactly when that had happened. How could I not remember a blow job? "You did this. You knew these thugs were hanging around your house. That's why you installed the security system, remember? If you were going to fuck your bodyguard on the couch, you could have at least shut the blinds on the damn windows." His chest heaved with deep breaths.

"We weren't fuck—" Gabe huffed out a sigh and dipped his head. "What do we do now? Is there any way for us to get ahead of it?"

Kevin set the photo on the desk. "I don't know. They said they'd give me until tomorrow to meet their demands and if I didn't, they'd take this info to those fucking news sites and maybe the police. They're even going to say that the firm is a front for human trafficking."

"Oh come on, that's ridiculous." Gabe scowled and walked to my side. "Jeremy, we'll find a way around this. I promise you." He grabbed my arm and kissed my cheek.

I glanced at Kevin, watching us, his gaze softening. He wasn't angry Gabe was gay, not at all. I'd been right on that account.

"It might be ridiculous and not true, but you know how a business can be slandered or even shut down by the conspiracy mill for this sort of thing. Remember the pizza-gate bullshit back in the twenty-sixteen election?" Kevin huffed.

Gabe stared at his father. "Yeah, but—"

Knocking clapped through the room. "Hello? Can I come in?" Jessica's voice filtered through the door.

"Come on in, Mom." Gabe threw a quick glare at Kevin, then strode to the door and flung it open.

As she entered, she peeked at Kevin, then brushed her hand over Gabe's forearm, wrinkling her brow. "Are you okay, honey?"

"He's fine." Kevin puffed out a harsh breath and rolled his eyes. "He's in love with Jeremy. I suppose there are worse things."

My heart skittered. Maybe I hadn't fallen out of favor with Kevin after all?

"Oh?" She ambled toward me, her gaze finding mine. "And you love my son?"

"I do." Reaching my hand out, I wove my fingers in Gabe's and pulled him next to me.

The ghost of a smile crept over her lips. "And here I

241

thought Gabe would be alone forever." She squeezed my fore-arm. "I'm glad he found someone, and you seem like such a nice young man."

"Jessica, we have more important matters to discuss right now." Kevin shifted in his desk chair. "We have to find a way to stop a scandal from erupting and ruining the name of the firm." His gaze found mine. "Even if the state decides there isn't enough evidence to press prostitution charges, this whole situation will put doubt into the minds of our clients." He shook his head. "Not to mention Jeremy's reputation as a lawyer, if he does become one." He arched a brow at me.

"I-I want to become a lawyer." A shiver ran through my chest. Would I lose my job at the firm over this? "Is this going to affect my employment?"

"Dad? You can't let that happen." Gabe rushed to the desk, planting his hands on the edge. "You can't. He's worked so hard for you all this time. He's one of your best employees, right? Otherwise, I know you wouldn't have given him the assignment of protecting me."

"Kevin, you can't fire him." Jessica stood right next to me and pursed her lips.

Kevin scowled, slowly shaking his head. "I don't know."

"How can we head this off?" I ran my gaze around the room, my mind ruminating over solutions. "What if we expose the mobsters first? What if we went to the police today and told them everything that's been happening?" I stepped toward him, my hands out. "Didn't you say you had a friend in the FBI you were going to talk to?"

"I did, but without any hard evidence, there's nothing I can do. The original messages they sent us are gone." He pressed his lips into a grim line.

"What about this?" Gabe pointed to the photos and envelope. "Isn't there a threat in here?" He lifted each photo, then took more out of the envelope, flipping through everything.

"It's only photos, Gabe. The message was sent to me in an encrypted email. After I read it, it disappeared. These guys are smart. They've got some cybercrime skills." Kevin rubbed the back of his neck.

"We should still go to the police." Gabe twisted to face me. "Don't you have a friend in the police academy? Maybe he can help us?"

With my pulse kicking, I stared at Gabe. "Yeah, maybe." Did I really want to admit to Grant that I'd fucked up my first and only bodyguard assignment and out myself to him at the same time? I had no idea how he'd take this. I'd look like an idiot to him.

Gabe grabbed my hand. "Jeremy, come on. It's worth a shot. He knows you, right? He'd believe you weren't working as a prostitute. He's got to be able to help us."

I breathed in deeply, thinking through his words. "Okay, I guess I can try him." I dipped my head, then shook it. "I have no idea what he's going to think of me." But did it really matter? I had Gabe's friends now, men who I'd felt a strong connection with. Men who I knew would stand behind us.

"Can we go home now, Dad?" Gabe chewed his lower lip, studying me. "We'll get in touch with Jeremy's friend and get back to you."

Kevin stood up and walked around the desk to Gabe's side. "Son, I know I've been hard on you. I'm sorry you felt you had to lie to me all these years." He glanced at Jessica, standing beside me with glistening eyes. He opened his arms. "I don't do this very often, but how about a hug?"

"How about you don't do this ever?" Gabe fell into his father's arms and embraced him. "I'm sorry for lying to you." Sniffling, he peeked at his mother. "It's okay, Mom. We'll figure this out." He freed his father and stepped back, then cleared his throat and wiped his eyes. "Holy shit, I was not expecting any of this today."

Kevin patted Gabe's back. "I know it's a lot. But you have finals this week to focus on, right?"

"Yeah." Gabe raked his teeth over his bottom lip. "If my grades fall a little bit, don't hold it against me, okay? I mean, it's not like I won't graduate and pass the bar."

"Just this once, I'll let it go," his father said. "I love you, son."

"Even if I'm gay?" Gabe smirked at him.

"Even if you're gay." He took a long inhale. "I have to admit, it was a shocker to find out this way." He shook his head, a chuckle rumbling from this throat. "Holy hell. And Jeremy?" His gaze shifted to me. "I had no idea."

"I didn't either. Well, I wasn't sure until I met Gabe." I dipped my head, then focused on Kevin. "Guess I figured some things out about myself." My shoulders relaxed. What a relief this must be for Gabe.

"Can I get you two something to eat? Have you had breakfast yet?" Jessica gave Gabe a small grin, then turned it on me. "I have some ham and cheese quiche I can heat up for you."

"What do you think, Jeremy?" Gabe grabbed my hand.

My stomach rumbled. "I'm starved, actually." Now that all the excitement was over, breakfast sounded great.

"Let's go have some quiche." Gabe kissed his mother's cheek, then led me out of the study and down the hall into the kitchen with his mother following. "Where's Aiden?"

"I think he's still in his room. I'm sure he won't want to come out until he knows the coast is clear with your father." She shook her head as she grabbed the quiche off the counter, then sliced it and set it on two plates. "You should have heard your father this morning after he found the package at the front door when he went out for his run. I thought the house was caving in on us."

"Shit, I'll bet." Gabe sat at a wooden barstool at the kitchen island while I dropped into the one next to him. Blowing out a breath, Gabe propped his elbows on the counter and set his face in his palms. "I can't believe this happened."

I draped an arm around his shoulders and leaned in close. "Yeah, but now your dad knows about us, and you don't have to hide anymore."

He lifted his head. "Yeah, but at what cost? I'm sorry, Jeremy. You don't deserve to have to deal with this bullshit." He twisted toward me. "You are not a prostitute, and you did nothing wrong."

Jessica heated each slice of quiche in the microwave hovering over the stovetop. "Would you boys like some coffee or orange juice?"

I glanced at her. She knew what was going on. Would she want to talk about it, too? "Yes, please."

Gabe rose from his stool. "I'll get it, Mom." He pulled a coffee mug down from a corner cupboard. "I assume you want both, Jeremy?"

"Yes, please." With a sigh, I slumped in my chair. We were going to have to work quickly to come up with a plan.

As Gabe made the coffees and poured our juice, he said, "So, Dad was upset, but he didn't seem as upset as I thought he might be about me being gay." He plunked my drinks in front of me.

Jessica twisted from the microwave and pressed her fingers to her lips for a moment. "I think he's mellowed out in his old age." She pulled a heated quiche from the microwave and set it in front of me with a fork. "Guests eat first." She gave me a quick grin, then popped another slice in.

Gabe leaned his ass on the counter and sipped his coffee.

"Do you think when this situation is over, he'll come to his senses and disown me?" He arched a brow at his mother with the hint of a smirk on his lips.

She cupped his cheek. "Oh no, honey. I think it'll be okay. I was as surprised as anyone that he accepted it the way he did." She dropped her hand and shrugged a shoulder. "You never know, sometimes people surprise you."

"It didn't surprise me." I cut a bite of quiche with my fork. "Maybe your dad *has* mellowed over the years." I chewed my food, thinking on what I knew of Kevin. "I just hope this is a new beginning for you both."

Gabe walked to my side, then kissed my cheek. "I think it is. I guess I should have listened to you all along."

NINETEEN

GABE

After having a quiet breakfast with Mom and saying our goodbyes to everyone, we drove home in silence. Jeremy had looked stunned and tired, and I didn't blame him. He was the one with the most to lose in all of this. He'd become the typical pawn in the high stakes game of a wealthy family.

I drove the car into the garage and parked, then climbed out. "You okay?"

"Yes, I'm okay. You don't need to keep asking." He puffed out an exhale and followed me into the house.

Silas, Cash and Milo sat on the sectional, eating cereal, and watching Family Guy. Silas twisted around, throwing his arm over the back of the couch. "Hey, what happened? We woke up and you both were gone. Couldn't have gotten much sleep."

"No, we didn't." I grabbed Jeremy's hand and led him to the open end of the couch, then dropped in. "You're not going to believe this."

"Okay." Silas smirked at me. "But you're going to tell me anyways."

"What, Gabe?" Milo creased his brows. "Is everything okay? Superman looks a little pale."

Jeremy huffed a laugh. "Yeah, well, apparently I'm a male prostitute."

"A what?" Silas dropped his mouth open with a broad smile and hit pause on the television remote. "You must be pretty good in bed." He waggled his brows.

"Oh, stop it, Silas. It's serious." With a shake of my head, I scowled. "The mobsters took some photos of us together and sent them to my dad. The fuckers outed me and they're blackmailing him, saying that my dad is paying Jeremy as a prostitute for me and not as a bodyguard. I guess my dad has no evidence to combat it." I hung my head. It was so far-fetched it was almost silly, but as my dad had said, all they needed to do was create a scandal to put doubt in the public's mind about the firm.

"They outed you to your dad? Does that mean your dad knows you're gay?" Milo's eyes grew wide and he set his empty bowl on the coffee table.

"Yep, he knows." I placed my hand on Jeremy's thigh. "Jeremy was right. He wasn't all that upset about it. I think he was more upset about me lying to him for all these years." I twisted my lips. "But I don't know, maybe this bullshit with the mob overshadowed it."

Slowly nodding, Cash said, "And the mobsters actually did you a favor, didn't they?" Cash gave me a warm grin. "How does it feel to be out to your father after all this time?"

"Great." I snuck a peek at Jeremy, his face pale, and eyes unfocused, staring toward the coffee table. "Hey, talk to me. Talk to us." I squeezed his thigh. He had to know we'd all have his back.

He blinked a few times and scrubbed his face. "I don't even know what to say. I think I'm in shock." He focused on me.

"We never had sex in public or with the curtains open in your room. How can they have photos of us?"

"Jesus, they took photos of you two?" Silas lowered his brows.

"Yes, but my dad says they hacked into his servers and deleted some data the firm had on them that would prove they were being threatened and the need for him to hire Jeremy as a bodyguard." I hung my head. Fuck, this was so complicated. The burden of proof would be on the law firm in this case. It was easy to see how assholes like this got away with shit.

"Wait, so your dad has photos of you two having sex?" Milo's eyes widened further.

"No, not having sex. Like kissing and making out." I chewed my lower lip. No wonder Mom had been upset when we'd gotten up there.

"Wait, making out where?" Silas side-eyed me.

"On the couch." I raised the edge of my lips. I knew what was coming next.

Silas grimaced. "Dude, no dicks out—"

"I know." I glanced at Jeremy. "There were no dicks out...I think." I thought back over the last month. When the hell was that? "Did you take a close look at that photo, Jeremy?"

"Huh? No, why?" Jeremy studied me.

"Maybe that wasn't even us. Maybe..." I pointed at Silas. "That was Silas and Cash. It was dark in the room and those two were watching movies when we were out."

Pink crept up Silas' cheeks and he peeked at Cash. "Yeah, well, we might have done...something in here."

"Silas likes to give head at weird times. I never know when he's going to go down on me." Cash released a soft snort. "It's not like I'm going to stop him. He's good at it." He shrugged a shoulder.

"Silas, you dog." With a chuckle, I shook my head. "They

got photos of you two and are trying to claim it's me and Jeremy." My heart skipped a beat. "Wait, that means they might not have the evidence they need to go after Jeremy." I cut my gaze to meet with Jeremy's. "Sure, they've got us kissing and holding hands, but that's not illegal in the prostitution sense of the word."

Silas held his hand up. "I'm in. I'll say whatever you need me to say to the authorities to prove it wasn't you two in the photos."

"Me, too. These jerks should be arrested for being peeping Toms." Cash crossed his arms over his chest with a huff.

With a sly grin, Jeremy leaned forward. "Holy shit, you know what? Maybe we can throw this back at them. We still have the videos of them hanging around the house. How about we use it to say they were trying to make sex tapes without our consent or something?" His gaze darted around the room. "It's illegal to photograph people in their own home without their permission."

"I think you're on to something. Even if they try to say my dad hired you as an escort for me, that's not illegal and we never did anything sexual in public." The heaviness on my heart lifted. "Dad should have known any photographs they took inside the house were illegal. He probably wasn't thinking clearly." No, he was too pissed off about me lying to him. It must have totally overshadowed his thinking. My heart ached for a moment.

"I think it's time *we* bring in the police." Jeremy pressed his lips together. "And I'm going to use Grant's connections in the PD to help us."

"Are you sure?" I flung an arm over his shoulders and lifted a leg over his thighs.

"I want to be out with you, Gabe, especially now. That means telling my best friend about us." He ticked his shoulders.

"I-I don't know how he'll react to the news, but if he has a problem with it, I still have all of you, right?" He glanced at each one of us.

"You're damn right you do." Silas reached over and patted Jeremy's knee. "You're one of the band wives now and we don't let people fuck with our band wives." He hooked a brow.

"Oh, Silas, you're so handsome when you get all protective." Cash fluttered his lashes at him.

Silas smiled and kissed Cash's cheek. "Thanks, gorgeous."

"This is pretty exciting. Gabe is finally out to his father and we're all going to put those thugs that have been creeping us out in their place." Milo clapped his hands over his chest.

"Damn right. Should we start with Grant first?" I tugged Jeremy closer to me. "I'd like to have a plan we can take to my dad."

"Yeah, it would be nice to show your dad that we can solve this situation for him." Jeremy dipped his head, resting his hand over mine on his thigh. "I do feel pretty bad about all this, and I want him to have faith in me again."

"He will. I'll make sure of it." I planted a kiss on his cheek. "Let's go and call your friend in my room." I was pretty sure he didn't want an audience for this.

"Okay, let's go." He stood up, then hauled me to standing and led me into my room.

"Good luck and let us know if you need us," Silas called out.

Warmth bloomed in my chest. I had the best friends ever. They'd never failed me and wouldn't now. I climbed up onto my bed, resting my back against the headboard while Jeremy did the same.

He held his phone out. "Well, here goes nothing." He dialed Grant's number and set it on speaker.

The call rang a few times, then clicked. "Hello? Jeremy?"

"Yeah, hi, Grant." He shifted his attention to me. "I have you on speaker right now with my uh...my principal. We have a situation I was hoping you could help me with."

"Of course. If I can help I will," Grant said. "The principal is your boss's son, right?"

"Yes, and his name's Gabe." Jeremy inhaled deeply.

"Hi, Grant. This is Gabe." I waved at the phone. Shit, it wasn't like he could see me, but I was meeting Jeremy's best friend.

"Hi, Gabe. So, what's going on?" Grant asked.

"My dad's firm is involved in a high-profile case, and it turns out he's being blackmailed by a defendant in the case." I bit the side of my lower lip. At what point would Jeremy come out to him?

"Okay, that sounds pretty serious. I assume you have proof of the blackmail? And what are the perps asking for?" Grant asked.

"Grant, there's something you need to know first." Jeremy winced. "I uh, I broke the cardinal rule on this job." His gaze flicked to me, then back to the phone. "I started a relationship with my principal, with Gabe."

Silence.

I stared at Jeremy. What a way to just come out and say it.

"Uh, Grant?" He furrowed his brows.

"I'm processing that statement. Gabe is, is male, right?" Grant asked. "So, you're telling me you're gay?"

"I'm telling you, I like men. Well, and women, but Gabe and me are in a relationship. I figured some things out about myself." He scratched his cheek.

"Gabe's band is Knot Me. They're all queer. Holy shit, Jeremy. You're queer?" He barked out a laugh. "I never would have thought."

"Me neither, but..." He grabbed my hand and held it on the bed. "Guess I am."

"Okay, so what does that have to do with this blackmailing thing?" Grant asked.

Jeremy twisted his lips, then asked, "You don't have a problem with me—"

"No, I don't care. I'm just surprised as fuck. That's all. I'm allowed to be surprised, right?" Grant chuckled. "And here I thought you were going to guard some hot *female* celebrity."

Okay, so Grant was cool with it. We needed to get back on track. "About the blackmail. We think we're dealing with a mob from Philly. We've caught men on cameras snooping around our house and now they've sent my father photos of me and Jeremy. We also think they hacked into my father's firm and removed any trace of their threats and accessed their account. One of the photos they had was taken inside our house. Doesn't that break the law?" The whole thing was becoming jumbled in my mind. There was so much to process.

"Wait, wait, wait." Grant huffed. "What are they using for blackmail and what are they asking for?"

"They said they'd accuse me and Gabe's father of solicitation with a bunch of those conspiracy news sites to slander me and his firm, unless his father gives the court evidence that would implicate his client to an extent that they're not held completely responsible for the..." Jeremy rubbed his brow. "Shit, this was supposed to be confidential, but there's no way to explain it without just telling you the whole thing. It involves the dumping of toxic waste and Desert Solar. The contractor they used is mob-based and dumped the waste in the desert to save money."

"You mean that spill out in Gila Bend?" Grant whistled. "Holy shit, that's big news. The feds are involved and everything," he said. "They're trying to spread fake news about you being a prostitute, Jeremy?" A laugh sprang from the phone. "God damn, man, when you go big, you go big."

A smile crept over Jeremy's lips. "Yeah, well, I guess I fucked up this bodyguard gig."

"No, you didn't. You're the best bodyguard I ever had." I lifted his hand and kissed his knuckles.

"Listen to you. Sounds like love is in air?" Grant asked.

"Yeah, we're in love. I have a boyfriend, Grant." Jeremy gave me a shy grin.

"You know? After all the bad relationships I've had with women, maybe I should switch sides. What do you think?" Grant chuckled. "Does Gabe have any gay friends he could hook me up with?"

I dropped my mouth open. "I might..." Milo came to mind, but the bastard had been hiding something on me and I wasn't completely sure of his status.

"Okay, so what do you want me to do?" Grant asked.

"We need advice and were hoping you'd know the best person to talk to on the force. I know it's only been a month." Jeremy pursed his lips.

"Let me make a few calls. My instructors are all pretty knowledgeable and I'm sure they can help." Grant sucked in a breath. "But, first of all you said these guys took photos of you inside your house. You need to get an investigation started on that."

"Yeah, well, the photos are actually of Gabe's roommates, and the mobsters thought it was us." Jeremy held the phone closer. "They said they'd tell the news sites that the firm is running a human trafficking ring and try to cause a scandal for my employer, too."

"Jeremy, everyone who knows you, knows you're a stand-up guy and not a prostitute and certainly not involved in human trafficking. I mean, that's just stupid. This will blow over," Grant said.

"Yeah, I hope so. I hope the firm isn't impacted too badly." Jeremy bit his lower lip.

"I'll get you the name of someone. First thing you need to do is have your roommates start the investigation into the private photos," Grant said. "I'll call you in a few hours. I'm there for you, buddy."

"Thanks." Jeremy's eyes glistened. "Talk to you soon."

"Yep, and nice to meet you, Gabe. Hope to meet you in person, maybe at one of your shows?" Grant asked.

"Definitely." I watched Jeremy end the call with my heart aching for him. While this situation had almost been good for me, it was terrible for him. "Let's pull all of our video together and have Silas and Cash prepared to start an investigation with whoever Grant tells us to call." I tightened my hold on his hand. "I love you, Jeremy. We'll get through this."

"Yeah, love you, too." He kissed my shoulder. "I'm so exhausted." He bent sideways and laid his head in my lap.

I combed my fingers through his long bangs. "Why don't you take a nap and let me handle the videos with the guys?"

He nodded.

A FEW HOURS LATER, between me, Cash, Silas, and Milo, we'd gone through all the videos and had catalogued which ones had the mobsters in them, the day and time they were at the house, and who was home at the time.

"These fuckers are not getting away with this." Silas sat across from me at the dinette with his face buried in his open laptop.

"So, you have no problem bringing these guys down?" With

a smirk, I glanced up from my laptop screen. It was rhetorical question.

Silas eyed me. "Fuck yeah. You know I'd love nothing more." He snickered.

"All we need is a person to talk to." I tapped my lips, thinking. "I'm going to let my dad know our plan."

"Okay." Silas shut his laptop and leaned back in his chair.

I glanced at Cash and Milo, sitting next to each other on the couch and reviewing videos on Milo's laptop. "If you two find anything else, tell me." I picked up my phone and dialed my father as they both nodded at me.

The phone picked up on the first ring. "Gabe, everything all right?"

"Yeah. I wanted to let you know, we have a plan." I puffed my chest out. I was going to show Dad my worth. I'd never felt closer to Dad than right now. He finally knew who I was and accepted me.

"Okay, what have you come up with?" Dad asked.

"We figured out that at least one of the photos they gave you, probably the most incriminating one, is not me and Jeremy, but my roommate Silas and his boyfriend, Cash." I glanced at Silas, his attention on me.

"Silas is gay, too?" Dad huffed out a breath. "I thought he had a girlfriend?"

"Dad, all my friends are queer." I rubbed my forehead. There was so much Dad didn't know. We were only on the tip of it. "He had a girlfriend, but now he has a boyfriend."

"Okay, well, let's get on with this plan," he said.

"Anyways, the photo was taken while Silas was with his boyfriend inside the house. That's illegal and Silas is going to start an investigation into it. We'll need that photo." I looked around me at all the guys with their laptops. "Between that and the video footage we have of their thugs at my house, I think we have something to combat them with."

"Yeah, I think you're right," he said. "If we can show you thought you were in danger, then it would make sense for me to hire a bodyguard for you."

"Yep." I hadn't thought of that angle before. "Jeremy has a friend in the police academy and he's going to give us the name of someone specific to start the investigation with. If there's an open investigation, then—"

"Then I can do some sort of a PR campaign myself and not give too much away, but be able to counter their claims," he said. "This might just work. We can even strike before they do, and I can let my PR person leak something as soon as tomorrow."

"Great idea, Dad." Warmth flooded my chest. Here I was, working with my dad to save not only my boyfriend from defamation, but his law firm. Jeremy had healed our relationship. I owed him so much.

"What do you think about coming out to the press about your relationship with Jeremy if it's needed?" Dad asked.

"I uh..." My gaze caught on Jeremy walking out of the hallway from the bedroom, rubbing his eyes. "I think that's a great idea, but we have to talk to his mom first. She doesn't know." We were supposed to be meeting her tomorrow. Were we still doing so with this mess going on? We had so much to do.

Jeremy stopped next to me. "Yes, we'll meet my mom tomorrow at the casino with Simone for lunch. She set it up." He pursed his lips. "I'll want to tell her about this mess, too, just in case it does blow up and she sees it."

I wrapped an arm around his waist and tugged him into my side. "Dad, set up whatever you need to. But I have a final on Monday morning, so after that would work." How the hell was

I going to be able to focus on my finals? Fuck, this week was going to suck.

"Okay." Dad sighed. "Let me know when you talk to a detective."

"I will, talk to you soon. Bye." I bit my lower lip, the hint of an ache whispering over my heart. "Love you, Dad."

Dad's breath snagged. "Love you, too, son. Goodbye." He hung up the call.

I stared at my phone. "Fuck, you know the last time I just came out and told my dad I loved him?" Tears pricked my eyes, and I snapped my gaze to Jeremy.

"Gabe..." He twisted into me, giving me a tight embrace, nuzzling my neck.

Milo, Cash and Silas all focused on me.

"Never. I can't remember ever telling him that. He's told me, like he did today, but I never said it back." I buried my face in Jeremy's neck and as I blinked, a hot tear tumbled down my cheek. Tightening my hold around him, my breath hitched.

"Fuck," Silas said as he, Cash and Milo all stood up.

"Group hug time," Cash said, wrapping his arms around me and Jeremy while Silas and Milo joined in.

"I love you guys." As more tears dripped down my cheeks, my heart burst with emotion. "And I'm not even drunk." I let out a ragged laugh.

"Dude, you know we love you." Silas chuckled. "It's sort of ironic that it took a photo of me giving Cash head on the couch to force you out of the closet with your dad."

"Oh, Jesus Christ." A hardy laugh sprang from my throat, and everyone joined in with giggles.

An hour or so later, we were all sprawled out on the couch, me resting between Jeremy's legs and against his chest in a corner, watching more Family Guy. The show had become our go to when we were all stressed out and needed to unwind.

Jeremy's phone buzzed on the coffee table, and I picked it up and handed it to him. "Is it Grant?"

"Yeah. Looks like he sent a text." Jeremy tapped open the message. "He sent the name and phone number of a detective, Roland Bilks. He says the guy knows our situation, knew my father, and he's on duty today." He blinked at the phone. "Shit, he knew my father."

"Really?" I sat up straight and studied Jeremy, his eyes glistening. "You okay?" Another thing we'd never thought of. Finding someone who knew Jeremy's dad and his family. Of course, the guy would want to help us. I shifted on the couch and Jeremy swung his leg around me.

"Yeah, I'm good." He bent forward and propped his elbows on his knees, then rubbed his forehead.

"You sure you're okay?" I glanced at Silas, shaking his head with furrowed brows. "Hey." Skimming my hand in a circle on his back, I leaned in. "Have you met this guy? Did your dad talk about him at all?"

"Not that I can remember. But if he did, I don't think I'd remember it. I'm sure Roland came to dad's funeral. Pretty much the whole department was there. I was in such a daze, I could have spoken to him..."

"Hey, it's all right." I pressed my forehead to the side of his hair. The situation was opening old wounds for Jeremy. "You've been there for me all day. Now it's time for me to be there for you."

Silas paused the show with the remote. "Dude, give me the number and I'll call him. Me and Cash are the ones that have to press charges, right?" Sitting at the other end of the couch next to Cash and Milo, he held out his hand and wagged his fingers at us.

With a nod, Jeremy stretched out and handed Silas his phone.

"What's going through your mind?" I pulled him into my chest, and he rested his cheek on my shoulder. Fuck, I'd been at odds with my dad my whole life. But at least he was still alive, and we were able to mend our relationship.

"I'll never be able to tell my dad about you." He threaded his fingers in mine and rested our hands over my thigh. "He would have loved you. He would have seen how smart and driven you are. How good you are for me." He freed a ragged sigh. "He would have seen how happy you make me."

Milo rubbed his eyes. "Damn it, Jeremy. You're making me cry."

"Me, too. Stop it." Cash swiped at his cheek.

Silas rolled his eyes. "You two scare me sometimes." He dialed his cell phone and tapped the speaker button.

The call rang once, then picked up. "Detective Bilks here."

"Hi uh, my name is Silas Brown, and I was given your name by..." Silas gave Jeremy a pointed look.

"Grant Nevens." Jeremy lifted his head and straightened his spine.

Silas gave us a quick nod. "Grant Nevens. I'm a friend of Jeremy Sweet and I need to report some peeping Toms and illegal photographs taken of me and my boyfriend in our home." Silas winced, then put the phone on mute. "Fuck, how am I supposed to say this?" he said to the rest of us. "It's awkward as fuck."

"Yes, Grant told me about the situation with you and with Jeremy. Can you give me your address? I have some time now to take a statement. I'm told you have evidence as well?" Roland asked.

Silas unmuted the phone. "Now would be awesome. Our address is twelve-thirty-two East Broadmor Drive in Tempe. We'll be here."

"Very well, then. I'll see you soon." Roland ended the call.

My heart lurched. "Shit, we don't have the photos here. They're at my family's house." I chewed my thumbnail and picked up my phone from the side table. "I'll text dad and have him text me a photo of it." I tapped out the message to my dad, hit send, and my phone rang with a call from him. "Hello?"

"Gabe, so you've got a detective on the way over?" he asked.

"I do." My heart lightened. Between all of us, we were finding a way out. "He happens to have known Jeremy's father, so I'm sure he'll do his best to help us." Not that it should matter, but police officers did tend to take care of their own. And Jeremy was one of them through his father.

Dad released a long breath. "Oh, that's good news. I've scanned all the photos, so I'll email them to you."

"Making backups?" I huffed a laugh. I wasn't going to let him forget that lesson any time soon.

"Yes, making backups of backups at this point," he said. "How is Jeremy?"

"He's all right. I'm taking care of him." Hooking an arm around Jeremy's shoulders, I kissed his forehead. "Don't worry, Dad. We've got everyone helping us. There's no way those assholes are going to tarnish his name or the name of the firm." I held my head high. Dad's law firm was finally starting to feel like my own. Like a legacy I could be proud of and build.

TWENTY

JEREMY

I snuggled into Gabe's hold and watched more Family Guy while we waited for Detective Bilks to arrive.

Gabe held his phone up to his face and opened his mail app. "Looks like I have the photos from my dad." He tapped a few times, tilting his head. "You know what? That is definitely Silas and Cash on the couch."

"Don't look at it too closely. You're creeping me out." Silas tsked, his arm wrapped around Cash, who was lying with his head in Silas' lap.

"Believe me, I'm not. Just looking at the hair. It's too long to be mine." Gabe chuckled.

The doorbell rang.

"Shit, must be the detective." As Cash lifted off his lap, Silas sprang from the couch and jogged to the door, then flung it open. "Detective Bilks?"

"Yes. And you are?" Wearing a white button up shirt and khaki pants, Roland stepped into the room and tucked a notebook under one arm. His graying hair was cut short, and his blue eyes were sharp.

"I'm Silas, the one who's in the uh…" He brushed his hand over the back of his head. "What should have been private time."

"Nice to meet you, Silas." As he shook Silas' hand, his gaze stopped at Jeremy, then he walked over to him. "Are you Patrick's son?"

I stood up. I must have met him before. "I am." I held out my hand. "Sorry if we've already met at the funeral. I don't remember much from that day."

Shaking my hand, Roland said, "It's okay. We did only meet the one time, but I could probably pick you out anywhere. You look just like your dad." He inhaled. "He was a good man."

My heart stung. I'd been told that a lot when he was still alive, but hadn't heard it in two years. "Thank you and yeah, people have told me I look like him." I freed his hand, then motioned to the dinette. "Should we all have a seat at the table?"

"Sounds like a good plan." Roland eyed the table, then sat at the head of it.

Silas and Cash dropped into chairs on Roland's right while Gabe and I sat across from them. With all the work we'd been doing together, we'd brought extra chairs in from the patio table outside.

After setting his notebook on the table, Roland opened it to a blank page and unhooked a pen from the top. "Silas, tell me what happened from the beginning."

"Shit, well…" Silas glanced at Gabe.

"The beginning starts with a case my father is defending." Gabe reached his hand under the table and threaded his fingers in mine. "My dad is a founding partner in the Phoenix Law Firm. He's defending Desert Solar in a chemical waste dumping case."

Roland nodded and scribbled in the notebook. "Go on."

It was my turn. "After the firm, which I also work at, received threats, Gabe's father hired me to be his bodyguard. Gabe's going to law school at ASU and needed to focus on his studies, so..." I hung my head. I wasn't sure where I was going with this. Maybe trying to find a way to rationalize falling for my principal? What would Roland think of me?

Gabe squeezed my hand under the table. "My father had me install a state-of-the-art security system along with cameras. So, we have video of everything. Well, mostly everything." He pursed his lips.

"So, you believe you have video of the suspects who took the photos?" Roland narrowed his eyes. "Do you have video of them taking the photos?"

"Uh, no, we don't have that." I winced. "We'd been catching some men in a black Mercedes, well, probably staking out the house." Which was pure conjecture on my part, I knew with my background in criminal justice, but I said it anyways. "But they got wise to the cameras and covered them a few times."

Roland nodded, tapping the end of his pen to his cheek. "When you say staking out the house, why do you think they'd do that?" His gaze snapped to Gabe. "Did they threaten to kidnap you?" He pointed his pen at Gabe.

"Jeremy? You said that wasn't real, right?" Gabe snuck a peek at me.

Heat crept through my cheeks. "No, like I said before, I just told you they were threatening to kidnap you to get you to let me stay here." Shit, he was still worried I hadn't been completely truthful about things. I focused on Roland. "No, they did not threaten to kidnap him."

With the edge of his lips twitching, Gabe nodded. "My dad said the threats were veiled, just enough for him to know he was being threatened, but not enough for him to actually call the police." He huffed. "He didn't want these mobsters to know we were worried about them. I think my dad was concerned about appearances, you know?"

Hooking a brow, Roland, said, "Mobsters? What mob? Do you know?" He looked at me and wrote in his notebook.

"I don't, but Kevin, Gabe's dad, said they were from Philly." I hoped I wasn't offering up any information Kevin didn't want me to divulge. I rubbed the heel of my hand over my tight chest and my mouth went dry. We should have gotten waters before we sat down for this. We hadn't even gotten to the embarrassing part, and I was already on edge.

"And so the photos that were taken, they must have thought they were worth something." Roland gazed at each of us. "What did they think they had?"

Gabe squeezed my hand again and brought our entwined hands up on the table. "While Jeremy was protecting me, we fell in love. They threatened to spin our very loving relationship into something foul. They're threatening to use the photos to say my father hired Jeremy as a prostitute for me." Gabe spat out the last words and his lips thinned. "You know his family. You know his father would never raise a son who would engage in illegal activities like that." His chest heaved with deep breaths.

I stared at Gabe. I didn't think I'd ever seen him seething with anger like this before. "Hey, settle down." I patted his hand over mine.

"No, Jeremy. It's not right. These thugs have had us scared for weeks. I'm sick of it and now that I really think about it, how dare they accuse the man I love of being a, a—"

"Gabe, it's all right. We'll get 'em. Don't you worry about that." Roland gave us a sly smile. "There's a certain mob from Philly we've had our eyes on and I'm sure this will add to the evidence we've already collected." He sat back and ran his hand over his short, graying hair, then dropped his pen on his notebook. "So, where do you come in with all of this, Silas?"

"Well..." Silas quirked the edge of his mouth and ran a finger in a circle over the table. "Turns out one of these supposedly damaging photos was not of Jeremy and Gabe, but was of me and my boyfriend, Cash." Silas twisted to face Cash.

Cash lifted his chin. "Yes, they took a photo of us in a very intimate moment and that was completely uncalled for." He smirked at Silas.

Roland rubbed the side of his nose. "Can I see this photo?" He huffed out a breath. "Don't worry, I won't judge." Holding out his palm, he snickered. "You have no idea the sort of things I've already seen."

Gabe rushed to the kitchen island, brought his laptop to the table, opened it, and typed, then spun it around to Roland. "It's this one. It's sort of hard to tell who's in it if you don't know us well."

Running his gaze over the laptop screen, Roland said, "I see. There's also a date and time stamp there in the corner." He pointed to the screen. "Where were you two when this was taken, Gabe and Jeremy?"

"We were out at dinner. We paid with a card, so we have proof." I furrowed my brows. Why did it matter where we were? He wasn't questioning the prostitution thing, was he?

"Okay." He turned the laptop toward Gabe. "I'll need the footage of the men who've been stalking your home and—"

"They also stalked us when we went out together. Some of the photos they took were of Jeremy and I out on dates." Gabe's gaze grew hard.

"Gabe..." I grabbed his forearm. "Taking photos of people out in public isn't a crime." Gabe was starting to let his emotions get the best of him.

"That's true, but knowing that can help map out a motive

266

for the big picture here, which was these men were looking for dirt on Kevin Johnson's son." Roland snapped his notebook shut. "I'll need to get in touch with your father. I assume he's open to that?"

"He is." Gabe's eyes widened. "You know who my father is?"

"Certainly. He's one of the best-known lawyers in Phoenix. Definitely one of the best trial attorneys I've ever seen." He tapped the table and stood up, then slid a card out of the breast pocket of his shirt and held it out. "My email is on the card. Send me a link to someplace I can access the videos and the rest of these photos."

Gabe's mouth dropped open. "Yeah, sure."

"We will, detective." I stood up and shook his hand. "Thank you, very much."

"You're welcome. You take care of yourself." He glanced at Gabe, then focused on me. "He'd be proud of you." He gave me a broad smile. "By the way, my son is gay, too. Finding out sent me to PFLAG and a whole world opened up to me." He walked toward the door with all of us following, then stopped. "I'd tell you all to take care of yourselves and each other, but it looks like you already are." He stepped out the door and waved behind him. "I'll be in touch."

As I shut the door behind Roland, I slumped my shoulders. At least he didn't say anything derogatory about my relationship with my principal. I followed Gabe and the others to the couch, and we all sat down.

Gabe, sitting next to me, grabbed my hand and kissed my knuckles. "You okay? That looked hard for you."

"Yeah, but it's done." I blew out a breath. "What's next?" I let my gaze roam over Silas and Cash, then Milo, all watching me.

"We wait. I'm not sure what my dad is going to do, but I'm

sure he'll think of something." Gabe's gaze dipped to our entwined hands, then focused on me. "I'm meeting your mom tomorrow, right?" His lips twitched into a half-smile.

"You are." I slowly nodded. "Do you have more studying to get done?" I needed to steer him back to his studies. It was going to be a busy week for him.

Gabe sighed. "Actually, it's getting late. Maybe we should go to bed, and I'll get up early tomorrow to study?"

Silas smirked at us. "Go to bed. That's a great idea." He waggled his brows at Cash.

"I get it. I'll just sit here and watch a movie." Milo picked up the remote and turned the television back on, then huffed and crossed his arms over his chest.

"Don't you have finals this week, too?" Silas stood and hauled Cash up with him.

"Yeah, but I'm ready." Milo sank into the couch.

"Come on, Gabe." I tugged him up and led him into his bedroom, then shut the door behind us. It was nice to finally be alone after all that had happened.

Gabe eyed me. "Are we sleeping, or?" He bit the corner of his lip, the bulge of his dick swelling behind his zipper.

I stepped to him and cupped his balls through his jeans, then claimed his mouth in a deep kiss, my tongue gliding across his. I could forget all this bullshit and enjoy him. Being with him was worth everything we'd had to endure today.

He let out a soft moan and thrust against my hand, then broke the kisses. "I want to blow you." He nibbled down my chin and nuzzled into my neck, his hands lifting to tease a nipple through my athletic shirt.

I dipped my head back, my cock jerking. "Yeah? I think I'd like that." I backed up to the bed, then climbed up and lay against the headboard, my balls aching with need.

"You have entirely too many clothes on." Quirking the edge

of his mouth he dropped his jeans and briefs, then shucked his shirt over his head.

"Yeah?" I unfastened my jeans and slid them down my legs with my underwear, then pulled my shirt over my head and threw everything on the floor.

Watching me, he slowly stroked his hard dick, pre-cum already beading at the tip. "You are so fucking hot, you know that?" He raked his teeth over his bottom lip.

"So are you." I wagged my fingers at him. "Come here." Now I couldn't wait for that blow job.

With a coy grin, he climbed onto the bed between my raised knees and looked me up and down, then licked his lips and ducked, flicking his tongue over the hard nub of my nipple, then sucking it into his mouth.

Sensation shot from my chest to my cock, and it pulsed off my stomach. "Fuck..." I squirmed and grabbed his sides, urging him lower.

He moved on to my other nipple, flicking and sucking, while fisting my dick and stroking it. "Love you." He licked down the grooves of my chest and stomach, then stopped with his lips hovering over the flared head of my cock.

"Love you, too." My breath hitched as pleasure sparked up my spine. Who'd have thought a little over a month ago I'd be here, in his bed, so damned crazy in love with him?

With a small smile, he dropped his mouth over my dick and moaned as he sucked and licked at the slit.

"Oh, fuck." My body shuddered and I arched my back with a groan. "Yeah, keep going." I threaded my fingers in his hair and rolled my hips, fucking his mouth in short thrusts.

He twisted his strokes and his cheeks hollowed with the force of his sucking mouth, making little whimpering noises. A thread of pre-cum dripped from his cockhead. He stopped and pulled off, his gaze finding mine, his pupils blown and lips red and swollen. "I need to fuck you, Jeremy. I don't know why, I just need it." He bit his lower lip. "Can I?"

"Yeah." I pulled the lube from the nightstand drawer and handed it to him. I'd do anything for this man, give him anything he wanted whenever he wanted it.

With a quick nod, he sat up on tucked legs and slathered lube over my hole, his brows tensing. "I don't know why, but all this shit, knowing that we're both going to be completely out and open, makes me feel closer to you than anyone I've ever known." He hovered over me on a straight arm and sank a finger inside me, then rubbed over my prostate and focused on me. "It's like I...I just *need* you, you know?"

My heart bloomed with warmth. "Yeah, I know." I cupped his cheeks as pleasure heated my skin and I shut my eyes for a moment. I wanted to feel him inside me like never before. "Put it in, Gabe."

His breath hitched and he stopped, staring at me. "You sure? I don't want to—"

"I want you to fill me up. I want to feel it all." Where the hell was this coming from? He'd opened up a whole new world to me and I wanted to explore it all with him. "Can you try it now?" I pulled my knees into my armpits and exposed myself to him. I could trust him with anything.

"Yeah." He slicked his dick with more lube, then lined it up to my hole. "Tell me if I need to stop." He locked his gaze to mine and his cock twitched against me, then he pushed the head in.

Burning lit up my spine and I gasped. I wanted more. "Go," I rasped.

"Fuck, it's tight. Relax for me." He pressed his mouth to mine and snuck his tongue between my lips, tasting me with lazy kisses, then pushed in further.

Breaking the kisses, I freed a sharp gasp as more burning

and intense pressure swirled inside me. Still, I wanted more. "Keep going, all the way."

As he slid all the way inside me and his balls hit my ass, he shuddered, and goosebumps broke out over his skin. "Holy hell, you feel good." He dipped his head to my shoulder. "I need to wait a minute." He breathed heavily against my neck.

I forced my body to relax, the burn subsiding, and held tightly to him, nuzzling the side of his head. This was what I needed. The pleasure-pain took everything else away. "Gabe, fuck me good and hard."

His dick jerked inside me. "You're going to make me come saying shit like that." With a soft chuckle, he kissed my neck, up my chin, then my mouth, the kisses growing hungry. "You ready?"

"Yes, I'm very ready." I clung to him as he pulled out, then thrust inside me, sensation jolting through every nerve ending, and I cried out. "Fuck, Gabe, fuck me," I said in a ragged voice.

Through deep moans and gasps, he quickened the pace, his hips pistoning over me. He panted against my neck and his fingers dug into my shoulders.

For a few minutes, we gripped each other and fucked, his thrusts losing their rhythm and his body trembling against mine. Heat built in my balls and spread over me as his dick pegged my prostate over and over. Could I come from this? Pleasure spiraled from deep inside me and my cock pulsed, my hot cum spurting between us. "Fuck, coming."

He fisted my dick and milked me, then his body tensed as heat filled my hole. "Oh God, coming, too. Coming so fucking hard." He pushed in, held it, then thrust a few times more and collapsed over me. "Holy shit." He panted over my chest.

I tightened my hold around his shoulders and kissed his hair, then brushed my fingers over his curls. I felt so close to him. Was it possible to love him even more now than when we'd started? "Love you." It seemed I couldn't tell him that enough.

"You, Jeremy Sweet, are the love of my life." He lifted his head and gave me a lazy smile, then tapped my nose. "Do you know that? Nothing could ever tear us apart. We are invincible."

"Like Superman?" I gave him a sly grin. Now that was a nickname I could be proud of.

"Yeah, like Superman." He hid his face in my neck and giggled softly. "My Superman."

THE NEXT DAY, Gabe had studied all morning and now we were strolling, hand in hand, inside the casino on the way to a nicer restaurant. I let my gaze roam over Gabe's deep blue button-down shirt, then down over his black trousers. He'd dressed well to meet my mom.

As we entered the restaurant, I perused the place for Simone, glancing across the interior in dark woods and low lights. The place was just as modern and plush as the bar Simone worked at, where Gabe's band had played when I'd first realized my feelings for him.

Simone waved at me from a table, a broad smile lighting up her face.

Across from Simone sat Mom in a flowered dress, her dark, graying hair cut blunt at her chin. Her eyes sparkled as they caught on me, and her mouth quirked into a warm grin.

"They're right there." I pointed at their table.

Gabe leaned in. "Um...we're still holding hands." He attempted to pull his hand away.

I tightened my grip. "No, I'm here to tell her about us. I'm not hiding a thing." Her seeing us like this might be the conversation starter I'd need.

Simone sauntered toward us, the high ponytail on her head bouncing over her shoulders, then stopped with her hands clasped over her chest. "Hey, Gabe and Jeremy. Don't you both look cute together." She hugged Gabe and then me. "Gabe, let's go check out the slot machines. I know which ones are paying out." She wagged her brows at him.

"Yeah, sure." Flashing his eyes at me, he pursed his lips. "Good luck."

"I'm sure it'll be fine." I freed him and strode to the table, then dropped into the chair next to her. "Hi, Mom." My pulse quickened.

She furrowed her brows. "Where is Simone taking your friend?" She twisted around, glancing in the direction they walked off in.

"Mom, I needed to talk to you alone for a minute. You'll get to meet him after." I chewed my thumbnail, looking her over. Would she be okay with this? But she had a queer friend. Of course, she would. Where do I start? "I've been uh, doing a side job for my boss. I've been working as a bodyguard to protect his son from some threats we received at the firm."

Her eyes widened. "What? Oh my." She glanced behind her again. "Was that your boss's son then?"

"Yes, it was." I studied her. She either didn't see us holding hands, or didn't think much of it. "Mom, I learned some things about myself while I've been with him." I should get to the point quickly before she started asking more about the reason behind me taking this side job. "I fell in love. With him. With Gabe." I winced. Was it too direct?

Her gaze locked with mine and her brows snapped up. "Wait. Jeremy, I don't understand. Are you saying you—"

"I'm telling you I'm bisexual, Mom. I fell in love with a

man, the one I'm protecting. He's my boyfriend now." I shook my head. I was confusing her. I scratched the back of my hair. "Am I making sense?"

She stared at me, mouth dropping open. "You're coming out to me." A warm smile crept over her lips, and she grabbed my hand, resting over the table. "My friend, Helen, once told me about the time she came out to her family, and it was awful." She tsked, her eyes growing glassy. "I want you to know that I love and support you." She bit the corner of her lower lip. "That's what I'm supposed to say, right?" She squeezed my hand. "But it's true. I love you, honey."

A grin played over my mouth as warmth swirled in my chest. "Yeah, that's what you're supposed to say. You did good, Mom." Leaning across the table, I gave her a quick hug and kissed her cheek. "Thank you."

"Can I meet him now?" Her brown eyes sparkled at me.

"Yeah, you can meet him." I slipped my phone out of my back pocket and texted for Simone to bring Gabe to the table.

TWENTY-ONE
GABE

With sweat slicking my palms, I stopped at the entrance to the restaurant with Simone at my side. "I've never met a boyfriend's parent before. Hell, I've never even had a boyfriend before." I glanced at her. Damn, she looked like a female version of Jeremy.

She patted my back. "Well, there's a first time for everything, right?" She wound her arm around mine, then stepped forward. "You love my brother, right?"

"Of course." As I walked with her, I glanced between Jeremy and his mother, both smiling at me from their chairs. My heartbeat thrummed in my ears. Fuck, this was nerve wracking.

"And you're good to my brother, right?" She arched a brow at me.

"Of course, I think he's the best thing that's ever happened to me." I kept my gaze affixed to him and my pulse calmed. All I needed was him to get me through anything.

As we approached the table, Jeremy and his mother both

stood up and Jeremy draped an arm around my waist as Simone released me. He kissed my cheek. "Mom, meet my boyfriend, Gabe."

"Hello, Gabe. It's so nice to meet you." She squeezed my forearm, her brown eyes focusing on me. "You can call me Margie." She took me in from head to toe. "I hear you're going to law school and will be taking over your father's firm?"

"I am." I edged into Jeremy's side. "Jeremy should be joining me at the law college in the fall." My attention drew to him. "I'll do whatever I can to help him through it." Was that the right thing to say? I didn't want to sound like I was smarter than him. "But I'm sure he'll do just fine." Fuck, I should shut up now. "Um, should we sit down?"

"Oh, yes." Margie took her seat with Jeremy sinking into the chair next to her and me sitting across from her.

"Let's get mimosas. What do you say?" Simone clapped her hands over her chest. "A little celebration."

"Yes, please." I nodded. That should help calm my nerves.

Jeremy found my hand under the table and twined his fingers in mine, then rested them next to my napkin. "Mom, Gabe is a drummer in ASU's marching band and he's in a cover band that plays at Simone's bar here."

"Oh, my, a drummer." Her cheeks flushed. "I always liked marching band drummers. I dated one before your father."

"Mom." Jeremy stared at his mother.

"I didn't know that, Mom." Simone unwrapped her napkin and set it in her lap, then called the waitress over and ordered our mimosas.

"Yes, well, I did have a life before I met your dad." Margie ticked her brows at Simone. "So, I guess like mother, like son." She giggled.

Jeremy rolled his eyes. "Oh, no."

The waitress dropped off our drinks along with menus.

After sipping my mimosa, I said, "Drummers have good rhythm, right Jeremy?" Did I really say that out loud? Biting my lip, I snuck a peek at Margie.

"They sure do." She held up her glass. "To drummers."

While me and Simone tapped our glasses to Margie's, I said, "And to bodyguards."

"Oh, yes." Margie chuckled, then covered her smile with her fingers. "This is just like that movie, isn't it? The one with Whitney Houston?"

"Uh, I don't know about that. I'm not exactly famous." I gave her my most charming smile. She seemed so easy going and from what I'd heard of Jeremy's father, he'd probably been like that, too.

"Yeah, well, there is something you should know, Mom." Jeremy's gaze followed the waitress as she set our drinks down.

"Can I take your order?" The waitress stood next to our table.

"Uh, can you come back?" Jeremy pursed his lips.

"Sure thing." The waitress sauntered off.

What the hell was Jeremy going to tell her now? This looked serious. I sipped my mimosa.

He threw a glance at me. "The people I'm protecting Gabe from are trying to use our relationship to tarnish the firm's name." He rubbed at his neck.

"Oh? How so?" Margie leaned closer to her son.

"Jeremy..." I squeezed his thigh. If my father found a way to silence these guys, maybe he didn't have to tell her about the case. "You don't have to—"

"But I don't want her hearing about this on one of those weird news sites or the internet or worse yet, hearing it from a neighbor." Jeremy huffed a quick breath.

"What's going on?" Margie glanced at me, then focused on her son.

My pulse quickened. So far, she hadn't put together that our relationship had gotten started in an unethical way.

"Mom." He freed my hand to grab hers over the table. "The mobsters are intending to blackmail the firm by spreading a rumor with some of the conspiracy pushers to say that my employment as a bodyguard for Gabe was a front for um..." He pursed his lips, his gaze dipping to their hands. "For prostitution. They have photos of us together and they were able to hack into the law firms accounts and found the extra payments to me."

Margie's jaw dropped. "You've got to be kidding me. Where on Earth do they get off saying something like that about my son?" Her gaze hardened. "It's obvious the two of you are in love." She waved her hand between us. "I mean, look at the way you look at each other." She huffed. "My, God. They can't get away with that. You can't just go and accuse people of something that isn't true and throw it to the internet," she said. "What if some of those idiots out there believe them? Can you file a defamation of character suit against them?"

Holy hell, she was *pissed off*. "Margie, my dad is working hard to stop them." My gut churned. But if Dad didn't stop them, would we be accosted by people who believe all that nonsense, like how the poor families of the Sandy Hook shooting were?

"Mom, do you remember a detective Roland Bilks?" Jeremy wrinkled his brows.

"Roland." She blinked and sat back in her chair. "Of course. He worked with your father on a few cases." She ticked her head. "He was a good man, a smart man. Your father spoke very highly of him."

With a long exhale, I relaxed my shoulders. Maybe there

was hope yet. "Detective Bilks is working on this case. He took our statements last night." I wasn't going to mention the private photo of Silas and Cash. "He should be speaking with my dad today, in fact." Everything had snowballed so quickly, I hadn't had time to think this mess through all the way.

Margie lifted her chin. "Well, if anyone can stop this, Roland can." She drank her mimosa. "Your father would have had none of this. If he were still alive, he'd take these mobsters on, and they wouldn't know what hit 'em."

My heart warmed. With how close Jeremy had been with his dad, I had no doubt she was right. "I wish I could have met him." I rubbed my thumb over the top of Jeremy's thigh.

"He would have loved you, Gabe, and he would have been very supportive of you two." She glanced at her daughter, watching us with wide eyes. "Right, Simone?"

With a smirk, she said, "Damn right, Mom." She held up her glass and Margie tapped hers on it, then they both took a sip.

"I can't believe the crap you're going through, Jeremy." Simone shook her head. "When did all this happen?"

"The last few days. Gabe wasn't out to his dad." Jeremy's breath caught. "Sorry, should I have said that?"

Tilting my head, I rubbed my fingers over the stem of my glass. "It's okay." My attention drew to Simone, then Margie. "My dad was pretty strict when I was growing up and me and my mom both thought he wouldn't tolerate me being gay, so I hid it." I sucked in a deep breath, my heart aching. I'd lost a lot of time with my dad because of it. "But this thing blew up and when he found out..." As my mouth quirked on one side, I slowly shook my head. "It was bad, but he accepted me." I let my gaze find Jeremy's. "He accepted *us*." I chuckled. "But I think it was because he admires Jeremy here so much."

"Gabe, he loves *you*." Leaning over, Jeremy kissed my

cheek. "He even said so. I heard him." He slung his arm around my shoulders.

"Yeah, but I've never seen my dad just shoot the shit with anyone the way he did with you that night at my parents' house." I grinned at Jeremy. My dad saw in Jeremy the same things I did. The same things I loved about him.

"It sounds like this mobster problem was a blessing in disguise. It brought my Jeremy to you, Gabe, and it brought you closer to your father?" Margie lifted her brows.

"Yeah, it sure did. I wouldn't change it for anything." I pressed a soft kiss to Jeremy's cheek and leaned into him.

"Are you ready to order now?" The waitress stepped to our table.

Jeremy smiled at her. "Yes, now we're ready." He picked up his menu.

THE NEXT FEW days were a whirlwind of studying, tests and passing out exhausted. When I'd texted or tried to call my dad, all he'd tell me was they were working on it and to focus on my finals. And so, I did, with Jeremy always vigilant by my side. No news had popped up anywhere about the firm or about Jeremy and me, so Dad and detective Bilks must have been getting somewhere with countering their threat.

On Thursday afternoon, I was sitting at the dinette studying for my last final with Jeremy relaxing on the couch, watching a baseball game. Silas and Milo were both at work.

Jeremy's phone lit up and buzzed on the coffee table.

"Shit." He jumped, then snatched it. "H-hello? Kevin?" He hopped up and paced the room, raking his fingers through his hair. "Really?"

No way was I not hearing this damn call. "Hey."

His gaze cut to mine, and he stopped. "Hold on, Kevin."

I wagged my fingers at him. "Put it on speaker and come over here."

"Oh." He strode to me and fell into the chair next to mine, then set the phone on speaker on the table between us. "Go ahead. Gabe can hear you now."

"Hi, Gabe," Dad said.

"Hi." My pulse kicked up. He needed to get on with it. "So, what happened?"

"Turns out, we're not the only ones these jokers have been blackmailing this way. You could say it's sort of their MO." Dad chuckled. "We were able to give the police *and* the FBI, I might add, the last bit of evidence they needed to make some arrests."

"So, me and Jeremy aren't going to be an internet sensation?" I giggled and grabbed Jeremy's hand, then kissed the back of it. No way I couldn't make jokes about it now. My heart slowed and I breathed in deeply.

"No, you are not, and neither is the firm," Dad said. "Jeremy, this detective Bilks really thought highly of your father and of you."

"Thanks, Kevin." Jeremy's cheeks reddened. "My Mom said he was a good detective."

"He is. I was very impressed with him."

"So, is this whole thing over now?" I glanced at Jeremy. How weird would it be to return to normal...and with a boyfriend. Damn. Who'd have thought?

"It is. Jeremy, your contract as a bodyguard for Gabe is over. I expect you at the office bright and early Monday morning." Dad let out a long breath.

"Not tomorrow?" Jeremy furrowed his brows.

"No, I have one final test and you can help me study for it."

My chest pricked. I wasn't ready to let him go just yet. How the hell was I going to handle not having him around every second of every day?

"I figured you two would need some time to acclimatize yourselves to a new normal in your relationship," Dad said.

Smart man. "I think you're right, Dad. I have yet to see Jeremy's apartment." I hooked a brow at him.

"Okay, then. See you Monday, Kevin. Looking forward to it." Jeremy locked his gaze to mine.

"See you and...love you, son," Dad said.

With a hard swallow and my chest aching, I came close to the phone. "Love you, too, Dad. Bye." It was getting easier to say all the time.

The call hung up.

"Get this test over with and we're going to spend a nice evening at my place tomorrow night." He gave me a sly grin. "I'll even cook."

"Oh, that sounds like heaven." Finally, we were free. I cupped his cheeks and placed a long, deep kiss over his mouth. "Can't wait."

I drove my BMW into Jeremy's parking lot, surrounded by modern apartment buildings, and looked around. This was a newer place, the buildings squared off in creams and grays and the landscaping full of cactus, lantana and Mexican bird of paradise, with a few mesquite and palo verde trees rising up around the pool area, behind a clubhouse.

As I pulled into an open spot by the clubhouse, I sat a moment in my car, the late afternoon sun peeking its way through the dark tint on my back window. It was hot as balls outside and it was only the end of May. I'd finished my last final and had spent most of the day without Jeremy by my side. How many times had I looked for him, or almost said his name, only to realize he wasn't there?

I peeked out my windshield to the second floor and the open stairs that would lead me back to him and my pulse sped up. It hadn't even been twenty-four hours without him, and I was still excited to see him. Yeah, this was true love for sure. Having him move in was the right call. As a grin played over my mouth, I shut off the car, climbed out and strolled up the sidewalk, the heat of the day assaulting my senses.

"Gabe!" Jeremy stood from the front balcony of the building and waved at me, a wide smile stretching his generous lips.

"Hey, nice place!" I strode to the stairs and took them two at a time, then jogged across the balcony to land in his arms. "Fuck, I missed you."

He kissed my head and wrapped me up in a tight embrace, lifting me off my feet, then burying his face in my neck. "I missed you, too." He freed me and placed his hands on my shoulders. "It was weird, wasn't it?" He gave me an open-mouthed smirk.

"It was. I kept thinking you'd be right around the corner or something." I scratched my forehead. He must have gone through the same thing as me. The heat prickled over my skin. "Let's get inside. It's hot as fuck."

"It is. Let me show you my place." He opened the door for me and stepped aside.

The scent of meat and garlic filled the room. "Oh, damn, that smells good. What are you cooking?" I perused the room as he shut the door, his modern, black leather sectional wrapping around the main room with a dark wood coffee table centering it. "Damn, that is a nice sofa." I nodded. It was nice everything. The guy had good taste in furniture.

"Yeah? Told you." He sauntered into a galley-style kitchen of white cabinets and stainless-steel appliances, open to the main room. "How about a bourbon?" He popped the cork off a bottle of Basil Hayden.

"Oh, hell yes." I walked into the kitchen and stood next to him, then ran my finger over the gray quartz countertop. "I don't know, you might be downgrading when you come to live with me."

He poured the bourbon into two low-ball glasses. "Gabe, you're worth it." He kissed my cheek, then held out my glass. "Besides, I was going to get a cheaper place when I went back to school anyways."

"What are you cooking?" I peeked at the oven. There was something on the broiler pan.

"Bacon wrapped filet mignon with garlic mashed potatoes and roasted asparagus." He held up his glass. "We're celebrating."

"Yeah? Like what?" My stomach rumbled. Damn, I was hungry.

"Yeah. We have so many things to celebrate. You're done with finals, we're boyfriends and you're out to your dad. Shit, is there more?"

I held up my glass. "We're going to be more than boyfriends, we're going to be partners, as Axel would say. I mean, you *are* moving in." I tapped my glass to his, making it clink. Was I going too fast here? Did I care? Hell no. It's what we did in Knot Me. When we found the one, we knew it and we owned that shit.

"Partners. I like that." He sipped his bourbon and set it on the counter, then twisted to the stove. "You go relax on our new comfy sofa over there and I'll get everything prepared." He opened the stove door and sizzling filled the room along with the scent of bacon.

"Fuck, am I hungry." I sipped my bourbon as I passed a tall dining table with six chairs, already set with cream stoneware, silverware, and black linen napkins. I picked up a napkin, examining it. "Are you sure you're not gay? Because the set up you have here screams, *gay man* to me. Not *bisexual, I've only been with women.*" With a snigger, I set it down.

"I watch a lot of HGTV." His face flushed and he pulled the steaks out of the broiler and set them on the glass stovetop. "Okay, maybe I *am* gay. Who knows?" With a wicked smile, he shrugged a shoulder. "Don't know if I'll ever be with a woman again..."

"You better not." I flashed a glare at him. Heat pricked my chest. "Don't even tease about that." I drank more bourbon, then stepped to the sofa and sank in. God, this was comfortable. I couldn't wait to move him in and get rid of that ratty old thing at the band house.

Jeremy worked swiftly through the kitchen, humming to himself and making clanking noises as he plated our food. "Okay, come and get it." He beamed at me.

I strode to the table, and he pulled the chair out at the head of it. "Thank you." I dropped into the chair while he took the seat next to mine. He was being such a gentleman. It was so sweet. My mouth watered as I laid my napkin in my lap and picked up my silverware. Everything was cooked to perfection. "Damn, this looks good."

"Thank you. Hope it tastes as good as it looks." He cut into his steak.

I stuffed a forkful of mashed potatoes into my mouth, the garlic and butter mixing with the creamy potatoes. "Oh, holy hell, this is good." I tapped my potatoes with my fork. "Your cooking was good at the band house, but this blows all of that away."

He wrapped his fingers around mine resting next to my

plate. "Gabe, I wanted to show you how special you are to me." He squeezed my hand. "I was thinking today, while I was putting my things away and cleaning up the dust that had collected after being gone for so long." His eyes grew glassy. "You and me, we went through a lot together. The last time I was in my home, I was a completely different man. I thought I knew what I wanted, but I had no clue. You showed me what real love is all about. And friendship...shit, it was like I was living in another world down there in the band house." He shook my hand over the table. "I have never in my life felt so loved, so safe and so a part of something bigger than myself." He sniffled, then swiped at his eye. "It's all you." He chuckled. "Okay, and your friends, but mostly you."

I stared at him a moment, my heart aching with warmth, my eyes stinging. "You gave my father back to me. You, a man who'd lost his." I blinked through the blur. "I didn't know what I was missing out on. You did."

He nodded, his gaze falling to our hands. "I'm glad you found your way to each other. You know, your dad is sort of like a father to me, too."

"Good, I can share." I leaned in and kissed his forehead. "I love you, Jeremy."

"Love you, too." He sniffled again. "Okay, let's stop this. We have good food and bourbon." He gave me a forced smile.

I glanced at the couch, a wicked thought invading my head. "And after, we have a couch to break in." I quirked the edge of my lips. Yeah, we were doing this.

WHILE JEREMY FINISHED the last of the dishes, I stepped by the couch, eyeing it, my dick jerking in my jeans. Every guy in the band had had their turn on the sofa in the band house but me. *I* would be the first one to christen this thing.

As my dick swelled, I tossed my shirt off, then shucked my jeans and underwear down and kicked it all into a corner of the room.

"Gabe? What are you doing?" Jeremy peered at me as he stuffed a pan into a cupboard.

"Nothing." I stroked my cock a few times, letting tension coil inside me. Would Jeremy have lube here? Would he even let me fuck him on his couch?

"Gabe?" He strolled into the room to stand beside me, then turned me to face him. Through giggling, he said, "You're not jerking off on my couch. No way." He pulled my hand from my dick.

"No? Then how about you blow me on it. Then you can swallow everything and not leave a mess." I smirked at him. Hell, I could be devious sometimes.

"Though I would love to suck your dick, where the hell is this coming from?" He stepped closer to me and wrapped his fingers around my shaft, placing lazy strokes over it.

With a moan, I dipped my head back and bit my lower lip as pleasure shivered up my spine. I had no idea where this was coming from. "If Silas and Cash can do it..." Was that it? Fuck. Weird, but so what. I locked my gaze on his, then unfastened his jeans, my mouth watering, and balls aching. "Oh yeah, someone is getting sucked here."

His pupils blew wide, and his breath quickened. "Yeah? I'm liking this. We can have dicks out in my place."

"We sure can." I freed his already solid cock, then dropped to my knees and sucked him into my mouth.

"Oh, fuck." He groaned and gripped my hair, then thrust between my lips. "Fuck yeah."

I pumped him with my mouth for a moment, then pulled

off him and shoved him onto his precious couch. *Our* precious couch.

He scrambled to lower his jeans to his ankles and kicked them off, then ran his tongue over his lips. "I don't know why, but this is really turning me on."

"Because we've only done it in my bedroom?" As I crawled between his knees, I licked his slit, then the sucked the tip of his dick into my mouth and gazed up at him as I teased him.

His eyes fluttered shut and he moaned, sinking into the couch. "Fuck, Gabe..."

As I stroked him with my mouth and fist, I cupped his balls, flicking my tongue up and down his shaft. I quickened the pace, my cheeks hollowing as I sucked him in.

After a few minutes, his thighs quivered and his hips jerked, his fingers tangled in my hair. "Holy shit, coming. Fuck, faster, oh God." He panted, curling himself over my head as his hot cum spurted to the back of my throat.

I swallowed it down, while a shudder of sensation drew my balls up and pulsed my cock. As I freed him, I jumped up to standing, crept over him and straddled his closed thighs with my knees, then grabbed my own dick and guided it into his open mouth.

With a firm grip, he fisted my cock and pumped, sucking as hard as I'd sucked him. Pleasure sparked through my body, and I fell over the edge. There was no stopping it. "Fuck, coming." Propping myself on straight arms on the back of the couch, I bucked my hips, forcing him to take me all the way in as each wave of my orgasm pulsed through me.

He gagged, then opened his throat for me and milked me to the end.

As it slowed, I pulled out of his mouth and sat on his lap, my balls nestled on top of his spent dick. "Holy shit, that was fun." I fought to steady my breath.

He swiped his mouth. "Yeah, except that you tried to choke me out." He let out a soft snort as his gaze met mine.

"Sorry." Heat rushed up my neck. "Or...not." I pressed a lingering kiss on his lips, then cupped his cheeks. "You dealt with it pretty well when you figured out how to handle it. I might want you to do that again."

"Yeah?" He smirked at me. "Maybe I'll do that to you next time." Hooking his arms around my waist, he threw me to the side, both of us landing facing each other. "You're staying over tonight, right?" He brushed his knuckles down my cheek.

"I am. I don't know if I know how to sleep alone in my bed anymore." My gaze searched his face, my heart blooming with emotion. "We're going to have to figure something out until you can move in."

"Yeah, maybe we'll just trade off places. You're off for the summer, right? No school or anything?" He grabbed my hand and kissed my palm.

"I am, but I have my gigs. I was hoping to work on some of the other casinos in the area to see if we could get a regular rotation going for the summer." I huffed a sigh. "Or maybe even see if I can get us into one of the casinos in the mountains, like Flagstaff or Show Low." The more casinos we played at, the easier it would be come fall when tourist season hit again.

"Okay, but you'll have more time to uh, go out on dates and stuff, right?" He gave me a coy grin.

"Jeremy Sweet, are you saying you want to take me out on regular dates and not sit around watching TV while I study?" I kissed the tip of his nose.

"I am. There are so many places I want to go with you, Gabe. I want to show you off." He raked his teeth over his lower lip. "Like, maybe even the gay bar?"

I nodded slowly. "Oh, the Club on Mill?" That could be fun, and we could probably get the rest of the guys to join us.

"Yeah." He held my hand up between us, gazing at them. "I want to slow dance with you. I want to kiss you in dark corners—"

"Ravage me in dark corners even?" Warmth crept over me. There were so many possibilities. My life and my future finally looked bright. "We will do all of it, Jeremy. And always together." I moved our hands and pressed a deep kiss on his lips.

EPILOGUE
JEREMY

ONE MONTH LATER

"Move it a little bit to the left." I stood inside the main room of the band house, sections of my sofa all in a haphazard pattern in the room. It was moving day and all the back and forth between our places over the last month was over. I was finally with my found family for good and Gabe had passed all his classes with straight As—my smart, driven partner.

"Make up your damn mind." Silas said, with a huff as he and Gabe lifted the corner piece of my black sectional and shifted it left.

Milo stood next to me, jutting out his hip and his fingers held over his mouth. "I don't know. I think the corner should be over there." He pointed to the other end of the room.

"No, that would cut the whole room off. It's bad energy." Caleb walked by us with a box in his arms, then ambled into the hallway to the bedrooms.

"What do you think, Cash?" Milo tagged his shoulder as he walked by.

Cash stopped with a smaller box in his arms and shrugged a shoulder. "I think it should go where they had it, but move it more to the right."

"You've got to be fucking kidding me." Silas dropped his end and straightened with long exhale. "I'm not moving shit until you all can figure out where you want to put it."

Axel sauntered into the room with a load of clothes on hangers flung over his shoulder. "What's wrong, Silas? Need to work out more?"

"You be quiet." Silas pointed at Axel. "Why don't you move some of this heavy shit for once?"

"Why should I when I have your muscles to do it?" With a sharp hum, he strolled into the hallway.

"Jeremy, how about we just put it where the old one was?" Gabe planted his hands on his hips and blew a lock of curly hair off his forehead.

"Yeah, we need to cover that cum stain on the carpet that Silas and Cash left." Remy snickered as he brought a larger box into the kitchen.

"How do you know it isn't left over from you and Axel?" Caleb walked out of the hallway. "Didn't I hear something about you sucking Axel's dick on the floor there the first time you were together?"

With wide eyes, Axel pounced on Caleb and covered his mouth. "Caleb, that was confidential information. Shut up." He turned his stare on Remy.

Remy shook his head, shifting his stance by the kitchen island. "Why am I not surprised?"

"How many dicks have been out in this room that weren't mine?" Gabe gave a pointed look to each of them in turn.

Everyone hung their heads except for Milo.

"Jesus fucking Christ, you guys." Gabe strode to me and draped an arm around my waist. "Guess we know what we're doing when they're all out."

With my cheeks warming, I let the corner of my mouth tug up. "Yeah, but we got to this couch first." Funny how a few months ago, I'd never dare to admit to something like that. But with them, I was safe and *loved*.

Milo faced us, his mouth dropping open. "Are you serious?" He stomped his foot. "When do I get my turn?"

Cash stepped to Milo and ruffled his hair. "Oh, I'm sure that boy you've had your eyes on will come around."

Snapping his gaze to Cash, Gabe said, "What boy?" He freed me and stepped to Milo. "Why does Cash know about this, and I don't?"

With a shrug of his shoulder and lifting his chin, Milo said, "You've been a little busy with Superman."

Gabe's gaze cut to me, then back to Milo. "Yeah, guess so. Can you blame me though?" He held his arm out. "Just look at him."

"Shit, Gabe." I wrapped him up in my arms and buried my head in his neck. "I love you and I'm going to love it here even more now. No matter where we put the couch." I breathed him in.

"I heard that." Silas moved the couch piece back to its original position. "There. It's covering the..." He flapped his fingers at the carpet. "Whatever the fuck that stain is and it's not blocking the energy from the front door to the patio doors. Are we happy now?"

"We are very happy." I squeezed Gabe harder and kissed his cheek. I'd never been happier in my life.

Milo carries an unrequited love for his firefighting best friend, Ryder. With a newfound self-discovery, will their friendship ignite into something more? Grab More Than a Spark Now.

Want to see what Gabe and Jeremy really look like? Claim your free character art.

THANK YOU

Thank you for reading **Protect My Heart**. Helping other readers find new books to enjoy is easy when you share a review. If you want to share your love for Gabe and Jeremy: please leave a review. I'd really appreciate it!

Another huge help is recommending my work to others. Spread the word by giving this book a shout-out in your favorite book rec group if you like.

Get exclusive content at Christie's Facebook reader's group:
Christie's Cocktale Cafe
Find Christie and all her MM Romance books online at:
CHRISTIEGORDON.COM
Connect with Christie on Social Media:

ABOUT THE AUTHOR

Christie Gordon started writing gay and MM romance books after finding MM fanfiction by accident and falling in love with it. She's always had stories in her head and always enjoyed writing, so she decided to try her hand at it and took up fiction writing classes at a local community college. She published her first MM romance book with a small press back in 2009. She enjoys writing about men discovering themselves, overcoming obstacles and finding love in the process, along with a happy ending. Visit her website for a complete list of her books.

Christie worked in the high-tech industry with a Bachelor of Science in Electrical Engineering and a Master's in Business Administration. She currently lives in the Phoenix, Arizona metro area but has also lived in the Bay Area of California and grew up in Minnesota. If she isn't writing, she's watching boys love dramas or creating digital artwork. She's also a mother of two young-adult sons, whose antics keep her on her toes. Her one-eyed rescue pug is always by her side, snoring the day away.

Made in the USA
Columbia, SC
19 June 2025